Raiden Out The Storm:
An (Off-The-Rails) Ice Era Chronicle
2:15 a.m.
C.M. Moore

www.trollriverpub.com
Raiden Out The Storm:
An (Off-The-Rails) Ice Era Chronicle (2:15)
Copyright © 2017 C.M. Moore
ISBN: 978-1-946454-48-5
Cover Design: Proebook Covers
Editors: Ravindra Banthia

Dear Reader,

Connor and Monica have worked very hard on this particular piece of entertainment. This book was brought to you by hard labor and love. Please respect an artist's work for the enrichment we try to bring you. I humbly ask that you don't outright steal this child born on paper and brought to you by love. If you come by this book by nefarious means and you are simply unable to give the change in your pocket for the purchase price, then take it with my blessing. But if you can purchase it and would like Connor and Monica to continue to bring you great books, please purchase a copy to support them.

Thank you,

Troll River Publications

Join the fun with giveaways, updates, and new release opportunities at: http://eepurl.com/dnoLrr

Dedication

I dedicate this book to my dog. I call him all the names you see in this book. His vet's bills get very expensive, but I love him anyway. Here's to cash in my pocket the next time he eats five loaves of banana bread, tinfoil and all.

Acknowledgements

To my better half, without you, this book wouldn't exist. Really.

To Meghan Ludwig… and her daughters, Kaelie, Elica, and Fiona, who told me to write my threesome book and not be apologetic. Thanks for calling me trendy.

To Whitney and April who are still looking for mistakes in my work. Couldn't do this without you.

To the Trolls in the Troll River Publishing House. When I need help, you come like Batman when the signal is up. I can never thank you enough.

To Dillon from the Starbucks in St. Cloud, MN. Thanks for breaking up my writer's block. You serve a mean cup of coffee!

To Kay, you give me time to write, and love, and inspiration… but mostly time to write. You are indeed the best.

To Amanda, tell your dad that it really is you being acknowledged. And if he keeps saying it isn't, we are going to acknowledge him next.

To Alison and Diane, when I see your comments on Facebook, it always cheers me up. Thank you for the support and the laughter. Also, I think all the items are sex toys. I'm not good at that game.

To Stephanie, I cannot tell you how much I appreciate your patience with me. I hope we will always be working together in some shape or form.

To my daughters, Sam and Capi. Especially Capi… thank you for helping me pick out the name of this book. Sorry it changed, blame Amanda.

And finally, to all the readers out there… I write to share this with you. You remind me to keep trying. I hope I don't disappoint you.

To all of you, again, thank you.

Dear Readers,

I'm writing a little note to you about my Off-The-Rails books, but as always, I'm a slow burn. I'll get to that. I promise. Stay with me.

When I first started writing books, it was simply a hobby with my wife Monica. Monica and I would sit across from each other at our favorite café and create. We'd laugh about our characters, we'd play God and toss problems their way, and mostly I loved the way her eyes would shine when a great idea would slip from her lips.

Nothing about that has changed. This is still our hobby, our love affair. I still sit with her and the books can only be created with her at my side. However, as I started to get drawn deeper into this world of ice and snow, I began to learn more about myself. I think that anyone who writes knows that somewhere along the way we can't help but pour out a little of our soul when we tell a story.

And so, the birth of the Off-The-Rails.

Off-The-Rails stories are not only male/female love stories. They can be gay, bisexual, a mix-and-match. In short... different. Things I'm exploring about myself. Things I'm exploring about life. I write these as my own experimental contemplations as well as painting a futuristic landscape that isn't black and white.

Today we live in a world as varied as a rainbow flag, different in ideas, as sexual preference, as in skin color. And since this series of books is set in the future, I can't imagine a world that doesn't still have gay couples, lesbians, or threesomes. To be honest, I don't want a place where these mixes and matches are missing. It would be gray. Diversity adds color.

My Off-The-Rails stories are partly here as companion novels to the times. They add range. I will never tell my fictional characters who to love anymore then I would tell someone on the street who they should be with. These stories may upset your moral compass a bit, but I promise you, I'm writing the correct story for the character at hand. This is their world, their journey, as much as it is mine.

But in case you're not a fan of the Off-The-Rails, don't be worried. 1:05 a.m., 2:05 a.m., 3:05 a.m. etc. will always stay male/female for those who prefer it. I get that sometimes that's just want you want to read. No one will ever have to read the Off-The-Rails to understand the main story line. Without reading the other books you will be able to follow me as we march closer to whether Earth turns into a ball of ice floating in the universe... or warming up the planet somehow and everyone surviving. The books with the time titles will always be the ones where Monica and I move the Ice Era along, but the Off-The-Rails will have their place too. I hope you're cool with that.

Warm regards,

Connor & Monica Moore

~C.M.~

Prologue
(Ashley Winsor)

Place: Train car on Bilander in the Northern Earth Dens, C.T.O.N.A.
Time: 2:05 a.m.

Ashley Winsor was the meanest devil-may-care harvester on any train that ran underground. She'd spent years perfecting her rough-and-tumble male persona. On the surface of the planet, she survived the ice and snow like she was born for the harsh weather. Deep in the Northern Earth Dens, no one crossed her. Ash was king. No one told her what to do, and no one she met knew she was a woman.

Until today.

Just as Ash had thought she would force Weaver to back down, the no-good harvester did something she never thought was possible. He used some type of weird magic on her. He changed her world forever.

Ash had followed Weaver and the young woman traveling with him out of the cave bar and onto the train platform. They were led by Raiden "Mutt" Muttson who ran from the riot when the betting had gone to hell.

Mutt, she knew from traveling the trains and the trekking on the surface of the planet. He was one of the many men who gathered items from the ice to sell. They ran in the same circles, but never crossed paths other than to sling an insult or two. The woman, however, was a stranger. Ash was sure she would remember someone with eyes the color of blood.

Ash jumped the train and held on to the cold metal door handle. She took a second to glance behind her to make sure her best friend, Stone, shadowed her. Her other traveling companion, Morgan-Roth, was nowhere to be found, but she didn't have time to hunt for him right now.

Stone was taller than most men, and his long strides easily kept up with her pace. Her friend didn't ask why they chased Mutt, Weaver, and the woman with him. Stone simply followed her. That was her favorite thing about him. He shadowed her, and he cared about her. Sure, they never said things such as they "liked" each other. And sure, they never touched, other than when they punched each other in the arm, but she knew he was fond of her. Stone might be a little dumb and a marshmallow at times, but so far in the last two years, he'd stuck around. Right now, she was happy he had stayed. She needed him to face Weaver and his chums. There was no way she would let them get away with starting a fight in the bar and making her look bad.

Ash pulled the door open and tossed herself and her pack into the train. She snaked through the cars after Weaver, thinking about how he ruined the betting at the bar.

Laying Odds was the only harvester bar worth a damn. Since she had started pretending to be a man, no one had dared screw her over like he just did. She was King Winsor. Weaver would soon learn what happened to people who messed with her. Ash may not like the kind of hard, crude life she had to live, but whether she liked it or not, that didn't matter. What mattered was she didn't lose her position. Her life might be tough, but she survived, and no one hurt her. She wouldn't let anyone hurt her again.

The door to the lounging train car opened. Stone lagged, but she trusted that he would catch up. She spotted Morgan-Roth with Weaver, the vampire girl, and Mutt. It appeared Morgan-Roth had switched sides. Ash shook her head as she tailed the group. She couldn't blame Morgan-Roth too much. He was a priest. If anything, his only allegiance was to God. Fair enough. Her only allegiance was to money... and Stone.

Ash opened the next door. Ahead of her, Weaver and the crew halted in the hall. The tall Indian stood next to the little woman with the red eyes. The lady tried to get a door open to some private quarters. So, they thought they could get her tossed out of the bar, make her lose money, and they would get to kick back and nap on the train? Fuck those thatched-cock-sniffers.

Ash reached the woman's side first. She snapped her hand out and gripped the red-eyed woman's arm. That stopped her from opening the door.

"I got an angry mob back there. I'll be strung up for the stunt you fucking pulled. I'm never going to be allowed into Laying Odds again." Ash would have to make an example of them. Maybe even shoot them. If she didn't, she would appear weak. *I am King Winsor*, she repeated to herself.

Weaver shoved Ash back. She let go of the woman's arm. Ash's chin rose. Weaver had some nerve, the faffing ham-stain.

"Don't touch Nova. If you have a problem, it's with me." Weaver took a step closer to Nova. Apparently, the harvester had finally met someone he wanted. Too bad she didn't give a shit. Ash glared. She didn't care a dike's damn about his precious *Nova*. She had her own ice to climb.

"Get out of my way, Weaver," Winsor demanded. She wouldn't back down, she couldn't. Her reputation was at stake. Her status was always at risk. If someone heard about even one time that she let an incident go, it could mean the beginning of the end. There was always a wanker waiting to take her down. She knew what it was like to be at the mercy of someone else. Never again.

Nova tried to turn the key in the lock. Ash reached around Weaver and grabbed her hand. Not going to happen.

"We've got business." Ash couldn't believe Weaver was blowing her off anyway. He was out money too. Didn't he care? "That's money lost."

"Don't touch Nova again. This is my last warning." Weaver threw Ash's hand off a second time. What was wrong with him? Did he forget who she was? Weaver and she had made bets and lots of money together for years before he quit harvesting. Maybe Weaver forgot that she was Ash Winsor.

"I rule the trains, Weaver, or have you been gone so long that you've forgotten? Do you think you're sunshine now that you have a vampire to fuck?" Ash's eyes jumped to the red-eyed elf next to them. She might be able to grab the key from the little woman's hand.

From behind, Ash heard the door open with a grinding sound. Stone pushed his way into the hall. With him, Mutt, Morgan-Roth, Nova, and Weaver all in the same hallway, Ash felt slightly claustrophobic. She shook that off. Stone was here. Being with her best friend was always a good thing.

"Stone." Ash's eyes never left Weaver. "Pitch Weaver off the train. Give him to the riot." See how he would like that.

"You made a bet. You lost," Raiden snarled.

Ash glanced to the young blond-haired harvester. Raiden Muttson bugged her. Mutt made her want to slap him and suck his bottom lip. She hated the feelings he inspired inside of her, so by default, she hated him. The glaring and the insults had worked for her so far. She wasn't going to change their dislike of each other. Change was not on the agenda today.

"I did no such thing," Ash snapped at the sexy Asian with the stupid ponytail on top of his head. Really, Mutt should cut his hair. She didn't mind the silver spike in his ear, but the hair could go. Her eyes went back to Weaver. It was time to concentrate. "I said the vampire could have her money. I never said anything about Weaver. I'm thinking to soothe my headache, it might be best to fling Weaver to the harvesters back there. I think the vampire and I will get to know each other while they rip you apart." Ash smiled. That sounded just like King Winsor.

If she were alone, she would have congratulated herself for coming up with a solution that would scare others in the future. Weaver was collateral damage. If she wanted people to stay afraid of her, she had to do things like this. "You're a hot piece of ass." Ash eyed Nova. She could use this woman to protect her identity as a man. "After I cover your eyes, you can show me what you do to get Weaver so hard, unless…"

Ash smiled but her brain came up with an even better plan. She could regain her lost money and not have to toss anyone off the train. That would show the other harvesters they couldn't screw Ash Winsor, and she didn't have to kill

Weaver. Honestly, she wasn't up to killing anyone. Some days being a king was exhausting.

She eyed the red-eyed girl. The woman said she had a lot of money. Ash could take that to recoup her loss.

"You want to pay me all your HOCs to go away. For the right price, I could piss off." Ash smiled. Problem solved.

"Is that a threat?" Nova asked.

"I don't threaten. I state facts." Ash glared. Unfortunately, Weaver didn't look scared. None of them did. Blast it, she would have to pull her weapon. Why couldn't they just bow down to her so she could go to her room? She was tired and hungry.

Ash grabbed Nova's arm so she couldn't use the key to get into the private quarters. They weren't leaving until this was worked out to her satisfaction. She used her other hand to go for the colt .45 on her hip.

Weaver glanced at her hand, and Ash paused. The energy of the hall suddenly felt dreamlike.

The train itself seemed to gasp. Ash felt rooted to the spot like an imaginary person had just nailed her feet to the floor. She tried to back up, but her muscles didn't even twitch. Ash was now a living statue, and she wanted to scream.

Her eyes jumped to Weaver. They widened when the Indian's long black hair began to move like snakes. The strands began to unbraid themselves and float outward. Ash wanted to launch herself away from the eerie silence and the spooky hair, but she couldn't. She tried again to scream or shout. There wasn't even a breath of sound that slipped from her lips.

No one moved. Maybe they couldn't. Ash could only see Nova and Mutt out of the corner of her eye. She wondered if Stone was okay. This kind of freaky shit would have him running from the train in no time flat. Weaver's eyes turned red like they were filling with blood. Bloody gross. Okay, so touching the vampire was a bad idea. Now what? Her gun couldn't be drawn. She was fixed to this spot.

Weaver held up both hands with his palms facing outward. He took a single step back. How come he could still move? His back stiffened as his hair waved in the nonexistent wind. The magical blow-dryer switched from low to high.

As his hands started to move back and forth, there was a supernatural silence. Weaver's hands made a zigzag pattern in the air, and then just as abruptly as the weirdness had started, it ended. The harvester's hands dropped. His hair went limp.

All at once, multiple things happened. Stone backed up, wrapped his arms around his middle, turned, and left. The door slid shut. Ash refrained from rolling her eyes. *What a marshmallow.* They just… Ash inhaled. Something about her was different. She grabbed her chest. Was she having a heart attack?

Morgan-Roth wiped his brow. "I've never not been able to move before."

Ash felt a tug at her chest. Her heart pulled her toward Mutt. She glanced at the lean blond. Raiden clutched his chest as well. What was this feeling? The sensation felt like she'd just eaten a rock and was trying to swallow it.

"What did you do to me?" Ash tried to sound tough. It wasn't going well.

Mutt's light-tan skin had gone pale. He stared at Weaver. She did the same thing.

"I told you not to touch her. I promised to protect Nova. I warned you." Weaver shook his head like a monkey-tit.

"I'll leave. Just fix whatever it is that you did to me." Ash glanced around. The outlandish urge to hug Mutt and ask him to hold her swamped her senses. She had successfully ignored her attraction to the cute harvester for years. Why was this happening now? "Put me back the way I was. I'll go. I promise." She had to get out of here and fast.

Ash wrapped her arms around her middle as she tried to stop herself from reaching for Mutt. She had the gift of never getting lost and always finding a safe place to be. Right now, her senses shrieked that the one spot she needed to go to be safe was in Mutt's arms. She might hurl. She bent over and forced herself to stay still. She needed a moment to sort this out. What now?

"I'm not going to change what I did. I've bound you to Raiden. You'll not be able to leave his side. You don't know it, but the heartstrings don't lie. If I were you, I'd be working on figuring out how to add Raiden into your life instead of attempting to take our money and kicking us off the train."

"What?" Mutt bellowed.

Ash felt panic rise until she couldn't see. She gulped back the fear and confusion, but the anxiety didn't dissipate. Weaver couldn't tie people together. Could he? After he stopped living the life of a harvester, had Weaver learned this magic? Another thought stuck her right between the eyes.

Did Weaver marry her to Mutt? That wasn't right. She and Stone were… she didn't know what they were, but she didn't want Mutt. She couldn't risk another relationship. Getting close to anyone was chancy. They might find out she wasn't a man. Too many thoughts jumbled in her head all at once.

"Did you say the rest of my life? I don't want Winsor for the rest of my life! I don't want anyone. You're a terrible person," Raiden sputtered. "Nothing about you has changed."

Ash agreed. Mutt was correct. Weaver should be tossed into a septic tank.

"I'm sorry, Raiden, but Winsor is part of your other half. Your match. I hope in time you'll work it out with *her*."

Ash's eyes went wide. That's it. She would shoot Weaver. He deserved it.

Before she could draw her gun, Mutt sprang past Weaver toward her.

His abrupt movement caught Ash off guard. Mutt was known around the trains as an easygoing follower. He'd been kept like a pet by a cruel harvester named Doug for the last year. She'd been keeping an eye on him since the first time she'd glimpsed him. Ash had never witnessed him take charge or fight. Everyone knew he had a fondness for diplomacy. His movement backed her up against the wall. She glanced around the walkway. She couldn't shoot Mutt. If she had to face the truth, honestly, she didn't want to.

Mutt's left hand struck the wall next to her head. She stared into his eyes. They were a pretty shade of light green. She'd never noticed that before. With his other hand, he shoved his fingers under the hem of her coat.

Mutt's fingers pressed directly between her thighs. He shoved up and into the thick fabric of her pants. That mother-fucking-willy-wimble just felt her up. By reflex, Ash swung. Her hand connected with Mutt's cheek.

His green eyes widened at her like she was the one who had just grabbed for his sausage. The bloody piss-pilot. Ash took a deep breath. She just needed to talk to him. Ash had to explain and convince him not to tell anyone about her lack of a dick. The one thing she must do was *not* panic.

Mutt backed up. He gaped at her with a jaw that reached for the floor. She opened her mouth to come up with a way to fix this situation, but before she could speak, Mutt turned on his heel and bolted through the door to the next train car.

As soon as the door closed behind Mutt, the panic, the fear, the confusion swamped her. Ash sucked in a deep breath, but all the air in the train wasn't enough to keep the tears away.

Chapter 1
(Raiden Muttson)

Place: Train car on Bilander in the Northern Earth Dens, C.T.O.N.A.
Time: 2:15 a.m.

Shock made his hands tremble so hard that he struggled to open the door to the next train car. Raiden jiggled his pack to hide the telltale sign as he entered the walkway. He didn't want any of the other harvesters to mark his distress. Showing any weakness on a harvester train was like waving a red flag in front of a bull.

As he marched forward, his mind refused to believe he was irrevocably tied to Ash Winsor. Raiden wasn't up to solving the complex puzzle of the woman who dressed as a man and was the toughest son-of-a-harvester on any train that ran underground. He should just go back and demand Weaver undo whatever he had done to tie them together.

"*Helvete*," he swore as he rubbed his neck. He tried to ease the perpetual ache in his shoulders. Glancing around the hall, he paused near the sleeping quarters. Someone had haphazardly stacked crates in the narrow passage. Raiden didn't want to go back the way he came in case he ran into Winsor. Was he running away? No. He just needed a second to think.

Raiden decided to squeeze past the leaning tower. As soon as he got halfway beyond the containers, his mammoth pack snagged on a particularly jagged piece of wood. Struggling to free the fabric, he stopped when it became evident that he'd made the situation worse. His hands dropped down in defeat.

Fan-fucking-tastic. Not only was he bound to Ash Winsor, but he was also trapped in a hallway. He wiggled his pack again. He couldn't deal with any of this. Not when he had other problems to tackle. He had to send money home to his father. In the back of his head, Raiden pictured the vacant grin his father always had whenever life went wrong. Is that what Raiden was doing now? Fuck that. No grin was on *his* face.

Raiden scanned the closed doors of the lodgings on both sides of the aisle as he shifted again. Two men came out the exit next to him. Their eyes flipped to his bag hung up on the cartons. They chuckled as they left through the opposite door. Raiden shook his head. Finding a place to think on a train full of gambling harvesters was next to impossible. If he had a key to a private room, then maybe, just maybe, he could hide there and reason out this problem. Hiding wasn't an option, especially jammed next to wooden boxes, so he just stood in the walkway of the last train car before cargo.

Taking a deep breath, he tipped his butt on the slats and slumped next to the items. Reaching behind him, he yanked on the thick canvas of his bag. Nothing happened. Two huge men came out of the quarters to his right. He noted that a game of Boxcar Dice was in full swing. No one paid him any attention. That was fine with him. Chances were decent they wouldn't help him get loose but rob him instead. Not that he had anything for anyone to steal. He'd sold all of his trekking gear for food. They disappeared through the door he'd just entered. He exhaled relief.

As he watched the harvesters exit, his mind jumped to the tall Indian. He should go back into that other car and insist that Weaver undo whatever mystical thing he did to connect him to Ash Winsor. Was this a forever connection? Would he be with Ash until he died? Were they married?

Raiden glared like he could produce his ex-friend with merely an angry stare. His bones throbbed in protest, but he disregarded the ache in his joints. Instead, he slipped one arm out of his right strap. He started to loosen the other band on his shoulder. Again, the dull twinge in his joints returned. He'd had the pain since he'd turned twenty-five. The soreness was never going to change, and he'd long ago accepted the agonizing pounding. He tried to concentrate on his bag. After a few seconds, he dropped his forehead into the fabric. He wasn't getting free anytime soon.

When the bag refused to give, Raiden reached for the jagged lumber. Once he could move down the hallway, should he go on to cargo or go back to see Weaver? He could tell Weaver he didn't even like Ash. Didn't Weaver and Nova see them insulting each other at Laying Odds? Raiden refused to spend the rest of his life in Winsor's shadow. She already had *two* shadows, Morgan-Roth and Stone. What would she need another one for?

Just as he heard the fabric start to tear, the farthest door opened.

Doug took up the entrance. Raiden yanked harder as his eyes met Doug's. *Helvete.* Not him, not now.

"There's my Mutt." Doug snickered as he strode forward. He leaned on the planks further holding Raiden hostage. The strap clinging to Raiden's bicep dug in as if in league with Doug. Raiden averted his head when the abusive harvester shifted even closer.

"I'm not yours. I'm not a dog, no matter how many people call me Mutt." Raiden's eyes flipped to the other man. "I meant it when I said I'm done."

"I'll tell you when we're done." Doug's breath fanned his cheek. Again, Raiden tipped his head back as far as he could.

"I'm not making any more deals with you." Even if he hadn't broken away from his prostitution-type relationship with Doug earlier, he would still have to do it now. Weaver had decided to change Raiden's life, and there didn't seem to be a whole lot of ways he could put it back the way it was. Not that he wanted to go back to Doug. No matter what happened, never again would Raiden end up in the same predicament with the foul harvester. He'd fight before he would let Doug have him back.

Raiden put his hands up to push at Doug's chest. The man didn't lean back even an inch. The familiar aching twinge in Raiden's knuckles had his hands dropping. The same sense that told him when a storm was coming told him Doug was a threat. He knew that even without the on-again off-again gift. Raiden could feel the connection in his bones demanding that he run screaming from Doug and cling to Winsor. He wanted Ash. Doug repulsed him in a whole new way. Raiden had changed the second Weaver united his heartstrings to Ash Winsor. Doug was history, whether the man wanted that or not.

"When my dick's getting sucked, you'll find that I'm a good friend, Mutt." Doug leaned close again, and Raiden could smell his rank breath and unwashed clothes. He didn't have time for this.

"You were never a good anything." Raiden struggled against the stacks, and another inch of his bag split. He'd have to get another one, not that he had the money to do so. He looked over his shoulder at the damage.

"But if you think I'll be nice to you now." Doug swung. The punch landed square in the center of Raiden's stomach. Raiden wasn't prepared for the blow. He didn't have time to block. "You'll find out I'm not."

Raiden gasped for breath. The strike momentarily knocked the wind out of him. Raiden cursed the tight space and underestimating the other man. Doug's meaty fists grabbed his shoulders and forced him upright. The harvester shoved him hard to the wooden frames.

Doug drew back for the second hit. Before he struck, the door behind him opened. He paused as his eyes flew to the entry.

Ash stood motionless before them. Her silver eyes were the only thing that moved. She glared at Doug as Raiden's shoulder surged with pain. Around her eyes, red rings had formed, and her nose and cheeks were puffy. She looked like she'd been crying. Winsor crying? That would be like seeing a polar bear dancing.

"Doug," Ash snapped. It wasn't a greeting. The name was cloaked in a sneer with abject hatred hiding just under the surface. She stepped next to Raiden but didn't acknowledge him. *Fanken.* She would let Doug pummel him.

"Look who it is." Doug's fist dropped as his eyes flipped over Ash's short black hair. "King of the assholes." The beefy man gave a mocking bow, and then his eyes popped to Raiden's. "Mutt and I were just talking about how life for him would be better on his knees." Doug's huge muscles rippled along his arms. He yanked on Raiden's pack, shredding the wedged strap.

Raiden stumbled and then caught himself before he hit the wall. He straightened and pulled on what was left of his other strap. His eyes narrowed at the malicious harvester.

Doug took a step closer. "Come on, Mutt, heel." Doug pointed to the floor at his side, an action which wasn't new to Raiden.

Raiden didn't have time for this snowblower right now. He only had the energy to deal with Ash. One snowblower at a time.

Ash placed her hand on Raiden's chest. The soft pressure was off from her ordinarily surly nature. Her palm was warm. He hated it. The light touch made him feel alive. Weaver categorically fucked them up on a few levels. She pushed slightly, and Raiden leaned back until he was pressed against the wall. She went toe to toe with Doug.

Winsor obviously wasn't afraid of the other man even if Doug was known to be a real mean fighter. The harvester was a few inches taller than her, but she tipped her chin up and scowled. For a second, Raiden had the urge to protect her. He clamped down on the unfamiliar feeling as his heart tugged toward her. No way. He wasn't about to coddle Ash Winsor.

"Mutt's got business with me. You wanna go? Cause I'll slice you from stem to stern then hang you like fleam."

That sounded much more like the Ash Winsor that Raiden knew. She probably wouldn't even appreciate his help. King Winsor had a stronger reputation than he did. He would only act if Doug hurt her. Raiden knew from the last year of trekking with the other man that the harvester was capable of violence.

"You're blocking the hall," Doug muttered. Raiden had never seen Doug back down before. Ash was known and respected. For the first time, Raiden wondered what she did to earn that mixture of admiration and fear.

"Sod off." Ash thrust her heavy coat back to reveal a gun on her hip. The pistol wasn't a small weapon either. "Raiden's with me now."

Doug mumbled a curse under his breath and then backed up until he squeezed next to the boxes. When he got to the far door, he hurried away like Ash might shoot him in the back. Raiden thought Ash looked like she considered it.

"Is that real?" Raiden couldn't contain the awe in his voice even though he tried.

"Why would I carry a fake gun, slush-head? What am I gonna do? Throw it at a polar bear?" she grumbled. "Let's go."

Raiden shouldn't have asked.

"Go where?"

"We need to talk. Follow me." Ash produced a key to her private room. It dangled from her fingertips. Of course, she had a key. Ash Winsor was a king on these trains. Correction, *queen*. Raiden hesitated.

Ash glared. "Now, Mutt."

She reached for the door next to her. Her sharp chin rose, and she commanded him like a dog. If she thought he would merely follow silently, she had the wrong idea. He'd just dumped Doug for this reason. He wasn't going through that again. He wasn't Stone, and she could threaten however much she wanted, but he refused to crawl for her. He had a spine. He wasn't a shadow. Raiden might be easygoing, but when it came to her, he wanted nothing more than to tell her to get lost.

"Sit on it and spin." Raiden whirled away from her, but her hand grabbed the back of his long leather coat. Her slim fingers looked fragile where they dug in near his waist.

"What do you want? An engraved invitation? Stop being a dribbling wanker. We aren't talking in the hall. You wanna meet Doug again?"

Raiden glowered. He wasn't sure what a "wanker" was, but he had the idea it wasn't a compliment. He opened his mouth to tell Ash to suck a Siberian sheep, but before he could, a door opened behind him.

A group of harvesters picked up the boxes. The noise level tripled as they laughed, talked, and clattered crates.

"Fine." He wasn't about to tell her that she was correct. Having a conversation in the hall was a bad idea. He was pleasantly shocked. She didn't push it. Instead, she spun around and opened the door behind her.

Raiden wiggled his stiff shoulders and then shook his pack. He wanted to leave just because she was so sure he would follow, but that competitive streak he had around her chose this moment to strike. If Ash Winsor could deal with this problem, then so could he. He had to face the idea that they might have to be together. There was no way Raiden would stick his head in the snow. He would hear Ash out.

Raiden gripped the strap on his pack as he entered her sleeping compartment. At this point, he could do one of two things. He could fight their connection, or he could accept it. His mom always said, "Kun, attack is the secret of defense, defense is the planning of attack." She would tell him to figure out the problem and then fight for what he wanted. As a child, she'd continually pestered Raiden that he was too relaxed about life. He'd disappointed her at every turn. That might have been her Japanese heritage talking, but it also might've been that he *was* more comfortable following along than leading. He'd never considered that a flaw, but she did.

The sleeping compartment they entered had pinned-up movie posters and book pages attached to every available space on all four walls. He slipped his pack off his back and set it next to a cot plump with blankets and pillows. A British flag was draped near the door to the toilet room. So, this is where Ash lived? It looked like the rest of the train, just a little cleaner. Raiden had the notion the room would be pink or have pictures of flowers because she was a woman. Dumb.

Ash dropped her pack and then wrapped her arms around her waist. He tipped his head to the side. *Fanken*, but pity enfolded him. She looked crushed. Big, bad Ash Winsor looked defeated. He wanted to comfort her. Screw Weaver. He had done this to him. Weaver had given him… what? Emotions? Love for Ash?

Before today, Raiden didn't care about anything other than sending HOCs back to the water base for his sick dad. If his father were here, he'd say, "He who enters the game must endure it." Dad would tell him to stay, give in, bend. If he didn't oppose the match, he could learn to live with Winsor. That felt a little too much like grabbing his ankles. He wasn't a trained dog, and he refused to let Ash lead him around like an animal on a leash. His father allowed his mother to run his life; then she left him. She left him in pieces, and he'd let her go in silence while she picked another man. That wasn't going to be Raiden's future. Especially after he had seen the devastation it had caused. If anyone would leave, he would. Whatever had to be done, he'd do it. Raiden had never thought being relaxed was a bad thing up until now. Now he couldn't sit back and watch this unfold. Now was the time to listen to some of his mom's advice.

Ash turned her back to him. She admired a poster of three men and a woman playing cards. She didn't turn around and face him even though she was the one who wanted to get into their dilemma.

Raiden didn't know what to make of her silence. He predicted an attack. Calling each other names is what they did. He was ready for the insults and the slurs. They would go back and forth about who was better. The swish of the train started to get under his skin. His eyes darted over a half-drawn child's doodle and then landed on the black hairs that curled at the nape of her neck.

Feeling uncomfortable, he locked the door behind him and then crossed his arms over his chest. He wasn't a doormat like his dad was, and he wasn't a dog. If Winsor thought she could run him ragged, she would find out real fast he wouldn't bend over and take it. He wasn't afraid of her even if she did have a gun. He'd never been afraid of Ash Winsor, maybe begrudging admiration, and deeply buried sexual tension, but never fear.

After a few more minutes of grating silence, she slipped her hands through her coat and let the thick furs fall to the floor. The thump of the heavy fabrics was overly loud. She rubbed her arms and still didn't turn around. The back of her in that enormous fluffy sweater gave him no clue as to her shape. She looked as barrel-chested as Doug. He began to assess her figure. When he realized he was hunting for her ass under all those layers, he mentally slapped himself.

Ash fiddled with the gun holster on her hip and then unstrapped a buckle from her thigh. The gun landed on the discarded jacket. She sighed. He stared at her ass until he realized he was doing it.

"I'm getting real tired of looking at your back, Ash. Face me like a man."

"I'm not a man, and that stays between us, got it?" She spun around and pinned him with a steely look. "You tell no one, Mutt." Some of her black hair flipped over her ears and onto her forehead. The dark locks softened her features and made her silver eyes shine. How the hell had he missed that she was a woman? Straight up dense. He *was* a slush-head. He should've seen her feminine qualities long before now.

She kept up the glare, yet a few tears tried to escape.

Well, this was off to a good start. He was attracted to her, even though he didn't want to be, and neither one of them could speak civilly to each other. His mom would say, "stand your ground"; his dad would say, "cower." He had the urge to follow her. He had to think, not just react. With Ash Winsor, nothing ever came easy. She was his own private puzzle.

"Calm down. I just meant if you want to talk, then I'm listening. I'll give you a second."

"Don't say 'calm down' like I'm an overwrought twelve-year-old girl. I know what's what. You're a real ironclad dick-wagon. And you can take your second and shove it up your—"

A knock on the door startled him and cut off Ash. Maybe it was Weaver to say he would fix this. Perhaps his friend was wrong, and he didn't belong to this woman. Raiden was positive he belonged to a woman who didn't use bizarre put-downs. What was a dick-wagon anyway?

Ash opened the door a crack.

"What is it, Morgan-Roth?"

"Stone hasn't returned yet. What do you want me to tell him when he gets back?"

Raiden's brow knitted together as he surveyed Ash's back. Stone was that young, handsome shadow that rarely left her side. He recalled that the pale stranger had gone as soon as Weaver lifted his magical tying-him-to-Ash spell he cast. He didn't know what to expect of seeing the tall harvester again. Would Ash tell Stone that they were together now? The idea played over and over in his head. What would he say?

Ash groaned. He felt like groaning too.

"Blast it. I'll deal with it later." Ash closed the door.

Raiden had the feeling he would be dealing with it later too.

After the door was locked, Ash turned to face him. Her silver eyes met his green ones before they dropped to the floor. She tipped her head into her hands. *Fanken.* Now he melted like ice near a vent, all because of a handful of tears that shimmered in Ash's eyes. He should've beat Weaver with an ax handle.

The urge to comfort her reared up and almost hijacked his body. He ruthlessly held his ground and planted his feet. His fingers tingled with a new mix of pain and the need to hold her. Raiden was used to the arthritis from his gift, but this sensation was different.

"Weaver said he'd unbind us if we left him and the red-eyed girl alone for the rest of the trip." Ash lifted her head. "You left before he explained that."

"If *you* leave him alone. I was fine with Weaver and Nova until you came busting in." He didn't know why he pointed that out. The desire to take Ash down, to soften her, never left him. Where did that even come from? He was supposed to be laid-back. She didn't make him feel that way. Ever.

"We're not slinging blame, you quacking-tit." Her husky voice was sexy. Her insult... loony.

"You might not be, but I think it's clear whose fault this is."

"Are we gonna dump all over each other, or are we gonna figure this shite out?" Again, her voice made him measure how close they were to the bed.

Fan-fucking-tastic. He got hot with her voice. He swore that had never happened before. Raiden reminded himself repeatedly to keep his head together and his dick in his pants.

"I don't want to figure any of this *shite* out. This might surprise you, but I don't want to talk to you at all. I can't live with you. This is a mess. I don't even like you." He had to argue with her, or he might let her order him around until she made him beg. He would be brushing her hair and feeding her grapes before long, just to hear her sexy voice again.

"This train ride went all to pot from the start. It's a bloody mess, it is." Ash's shoulders fell, and she tipped her chin up. "I could live with you if I wanted. That's not the point. I just want you to stay here and not tell anyone that I'm a woman. I want you to promise. Do you think you can do that, Mutt?"

If she called him "Mutt" one more time, he would shake her until her teeth rattled. Her words nudged him. She could live with him? Did she want to be with him? She didn't say she *didn't* want him.

The idea of Ash Winsor picking him of all people made him feel ten feet tall. Funny, but that had never been something he'd felt before. Pride had him lifting his head.

"What are you saying?" Raiden took a step closer. What was it about Ash that made him grind his teeth together, but at the same time, he wanted to impress her? His eyes dropped to her lips. He'd never noticed how pink they were. They looked smooth. No, no, no. He wanted to shake her, not kiss her. His eyes went back up to the shiny silver orbs. He needed to get the hell out of this room. Raiden needed air that didn't smell like her skin. A second to clear his head would be ideal.

"I'm saying I want you to stay in this room for the remainder of the trip and not tell anyone I'm a woman. Seriously, does that spike in your ear block your hearing? Maybe I should give *you* a second. Obviously, you're not the fastest train on the tracks."

He wasn't staying in a tiny room with her, especially with a bed less than a foot away. They'd talk, and then he would leave. Raiden ground his teeth, but again the sentence that she could live with him poked his ribs like a spring in an old mattress.

"I hear you," he snapped. "I meant… you could live with me if you wanted to?" His stomach did a funny flip-flop. Would they have kids? Would she want to hold him at night? Would they fall in love? All those ideas were phantasmal. That wasn't the kind of life Raiden ever pictured himself having, especially with someone like Ash.

"I could if I wanted. I can do what I want. I'm Ash Winsor."

"Of course, you can," Raiden said dryly. So, Ash was making a point. He should've expected that.

"Ash Winsor can do what he wants." Ash's eyes traveled down his face and landed on his mouth. "I don't want to be attached to you though. I don't like you."

"I don't like you either."

Her tongue darted over her lips.

Raiden couldn't believe it. His eyes widened. He hadn't slept with a lot of women, mostly men, but he knew that look, and the gender wasn't relevant. His cock swelled. One look? Really? She could turn him on with one look? Weaver would have hell to pay for this.

"Right." Another lick of her lips. *Skit.*

"If I wanted to trek with you, I could." Raiden tried to sound harsh to make his point that she didn't get to call the shots, but his tone came out all wrong. His voice softened. He tried not to swallow his tongue.

"Oh, so you can trek with me? You're a tough guy?" A sexy grin graced her lips. Was she laughing at him?

"I can do what I want. I'm Raiden Muttson," he mocked. What would happen if he touched Ash Winsor? Where would this go? He took a step closer. Her body heat held that distinct scent, spicy and clean. It was simply curiosity. He inhaled deep.

"Here's the deal, tough guy." She gave a shrug, then another easy grin. Her eyes captured his. "I'm stronger than you are. I can handle when life gets tricky. You can't." She met him halfway. "You can't keep up with me. You'd never be able to follow where I lead."

Raiden felt like he was facing an avalanche.

"Can it, Ash. I can do whatever you can do." One minute he was ready to slap that I'm-better-than-you look off her face and the next his hands snatched her shoulders. He should've never touched her, but it was too late now. He pulled her chest to his until her lips were a breath away. Her big sweater gave, and he could feel some of her curves. "I'm as strong as you are, and I could follow you wherever."

He didn't mean that he *would* follow her. Raiden was determined to prove he wasn't afraid. He could handle big, bad Ash Winsor.

"I don't like you," she repeated, but she sounded like she reminded herself, not him. Her eyes studied his lips as her hands slipped to his shoulders. He let go of her arms long enough so she could push off his coat. The dense layers hit the floor with a thump.

"I don't like you either." Maybe they kept saying that because they wanted the words to be true.

"Traveling together would be a real blizzard. I've Stone to consider. He's my best friend." Her hands crept up his stomach under his heavy flannel and undershirt. They made a straight path to his nipples. Her warm palms stole over his pecs. He could feel his heart beat into her hand, and his breathing turned into a pant. The tingles under his skin magnified. The ache in his shoulders lessened.

"The shadow," he breathed. The handsome stranger who'd started trekking with Ash about two years ago. He'd never seen her without him.

"Are you scared of Stone?"

"I'm not scared of anything you have going on, Ash Winsor. I never have been." Raiden was losing the fight. He wanted her. Now.

"Are you saying you're gonna follow me?"

"I'm not saying I'm going to follow you, Ash, but I'm staying here right now."

"Stay and do what?" Ash lifted one eyebrow.

"I'll give you a second to figure it out." Raiden's mouth dropped to her lips.

Chapter 2

Ash's kiss was passion incarnate. There was such spirit in her. Her mouth was unlike anything Raiden had ever tasted. Her lips awakened his body like a dormant polar bear. How did Weaver do this to them? Raiden was past caring. He just needed to sedate the growing fire in his blood. Heat poured from her and into him as their lips fought for dominance. His body basked in their growing inferno.

Raiden pulled her tighter into his embrace with her hands crushed to his chest. His arm wrapped around her waist, shoving up her sweater. There was just too much damn fabric. His other hand slipped up her back to her head. His fingers tunneled through her thick hair. Raiden's senses went haywire. He could smell her, taste her, feel her. She became his drink of choice. His lips sipped on hers.

Silently, he commanded her to open her mouth. He was surprised yet again when she yielded to him. She parted her lips, and his tongue snaked inside to slide past her teeth.

The tingling under his skin spread to his whole body. These past few years, he'd only ever known pain. Never had he felt this kind of burning. His heart jackhammered in his chest as he licked her tongue in slow, deliberate movements. The constant ache in his joints eased away becoming a distant memory as he kissed her. She tasted like pure want. He made up his mind, in this one moment, he would have her. They wouldn't solve the separating problem right now. They wouldn't talk about how they disliked each other. All of that could come later, much later. Right now, passion ruled.

Her lips parted further. A soft moan poured from her as her arm curled around his shoulders. She tugged at his top. Yeah, he wanted the shirt off as well.

"Mutt, I…" Her lips separated from his for a moment, and then she kissed him again. It took all his self-control to pull away. He lifted his head and gulped.

"Ash. Don't do that. Not here, not like this." His breath came out in a pant.

Ash's bright silver eyes widened. They looked like little silver moons.

"Don't do what?"

"Don't call me 'Mutt' when we're like this." His hand went to his shirt, and with a quick tug, he yanked off his button-up and undershirt. As he tossed the clothing to the floor, his eyes traveled over her face. Her eyes sparkled with lust. She studied his chest and abs, and then tipped her chin up connecting their eyes. Everything about Ash screamed strength, but it was the brief flash of insecurity in her eyes that made her beautiful. It made her real. That look made her his.

"Raiden." The way she sighed his name captured his body and caressed his skin. Who knew that his name on her lips could win him over?

Raiden grabbed the bottom of her baggy sweater and lifted the top over her head. She seemed shocked at his actions, but she didn't move away. Instead, she wrapped her arms around her middle, and under her dark skin, he detected a faint blush. His eyes dropped. Ash's entire chest was bound in long strips of black fabric. The dark-black bands made her brown skin seem a lighter shade.

"Ash?" He tried to capture her eyes and failed. "It's okay?"

She wouldn't look at him, but she nodded. He used two of his fingers to tip her chin up. Her eyes stayed stubbornly downcast. He would never tell her this, but he secretly liked when she jutted out her chin like she was better than everyone. Her strength was a trait he coveted, and he never wanted to see her without her steel spine. When her eyes met Raiden's, he smiled at the uncertainty there. His thumb feathered along her jaw.

"Take it all off, Ash. Let me see you."

"Now who's following who?" She raised one eyebrow.

Oddly, no argument or insult flared out after that sentence. Instead, her hands went to a small plastic clasp at the center of her chest. She obeyed him. The fastener unsnapped, and then she unwound the stretchy black ribbon.

"Ash, you're..." Raiden exhaled. He didn't have the words for how beautiful she was. "*Vacker*," he mumbled as he reached out and began to unwrap her like a present. His mouth filled with saliva like he was about to eat a treat. He licked his lips and swallowed. The fabric was warm where the strip snuggled against her skin.

"*Vacker*?"

"My father is Swedish. I just remember some of the words. *Fanken*, *Helvete*." He cleared his throat. "I only meant that you're beautiful, Ash."

"When it's us, like this," Ash gathered the last piece of cloth to her chest, "you can call me Ashley," she dropped the binding, "Raiden."

When she said his name in that same breathy way, the sweet tone made his cock try to rip through his pants to climb into her body. If he ever got inside of Ash Winsor, he was positive he would never want to leave.

"Ashley," he whispered before he kissed her again. Heat exploded inside his body. Fire poured into his veins until his hard-on pressed agonizingly against his zipper. He'd never felt this inflamed, and they hadn't even done anything yet.

Pulling away from her mouth, his eyes dropped to her now-exposed chest. All he could do was ogle like a virgin, and he was no virgin. Ash Winsor had a pair of the most perfect tits he'd ever set eyes on. Was this a dream?

"Are you only into men?" she asked.

Raiden figured she misread his hesitation. "I like women and men." He smiled as her nipples puckered under his intent stare. Topped with dark areolas, Ash's breasts looked like they begged for his mouth. Her chest tapered down toward a smooth, flat belly.

"Stone is like you." She ran her hand over her chest. "Is something wrong?"

"Nothing. No." Raiden gulped. His hands itched to feel the weight of such amazing globes. They would overflow his hands. He had to taste them. Soon. "It's only that if someone had told me that this was what was under your coat all these years, I would've called them a coal-eater."

Ash grinned.

Raiden's hands flew to precisely what he wanted. He shaped her breast into his palm. The skin was both soft and firm and so, so hot. He tugged at her nipple with his fingertips as she arched her back.

"*Tack.*" Raiden drew her to him again and brought her pebbled nipples tight against his naked pecs.

"I'm not going to ask." She laughed.

He chuckled, and then his mouth zeroed in on hers. His tongue slid past her lips to tangle and taste. Hesitantly, he felt her hands rise to his neck, then into his hair. She tugged, and his ponytail came undone. Everything inside of him was undone. His locks brushed his cheeks. Frustrated, he quickly used one hand to flip the strands back.

"I hate letting go of you for even one second."

"Then don't."

Somewhere, far away, was the idea that he and Ash Winsor were enemies. All he could think about was her sexy skin and her nipples rubbing against his light mat of blond chest hair. He fought for his sanity and then decided he didn't need it. This wasn't Ash Winsor, king of the harvesters. This was Ashley, his woman. Just her and him and now. The tingling under his skin told him all he needed to know. He was going to have sex with her. He knew it like he knew when a storm was on the surface of the planet.

Ash and he sipped from each other until he was drunk. Moans floated around the room, his then hers. He pressed her toward the cot until her butt hit the edge. He wanted her under him, maybe forever.

He licked her lips and then sank back into her mouth. He'd never been this aggressive in the bedroom, but he couldn't seem to stop. Another sigh from her teased his ears. His hands stroked her shoulders, first testing the inviting skin, then demanding more of the connection. She murmured her approval, and he drifted lower. Pressing his pelvis to hers, he had to touch every inch. The longing to make her scream and come clawed through his system until it was all he could think about. Raiden's soul demanded to feel her smooth thighs wrapped around his waist.

His hands ambled back to her chest. Once again, he tugged at her nipples with his fingers and then with his mouth. He couldn't get enough of the way she offered herself up to him. He lapped at her torso, while her hands jerked his belt. Raiden had never thought of himself as forceful, but in about two seconds, he would pin her to the bed.

Raiden let her free his buckle. Next, her nimble fingers unbuttoned his jeans. As she did, he nuzzled her chest heading lazily toward her pants. His hand gripped her belt just as his teeth grazed lightly over her perky nipple. She arched her back toward him. He had her pants open and descending toward the floor before she even noticed it. When she finally did pay attention that he had her nearly naked, her eyes went wide.

"What're you doing?" she squeaked, as she quickly reached down and grabbed the fabric. She pulled her pants up to her knees. "Gash."

"What do you think I'm doing?" Raiden paused and pushed back his hair. He bet Ash was the kind of girl that wanted to be on top. Well… she could be in charge—for a little bit. That he could give in to. "Do you want to take your clothes off by yourself? I can watch."

The idea made him grin. Watching her strip would be more fun than winning Boxcar Dice.

"Raiden, I…" Ash bit her bottom lip.

He wanted to lick her teeth. She wouldn't look at him. He was starting to hate that. Raiden liked it better when she glared with that I'm-better-than-you look.

"What?" He tipped forward until he was in her line of sight. "You want to be on top?" He placed a hand on both sides of the cot next to her thighs. "You can ride me. Get it? Ride-in?" Raiden inhaled again. Damn it all, she smelled like sunshine.

"Funny. No, it's just that I…" She finally looked at him. Her eyes glittered like polished chrome. "Blast it, I'm sputtering like Stone." Ash groaned, "Raiden, I…"

"What?" He pressed her shoulders back and dipped his head. He let his tongue travel all over her breasts again. When he hit her nipple, her back curved toward his mouth. A smile hung on his lips. He loved that. "What, Ashley?"

Her heavy jeans were still clutched in her fist and had risen to mid-thigh. He reached for her flexing fingers. She let go of the fabric, and slowly Raiden pushed them down. They hit her bulky boots.

"I've not…"

"What?" His eyes narrowed as he reached for her boot laces. "You've never had sex?"

She searched the ceiling. The silence made him nervous.

Ash Winsor was a virgin? That couldn't be right. He tried to recall someone bragging about Ash Winsor's sexual prowess. He remembered the whispers that *he* was the best lover on the trains. Raiden shook his head at how stupid he was. People had used the word "he" when they gossiped.

They all lied.

"Are you a virgin?"

"I'm not a virgin. It's just that I've not done this in a long time." She paused and then bent her head. She shoved off her boots and then peeled off her socks. "A long, long time." She glanced up as she shimmied out of her pants. "I was hurt the last time." Her jeans pooled to the floor exposing long, sexy legs. Her back straightened suddenly.

She glared as she lifted her chin. "Don't hurt me or I'll shoot you."

Raiden grinned. Her words stroked the ego he didn't even know he had. A long, long time? And she chose him? Even if this was just because of Weaver, he felt special. That tingling returned full force. His cock cheered.

"I'm going to make you scream, Ashley."

Her eyes narrowed, and her chin lifted a notch higher. "I'll shoot you."

"I meant it in a good way." He sighed. There was a sweet scent to Ash that he'd never noticed before. Her fragrance took him over. Her inexperience took him over as well.

"No one screams in a good way."

"I'll show you." Raiden pressed her back onto the cot until she was flat. Her legs dangled toward the floor. "You'll like what I do."

"I never pegged you as cocky."

"I've never pegged you as timid." He glanced at her underwear. What covered her mound were men's briefs, black with a gray elastic band. The masculine underwear made him grin.

"Timid about sex?" Her eyes searched his.

"About anything." Raiden hooked his thumbs into the band of her underwear and brought them to her knees. They slid off and hit the floor. He pictured those long legs wrapped around his waist.

"I'm not timid," she said raising one eyebrow.

"I know. Big, bad Ash Winsor." Using both hands, he massaged his way between her legs. He worked his way up toward the small patch of hair hiding the little button that would make her pant, scream, and come. He would touch Ash until she would want to start calling him king. Her eyes never left him as he leaned closer.

Tipping his head down, he stopped to, once again, breathe her in. She smelled like warmth.

"Should I shower?" She squirmed under his intent gaze, and her hand covered her chest. "I'd make a dog joke about the sniffing, but I think you're kinda touchy about the name."

"I'm not sniffing you; you just smell good. You smell like the kind of heat that could warm a man after an entire day of trekking on the surface of the planet. I've never noticed it before." His hands crept up the inside of her thighs. His thumbs stroked in lazy circles.

"You smell like fruit." Her hands rose to his hair and tunneled through the locks.

"It's called Mango Passion soap."

Ash giggled. "You wash with soap made for twelve-year-old girls."

"And you like it." With his fingertips, he gently pushed her legs further apart. "I guess, we've never been this close to each other before to notice."

"True." She wiggled again. "Should I just sit here?"

"Yes. You're amazing, Ashley, just like that." Raiden stroked through the patch of damp curls between her legs. He kissed her shoulders and nibbled on her neck. "You're so hot, like fire. Ash doesn't fit you." His breath came out as a pant over her skin. "Ash is too cold. A fire that's burnt out."

"Stone calls me Torch when we fight." Her eyes captured his when he lifted his head.

"Torch. That's better. You're more like a little torch. So hot." Raiden used his fingers to once again pet the glistening curls, but now he pushed her lips apart as he dropped to his knees.

"Bowing to King Winsor?" She grinned at him. "You want to beg me for something?"

"We'll see who's begging when I'm done."

His fingers pushed until her damp slit greeted him, swollen and waiting. Leaning his head forward, he licked languorously against her clit. The nub peeked out at him, asking for attention. Ash moaned. She tasted as good as she smelled. Better even.

Raiden used his tongue to investigate her tight channel, and her taste exploded on his tongue a second time. He might be able to get drunk off her cream. With long, broad strokes, he worked into her with first his tongue then his finger. He slipped into her slit up to his first knuckle. His thumb flicked her clit back and forth. His tongue followed. Ash's hips lifted, and another moan escaped her.

"I promised to make you scream," he whispered. "A moan is good but not good enough."

Raiden worked his finger into her tight body further and rubbed back and forth. Her wetness gathered and dripped. Her moaning continued. The muscles inside her body started to clench. Her head flipped back and forth as her hips began to rock on his hand. He sensed her climax was close. She repeated his name as he built the tempo. Without warning, she went over the edge.

Ash begged him not to stop as her back bowed and she shuddered. The cream that coated his fingers was better than anything he'd ever tasted. He licked the rest of her excess and then clutched her ass. He kissed the insides of her thighs as she murmured his name.

"Saying my name was good, and the begging was hot, but that wasn't a scream."

"I didn't know I could come like that. Fuck Weaver."

"Could you not say his name right now?" His eyes met hers and a grin spread on his face. "I'll just have to try again. I promised screaming, didn't I?"

"But I just—"

She didn't finish her sentence when he licked her clit again. He petted the curve of her ass as she wiggled. Yes, he would make her even wetter, and then he would slip inside of her and satisfy the iron pole in his pants. His damn cock pressed so uncomfortably he considered stopping, but he'd said screaming. He could do that. That competitive streak jabbed at him. He wouldn't disappoint Ash Winsor, and he was no liar. She would cry out. Raiden would apply every bit of knowledge he had to make that happen.

Raiden slipped his hands from her ass toward her slit once more. He was amused by the pale tones of his hands on her darker skin. He rubbed again, fluttering his fingers along her glistening inner thigh. She moaned and then groaned when he sank one finger in. The digit went deeper this time, and she squirmed.

"Don't hurt me." Her hand reached down and grabbed his wrist. Her small fingers dug into his arm.

"I won't. I'm no liar, little torch."

Ever so slowly, she let go and settled back on the cot. Raiden lifted her legs and placed them on his shoulders.

Raiden dipped his head and fastened his mouth to her clit. He sucked relentlessly, refusing to release the sensitive nub. He felt her thighs shake, and he wanted to smile. Her moans got louder. He'd have her screaming.

He built her orgasm like a man building a fire. He slipped a second finger inside next to the first. He twisted them slightly and hunted for the spot that would win him a shout. He held her clit to his lips and flicked the tip with his tongue. Again, the squeezing of her muscles began. She bucked, but he kept the suction. Finally, he rubbed just the right spot.

Ash's hips rose off the bed, and she ground on his face. She screamed his name over and over again. Her hand landed on the back of his head. More of her liquid heat coated his chin.

After a few minutes, she flopped backward. Raiden was finally free to study her.

"There's the scream I promised. You're amazing, little torch."

"I'm not little. I'm six-foot." She giggled. The sound of her giggle made him smile. It was a strange sound like the laugh was rusty, but he wanted her to make it again. *Skit*, he wanted to see Ash Winsor happy.

"Doubt it. You're not the same height as me, but I won't fight with you." He stayed between her legs and kissed the back of her knees. His mouth feathered upward. "What do you say to another round?" He tugged at his too-tight jeans.

She leaned up on her elbows. "Another round of fighting with you?" Her eyebrows came down. "I don't want to do that, Raiden. At least, not right now."

He chuckled.

"No, not arguing." His fingers brushed at the damp curls still coated with his saliva. "Although, good to know that we can argue later. I'm sure you have plenty of insults for me." He slipped his fingers between her lips. "Now who needs time to figure out what we're talking about? I'll give you a second."

Her eyes widened. "I don't need a second to—"

A knock stopped her sentence. Both their eyes popped to the door. He had just gotten Ash to light up like a torch filled with ethanol and acetone. He didn't want the interruption. What now?

Chapter 3

"Get the door, Mutt." Ash hopped from the cot and rushed to the bathroom. The door was closed before Raiden could get annoyed at her high-handed order and the name. He supposed he was just going to have to get used to her arrogant side. Well, she could instruct him all she liked, but when it came to sex, she caved like thin ice. When it came to the bedroom, dare he think it, Ash was *docile.*

He rose and kicked his discarded coat to the side as he reached the door. The knock came again just as he opened it enough to peer out.

"I gotta piss." Morgan-Roth stood in the hall leaning on his heavy-duty carved walking stick.

Raiden kept himself from slamming the door at the intrusion and dropped his arms to his side. Morgan-Roth hurried past him. The other man's eyes bounced around the room to the clothes on the floor and to Raiden's half-naked frame.

"Open up, Ash. I gotta go." Morgan-Roth used one knuckle to tap on the door.

The door opened, and Ash stepped out wearing Raiden's shirt. When did she snag that? Ash tugged on the hem where the fabric fell to her thigh.

"I thought I told you to guard Weaver?"

"And pee on the floor?" Morgan-Roth plowed past her and shoved her out into the room. She stumbled, and Raiden caught her in his arms as the door to the bathroom closed.

"Gospel-pusher," she called behind her.

Her beautiful eyes rose to his, and she leaned back. Ash pressed her body closer, and Raiden took the invitation. His lips met hers.

Before he could think about how Morgan-Roth was in the toilet room, he kissed her like he would never stop. He felt dizzy, high, and hot. When he kissed her like this, the pain in his joints faded away. She ground her hips against his erection as he gripped her ass. *Helvete*, she hadn't put on her underwear. Her hand found the outline of his cock trying to break out of his partially open jeans. His body pleaded. Ash's hand closed over the underwear where his dick strained and twitched. Her eyes fluttered opened as she pulled her mouth away.

"That's not gonna fit."

Was she nervous? Her unease was sexy. He wanted to be the man to chase her apprehension away. He grinned.

"It'll fit," he murmured into her hair. "I'll work it in nice and slow and have you screaming again. All night, Ashley."

A cough had Ash flipping her head to look at Morgan-Roth in the doorway. The other harvester's massive muscled frame took up the entire opening.

"Before you go fitting anything anywhere, I've something I want to say to you both."

Raiden always thought it appeared like Morgan-Roth's shirt was about to rip at the seams. His body reminded him of a comic book he'd seen on the surface. The Hulk was green, however, not dark chocolate. He supposed he couldn't tell "The Hulk" to mind his own business.

"Fine. Say it, then go." Raiden's eyes pointedly snapped to the exit. He didn't need Ash's companion spoiling his night.

Morgan-Roth entered the tiny room making the cramped space feel even smaller.

Raiden tipped his head to the side as he pondered why the harvester would even care what he and Ash did. What did it matter if they fucked?

"Are you and Ashley in a devoted, steadfast relationship now?" Morgan-Roth's eyes studied them in turn.

"Devoted?" Raiden's eyebrows rose. Talk about killing the mood and trying out a comedy routine all at the same time.

"Steadfast?" Ash unwound herself from his arms. Raiden reluctantly let her go.

"Committed." Morgan-Roth's deep voice rumbled.

"Committed like I'm in an insane asylum." Ash heaved an aggravated sigh and then climbed up on the cot and crossed her legs. "Fine. Let me have it, Mo-gee; then go and watch Weaver and leave us alone."

Morgan-Roth crossed his arms over his chest, and the fabric struggled to keep the muscles covered.

"Have what?" Raiden glanced at the two of them.

"The speech." Ash tossed out her arms. "Go on."

"You sit too." Morgan-Roth pointed to the cot.

Sit? Raiden didn't know enough about Morgan-Roth to let his guard down that much. Was he the kind of man

Raiden should trust? The only thing Raiden knew about the harvester was that he often traveled with Ash. Some said they were siblings, two hard-core Fletcher Davis' kids together. Others said they were lovers. People could only speculate about Morgan-Roth—and Stone. The three of them didn't give out information.

Raiden leaned his butt against the cot as he considered "Mo-gee." Only Ash could probably get away with calling a big man like that a silly nickname. Morgan-Roth tipped his head to the cot and pursed his lips when Raiden didn't sit. He felt like a naughty child.

"I'm glad I caught you before you had sex."

"Who said we didn't?" Raiden lifted one eyebrow.

"The still-hard penis in your pants says you didn't." Morgan-Roth shook his head at Raiden's crotch. "Anyway, I've been praying about the two of you together, and I've decided it would make me feel better to know your intentions."

"My intentions?" Ash scoffed.

"You prayed?" What a strange thing for a harvester to say. People didn't pray unless an avalanche was about to fall on their heads.

"I've seen you both squabble over the last two years." Morgan-Roth studied his wooden walking stick. "You'd insult each other and gripe, yet I could tell you were drawn to each other like you couldn't help it. Moth to the torch, if you will."

"I suppose I'm the moth here?"

"It's not me." Ash snickered. "Torch." She pointed to herself.

"And if this is just going to be sex, I want you both to know that I'm disappointed. I expect more from you. I want you to put away your resentment and grow."

For the first time, Raiden noted a cross carved into the side of the massive cane. Morgan-Roth's huge hands traced the religious symbol.

"Oh, come on, Mo-gee; don't use the disappointment-learn-to-grow speech on me. I'm not Stone."

"I know who you are." Morgan-Roth's eyes narrowed at Ash, and then he turned to him. "So, do you plan to work this out? Are you staying? Loyalty? Fidelity? When life gets difficult, you can't run away."

"You want the moth to give loyalty to the torch? Moths die in the flame." Raiden wondered if he should lie or tell the truth. He'd gone back and forth on whether he should work out his situation with Ash or convince Weaver to split them up. Those thoughts had been in his head all the way up to the moment he and Ash had kissed.

"Is that a yes or no?" Morgan-Roth asked.

The ache in his joints returned with a steady throb. Raiden didn't know what to say.

"What are you going to do?" The harvester eyeballed him.

"I might fuck Ash then figure out a way to split." The words left his mouth before he could stop them. Raiden sucked in a sharp breath. He hadn't planned on saying that. He had to fix what he'd just blurted out. Raiden thought fast. "I don't even know if I like Ash. All we've ever done is clash. She's hot though." Raiden snapped his mouth closed. What the hell was happening?

"I'd hoped you were deeper than that." Morgan-Roth wagged his head slowly.

"I thought about fucking Ash even when I thought she was a man. She gets to me, not just her looks. Ash is more than just her gender. It's her strength I like." Raiden closed his eyes as embarrassment made him want to jump under the train. Why couldn't he keep his mouth shut? He'd never said that out loud. Not to anyone. Ever.

"Really?" Ash asked, and his eyes popped open. "The moth has a hidden desire to get close to the flame." A smile lingered on her lips. He glared at her.

"Did you give me a truth serum or something? Treacle?" Raiden glanced back to Morgan-Roth. "What the hell was that?"

"Morgan-Roth can make you say what you think even if you don't want to." Ash shrugged. "It comes in handy in the confessional."

"Confessional?"

"Mo-gee is a priest. I thought you knew that."

"Franciscan." Morgan-Roth smiled with bright white teeth. Raiden shoved his hair away from his face. The guy was a priest? What the hell was a religious dude doing on a harvest train?

"I guess, all the guys who said you were a Fletcher got it wrong," he blurted and then shut his mouth again. He'd better stop talking before he made an ass of himself, or maybe it was already too late.

"Fletcher Davis was my father." Morgan-Roth shrugged again. "But I came to talk about you two, not who I am." He turned to Ash. "And you plan to have sex then leave?"

"I'm attracted to Raiden. I thought I'd get off then see what Raiden wanted to do. I thought I could get Weaver to separate us before we got off the train. It's too painful to have the same relationship I have with Stone. When people get close, it's risky." She wouldn't look at him.

The two of them had the same thoughts about separating.

Raiden wondered how he felt about her admission. Every joint in his body throbbed in opposition to the idea, but he ignored the pain. What did he want to do? His eyes started a journey at the top of Ash's black hair and then traveled leisurely to her toes. Leaving her is what he wanted to do, wasn't it? Why did hearing the intention from her lips make him second-guess the idea?

"It makes the most sense," Raiden said slowly as his eyes met Ash's. "We've never even said a kind word to each other. I don't think we can get along. We should get Weaver to unhook us." That was logical.

"I don't know what I'm going to do." She exhaled. "But I don't see any reason I can't have a little bit of pleasure. Gash, Mo-gee, can't a girl have one or two orgasms? I think I've earned it after being celibate for two and a half years."

"Two and a half years?" When she said a long time, she meant it.

No one responded to Raiden's outburst.

"I've been praying, and I think God sent Raiden to help you and Stone. This world is complicated, and you both need support."

"Fan-fucking-tastic. Stone is just the guy I want to help." Raiden glanced at the door. What did he need to do to get rid of Morgan-Roth? As far as Raiden was concerned, his sex life was none of the priest's, or Stone's, business. If he and Ash stayed together or split up, that was between Ash and him. Besides, Ash and he were on the same track. They both planned to come and then walk away. If he left now, or she left him later, it didn't matter. The leaving is what would happen eventually. He refused to expect anything different. Holding on to hope where love was concerned would make him as big of a gullible dupe as his father.

"God has nothing to do with Weaver being an asshole. He was always that way," Ash snapped.

Raiden couldn't argue with that. Weaver was a terrible person. He doubted the Indian had sincerely changed.

"You know I'm leaving, Ash, but I've been dragging my feet. I must keep searching just like you, but I know that you and Stone haven't got it all worked out yet. So, I've stayed, but I think Raiden is the bridge that you and Stone need."

"I don't need anyone." Ash crossed her arms over her chest. "I especially don't need a bridge."

"So, now I'm a bridge and a moth." Raiden crossed his arms over his chest. "I guess, it's better than *Mutt*."

"Ash Winsor." Morgan-Roth's voice became deep and heavy. "I want you to make a deal with me. What is it that you and Stone always say to each other?"

"If you wanna win, you gotta bet." Ash scooted to the end of the cot. "What's the deal?"

"Bet on Raiden. Get to know him. Give this time. If you truly don't belong together, only then should you split up. I'm disappointed to think you'd use each other for sex and then move on. That's not a healthy way to live your life, for either one of you."

Ash glared. Raiden couldn't look at the priest. The word "disappointed" coming from a priest made him feel two feet tall.

"Fine. I'll give it a day." Ash gave a casual shrug. Raiden laughed and then covered the snicker with a cough.

"A day?" Morgan-Roth's face soured. "I mean it. Get to know him. Let Raiden help." His eyes flipped back and forth between Ash and him. "Let someone take care of you for a change."

"Two days." Ash's eyes jumped to him. "I won't kill him for two days." She smiled.

"I might kill you." Raiden grinned back. Ash snorted.

Morgan-Roth tossed a dirty look their way. "I'm thinking at least a month."

"A month!" they said in unison. Ash gazed at him and he stared back. No way. That was impossible. The more Morgan-Roth talked, the more he realized that Ash and he was a bad idea. Ash was prickly and standoffish. Raiden thought relationships never worked. Plus, Ash has some weird relationship with Stone. All in all, Raiden knew this would be a train wreck in a few days.

As Raiden gazed at Ash, he began to fully recognize that he knew very little about her. Her life appeared to be much more complicated than he first thought. He shouldn't get involved. Raiden was a relaxed go-with-the-flow harvester who barely had enough HOCs to buy food. He was a vagabond, not a pillar of strength. They could fuck, but that was it. He would leave before either one of them started to care.

"A week," Ash snapped. "That's the best I can do."

"Two weeks." Morgan-Roth headed toward the door like he already knew Ash would say yes. Well, Raiden wouldn't agree to that. Did Morgan-Roth just think that he would follow Ash around blindly? He didn't follow anyone. If he was honest with himself, he let the train lead the way.

"Ten days." Ash sighed. "But after that, if I decide to break the bond, then I'm gonna do it. If Stone isn't okay with this, then I'm out."

Morgan-Roth stopped in the doorway. "Raiden? I would like your word. Ten days."

"No." He felt awkward under the priest's steady gaze. *Helvete.*

"What's ten days? I believe that you'll be happy with Ash and Stone. Besides, you'd have someone to trek with other than Doug."

Raiden winced. Did Morgan-Roth know how Doug used him? Did other harvesters know? He was ashamed that someone had found out how low he'd stooped to get money. He gave an exasperated exhale. What was the best way to tell a priest to take a hike? Especially a priest who looked like he could kick his ass.

"Why do you keep tossing in Stone like he's part of the deal?"

"He *is* part of the deal." Ash shrugged. "He's my best friend."

"He's probably your *only* friend." Raiden grinned at her. She leaned over and shoved his shoulder.

"Ten days." Morgan-Roth's deep voice dared them to argue. "I'll expect you to keep your word."

"I can do it," Ash stated. The way she said it, made it sound like Raiden couldn't. If Ash Winsor could play nice with him for ten days, he could as well. He never thought he'd be in a relationship, and basically avoided them after watching his parents split, but this time he thought ten days was possible.

"If Ash Winsor can do ten days, then I can."

"Whatever, slush-head." She shoved his shoulder a second time.

"Then you have my blessing." Morgan-Roth smiled as he opened the door and stepped into the hallway. "You'll make a great bridge."

Chapter 4

As soon as the door closed behind Morgan-Roth, Raiden looked to Ash.

"He's a wet blanket."

"Yeah."

Raiden climbed up on the cot next to her and leaned his head against the wall. His dick was now at half-mast, and he contemplated getting his motor running again. Ash's room was nothing but intrusions and interruptions.

"Should I expect Stone next? Is he a monk?"

"No, slush-head." Ash laughed and punched his arm. "Stone is off somewhere fucking, I bet. If it's human and says yes, he does it. He'll be around later." Ash's tone didn't sound happy that her friend might be having a good time. Raiden studied every nuance of her face. Was that jealousy?

"What's the deal with him?"

"Nothing." Ash shrugged and dropped a mask of indifference over her features. "He thinks I'm a man."

"After two years? How come he thinks you're a man, but Morgan-Roth knows the truth?" Maybe she didn't trust

Stone, then again, if she didn't trust him, then why trek with him?

"I met Morgan-Roth the day I was raped. He's seen me without my gear. He's seen me as naked as the day I was born."

The silence that descended between them after that sentence stole the last of his hard-on. It also bunched his muscles ready to kill whoever touched his woman. He gulped down the shimmering fury and unexpected rage. He took a deep breath and then glanced at Ash. She had her head tipped back on the wall, and she stared at the ceiling. Hollering about the fucker who hurt her probably wasn't what she wanted. He didn't know much about women, especially a woman like Ash, but he understood listening. Before he had to leave his dad, listening was all he could do.

"You don't have to talk about it unless you want to."

"I can talk about it. I'm a lot better now. Sometimes it feels like it happened a lifetime ago to a different person. I'm not the same woman I was. I've spent heaps of time thinking about it and talking to Mo-gee, and I guess, I learned to deal with what happened."

"Who hurt you?" Did he want to know so he could find the guy and kill him? He might. "Does Stone know any of this?" Raiden had the notion that if Stone knew, her "best friend" would have killed the man by now.

"No, Stone doesn't know. If I told him, I'd have to explain about me and hiding my gender. Stone tends to run at the first sign of trouble. It's complicated, and it's better this way."

Raiden didn't think it sound that complicated.

"Just Morgan-Roth knows?"

"Yes, Mo-gee knows. The guy's name was Felix Fletcher. We had a thing. I was young, and I thought he was the brill." Ash offered him a sad smile.

"Brill?"

"Brilliant."

"The guy was a Fletcher? Like Morgan-Roth?" Raiden had heard that Fletcher Davis had kids out there. Morgan-Roth was the first person who admitted that was true. Harvesters on the trains gossiped that the H.S.P.C. had it out for The Originals. People said that the Fletchers still ran the organization, and no one claimed the name. Raiden glanced at Ash. He'd never heard of anyone meeting a real-life Fletcher before now.

"My uncle knew Felix was a Fletcher. Everyone knew. My uncle even warned me he was bad news, but I didn't care. In the beginning, my uncle made sure he didn't know I was a woman. We agreed that was the way it would be. My uncle wanted to protect me as much as he could when we started to ride the trains. Eventually, I thought I knew what was best, and I told Felix I was a woman. We started a relationship, if you could call it that. Mostly he was a smarmy git, and I slept with him pretending that he loved me and that I'd be the one to change him. I don't do stupid shite like that anymore. If you have a badger, you can't hope it's going to change into a fish."

"I take it Felix didn't change."

"No one changes. They are who they are." Ash paused and then looked at Raiden. "The snow was on the ground from the start. One day, I told him I was worth more than the way he treated me. I kept thinking if my parents were alive and they saw what an ice storm my life had become and how he used me, they'd be sickened. And so, I kicked him to the platform."

"He didn't like that." What happened with Doug crowded into his brain. He pushed the memory out.

"It wasn't pretty. A year later, Felix came back, and he assaulted me." Her voice dropped to a painful whisper. "I never thought he'd return. It was horrible." She swiped at a few tears on her lashes.

"I'm sorry, Ash."

"Blast it, I don't need pity."

"It's not pity. Trust me when I say I know what it's like to underestimate someone. To misjudge a relationship."

Ash nodded. "Yeah, I should've never underestimated Felix."

"And Morgan-Roth was there?" Raiden tried to figure out how the priest fell into all of this.

"That night, Felix took something precious from me, and I fell apart. That same evening, Morgan-Roth showed up to stop his brother. He was too late. While he closed the cuts on my face, Mo-gee told me he wanted to make up for what Felix had done. Morgan-Roth said he would help me as best he could. We got off to a rocky start. I didn't trust him, priest or not."

"I don't blame you." Trusting a Fletcher took courage, but trusting the brother of your rapist took Herculean strength. A new respect for Ash Winsor grew. She was more than what she appeared when she walked around all cocksure of herself on the trains.

"Even though they share the same blood, I still learned to see past Mo-gee's last name. If he's asking me to put up with you for ten days, I can. I owe him for the help he's given me for the last two years. He's been trekking with me since Felix beat me up."

"And Stone doesn't know any of this?" Raiden couldn't understand that. If they were so close, why not tell him? She said "best friend" every time Stone was brought up. "Don't you trust him?"

"I trust him. It's just that Stone scares easily. It's better this way. I lead. He follows. We don't have to be any more than that for now." Her hand slipped to his, and silence settled between them like a thick fog. He tried to take a deep breath and concentrate on her palm pressed against his. The tingles in his chest returned. The ache in his shoulders subsided. He tried to push away the growing feeling and the way his blood rushed.

"You should tell your shadow who you are," he said to get his mind off her smooth skin.

"I'm going to tell Stone tomorrow."

More silence sat between them. Raiden shifted uncomfortably, but not because of his joint pain.

"Does this make what we have been doing off limits?" Raiden rubbed his thumb back and forth over the back of her hand. His body was working overtime to convince him that Ash was still his. Didn't he just promise a priest to be with her? His stomach fluttered as he stared into her silver eyes. "I don't know where to go from here. After what you told me, maybe sex isn't a good idea. We can just talk."

"Talk?" Ash gave a husky laugh. "What are we? Twelve-year-old girls giggling at a sleepover?"

"I feel like I'm pushing you." Raiden was a decent person. He should get up and leave.

"You couldn't push me anywhere, slush-head." Her hand let go of his, and she stroked his thigh. "I do what I want. Ash Winsor is king."

"Of course, you are. You're king of the trains." Raiden laughed then sobered. "What now?"

"Is the moth still attracted to the torch?" Her voice held hesitation. "Even after what I told you?" Ash turned to face him. Her silver eyes examined his face.

"Yes." He ran his fingers down her cheek. "Do you still want me here, like this? Should I stay?"

"I feel restless when I'm around you, Raiden. Most of the time it was just easier to tell you to go to hell, but right now I don't want to fight with you. I want to feel you. I want you to stay." Her eyes dropped to his mouth. "I'm a nutter, I know."

"I don't think you're crazy. This energy is because of Weaver." He wasn't sure any longer if that was true or not; however, he did understand what she was saying. He didn't want to argue with her. The tingling in his body wouldn't lessen. Raiden yearned to be inside of her. A part of him had been interested in Ash Winsor from the first second she'd stepped up on the platform with Stone by her side.

"I don't know if it's Weaver. You got under my skin the first time I set eyes on you." She paused. "And apparently that's the same for you."

"I don't know what you're talking about." Raiden looked down at his lap.

"You wanted to fuck me even when you thought I was a man?" Ash phrased it as a question, but she smiled like she was teasing him.

"It's just Weaver." Raiden pushed back his hair.

"Weaver or not, I want to satiate it. Is it possible we can just shove all this rubbish to the side for a few hours?" She tugged on a few strands of his hair. "I can be with you for a few hours. Ashley, not Ash Winsor."

"I can do whatever you can do, Torch."

"I think we just made our first deal, moth." Ash grinned. "Should we shake on it?"

"Kiss on it."

"Slush-head—"

Raiden cut her off, capturing her mouth with his.

He licked her gently and then stared into her eyes. He eased into her, into her mouth and body. He kissed her lips until they fell apart even further. Raiden nibbled at the lower curve, and her ragged response spurred him to tug her down onto the mattress.

Watching her lashes flutter, he smiled when her hands clenched on his upper arms, digging her fingers in like she would never let go. That tight grip of her hands stirred his heart. It might be Weaver, he was sure it was just the bond that jerk created, but right now it felt real, too real. The tie was deeper than flesh. The connection was deep enough that it made his bones relax.

Raiden didn't know what he was doing anymore, so he gave in. He followed Ash's tongue and kissed her until his whole body felt like his limbs floated. Ash's breathing was harsh and irregular. Her tantalizing full breasts rose and moved against his naked chest. He wanted to fill his hands with the globes under that shirt. Feeling her pebbled nipples against him and feeling his tongue sliding over her skin once more would be heaven. He wanted to devour her and let her absorb him.

For once in his life, the throbbing ache in his body vanished. He would follow Ash anywhere if this pain disappeared.

"Raiden." Her soft plea washed over his ears. He was probably moving too fast. He needed to slow down, but her skin felt so damn good.

"Ashley?" He lifted his head, and her eyes dilated with desire. The silver turned black with arousal. Slowing down seemed impossible.

"If someone knocks on the door again." She cupped his cheek with one hand as her thumb ran along his lips. "Don't answer it. Deal?"

"Deal." Raiden swallowed hard. "I'm not opening that door for anyone." He could feel her heating in his arms. There was no way he would let even a harvester offering him a thousand HOCs in here.

Raiden nipped at her lower lip, and she smiled. His hand moved to her shoulder and then journeyed down her back. His other hand tugged at the bottom of the shirt. As his hand caressed her stomach, he watched her eyes. Her expression, every wave of emotion that flickered over her face unguarded. Vulnerable, open Ash was sexier than he could ever have imagined. Knowing she wanted this, that he was going to take care of her, was overwhelming. He didn't want her afraid of him. He gripped her shirt and lifted.

Once naked, a quiver passed down her spine. He noted the slight ripple. That small movement fanned the flames between them. Inside his body, heat and longing grew out of control. The tingling under his skin became unbearable. He wanted to rip off his pants and shove himself into her tight warmth. But now knowing her past, he ruthlessly leashed the unruly passion.

Touching her was addicting, and the more he petted her soft skin, the more he wanted to stroke. He fluttered his fingers over the satin of her thighs before pressing his fingers between her legs. Her lips parted the same time her thighs did. She drew in air sharply.

"Don't hurt me."

"I won't hurt you, Ashley," he whispered as his fingertips brushed her clit. "You're so much stronger than me, remember? Big, bad Ash Winsor." He wanted to remove the worry that still lingered.

"That's right, tough guy." She paused. "Why do you still have your pants on?" Her eyes raked his body, and he smiled. She might be nervous, but Winsor wasn't a chicken.

Quickly, he rose and dropped his jeans and underwear to the floor. His cock bounced forward, thick and heavy. The swollen head pointed toward the ceiling. Ash's silver eyes went smoky.

"I thought Chinese dudes had small dicks. That's what harvesters say."

"My dad's mostly Swedish, and I'm half Japanese."

"Yeah, well, whatever you are, that's not gonna fit." Her eyes raked his body a second time. She looked at him like he was an idiot.

"It'll fit."

She didn't say anything more, and Raiden expected her to make some sort of demand from him. Instead of speaking, she scooted to the middle of the cot and then set her head on the pillow. He admired her strength. Ash Winsor was no coward.

Raiden climbed up on the bed and pinned her to the mattress. His cock slid between her parted thighs and rubbed along her damp skin. She was so wet he thought he might lose his mind. He groaned as he hugged his arms around her. His erection wedged between them perfectly. She was so hot. The heat radiating off her took his breath away and made him euphoric. He was ready to burst because of the first interruption and now the waiting, but he could stand it. He held himself in check and worked to forget the itch under his skin. As she licked his lips, he closed his eyes. He could still taste her on his tongue. He wanted her to come again, and he wanted her to scream a second time—while he was deep inside of her.

"I like the way you feel against me." He kissed her shoulder and then nuzzled her neck. That smell of sunshine still lingered on her skin.

Ash tilted her head and offered a grin before gliding her palms up his shoulders. "What are you waiting for? Do I need to give you a second?"

"I don't need a second." He grinned before he took her mouth in a dizzying kiss. He loved her mouth, so supple. He loved the way she yanked on his hair. She pulled him to her hard like they could kiss for hours. Raiden shifted and then lifted his upper body until he braced himself on his arms. He stared at his cock as the head nudged against her wet slit and held his breath. She didn't tell him no.

Ash parted her legs, then grabbed his wrist. Her fingers dug in, and he didn't know if she held him close out of passion or fear.

"Do you need a second?"

"I need this, here and now."

Raiden glided inside of her slow and easy, while he clenched his teeth. Her channel was so incredibly tight he thought he might pass out. He needed to breathe. She pulsed and squeezed around him, and he was sure he had never felt anything this hot or this stimulating. He lifted his gaze to her face praying he didn't see pain. Her lips were clamped shut, and her eyes searched his. He rolled his hips, and she let out a heady moan.

"I'll make you scream."

"Okay, tough guy. Make me scream."

He smiled. She still held firmly to his wrist, and her nails dug in deep. He pulled out part way and then pushed in a little deeper. She arched her back. He could tell she liked that.

So did he.

He pressed down harder on top of her, as he used his hand to cup her ass. He gripped the firm flesh and lifted her so he could fit her even more tightly to his body.

He thrust again, and she let out a louder grasp. Her channel rippled in response and stretched around him. He had to close his eyes and take a calming breath so he didn't come with just that movement alone.

"More, Raiden, move," she commanded.

"Yeah, Torch, I know."

He kissed her and was quickly lost in the feeling of her breasts rubbing against his chest. Her nipples dragged along his pecs, and they convinced his hips to roll forward. He had to get closer to her core. She moaned, and he knew he wouldn't stop until she screamed. He wouldn't let Ash Winsor down. If she had waited years for this, then he would deliver mind-blowing sex.

Bending his head, he licked one nipple, then the other. He was hooked on the sound she made when he sucked. Somewhere along the way, her cries of pleasure became his new direction.

Raiden began to gently rock her into the cot. Her hips lifted to meet his. He couldn't stand the slow pace any longer. He started to pick up speed. His hands tightened to pull her closer to his pelvis, and he knew at any second he would shoot. He gulped down the building climax and slid in deeper and deeper. She was so wet he thought he might be covered with her juices for days after this was over. He would be so deep inside of her he would never be able to get out again. The idea scared him, but it didn't stop him.

Raiden intensified the friction. He positioned her, so he could rub her clit with every thrust. Again and again, her head tossed against the pillow. She closed her eyes, and her hips lifted out of his hand. She cried out for more, and he gave in. Whatever Ash Winsor wanted, she could have.

Grinding against her, he felt her inner walls contract around his erection. She milked him while her hand found his back. Her nails dug into his hips. She shouted his name just as she exploded.

He wanted to watch her come. He tried to make her scream, but he lost his mind. Her lips parted in a pant, and he kept up his ruthless pace. Her head tilted back, and her eyes shut. She looked like he felt, in ecstasy.

Even though he wanted the feeling to never end, he couldn't hold out any longer. Without his approval, his climax tore through him. The force of his orgasm sent every nerve ending in his body on fire. He tingled from head to toe. The pain in his joints that generally hounded him turned into a flash of electricity. The zing burned up his spine. His bones finally thawed.

Raiden buried his face in the crook of Ash's neck as the searing, intense pleasure zipped down to his toes. Never had he felt an orgasm that powerful and involved before.

He groaned as aftershocks made him tremble. Sweat flattened down his hair, and he brushed at the locks. Raiden continued to rock, feeling her shift under him as he emptied the last of his come.

Sex had never been like this. What did Weaver do?

Spent, he licked her salty skin and kissed her jaw. He rolled them onto their side, staying connected. He had a hard time letting her go. After sex, he normally got up and left. On a harvester train where the relationships were rarely concrete, it was expected that the person didn't linger, but he couldn't bring himself to do that. He toyed with her short black hair as he inhaled their combined scent in the air.

"Do you want me to leave?" He prayed she would say no. He didn't know what being together looked like, but he hoped he could hold her for at least a few minutes. It felt right to have Ash pressed next to him.

"I thought you said when a moth gets close to a torch, it dies." She lifted her head. "Are you dead?"

Raiden laughed. "Yeah, I'm dead. I don't want to move."

"That's too bad. I hoped you'd make good on your promise." She smiled at him then moaned when he shifted closer to her. "I didn't scream."

Raiden chuckled.

"I'll make good on it." His dick already started to twitch with just that thought. He pressed even closer to her as his eyes tried to flutter closed. His back burned where her scratches were etched into his skin, but the rest of his body felt fantastic. He floated on clouds. "I need a second."

"I'll give you a second to catch up." He heard the smile in her voice just as he closed his eyes.

Chapter 5

A warm hand slipped around Raiden's waist. The feel of the hot palm brought him to consciousness. He sat up disoriented. After shoving his tangled hair out of his face, Raiden glanced to Ash Winsor. She rolled away from him and faced the wall. Everything that had happened last night came screaming back to him with crystal clear clarity. *Helvete*. What was he going to do? He was attracted to her. He wanted her, but this feeling might only be because of what Weaver did to them. These emotions might not be real. Deep down, he wanted a significant connection, a long-lasting relationship. Not just ten days of pretending. He couldn't end up like his dad. Raiden would rather be alone.

"Ash." He shook her shoulder. They should talk. Morgan-Roth had said they should get to know each other. He would start right now. He didn't care if she called him a twelve-year-old girl. Maybe he could make this meaningful, not love, but a bond close to that.

"Lemme be." Ash rolled over onto her belly and buried her head under her pillow. Well, that was no way to start a conversation.

"Ash?" He shook her again. She gave him the finger. Fan-fucking-tastic. Apparently, she wasn't a morning person, and he was. He needed to work out what they would do for the ten days. He rubbed his eyes as he rose to his feet. Okay, so they would have to learn what the other person liked and disliked. They could talk about what they wanted out of life. He wanted to travel and send money home. He didn't have a lot of aspirations. Maybe that would be alright with her.

He bent over and scooped his underwear off the floor. Just as he had the briefs up, a knock sounded at the door. Raiden should've figured their peace wouldn't last. Ash's room was busier than a water base gate.

Raiden crossed to the entrance of the sleeping room and paused with his hand on the handle. If this was Stone, that meeting would be a disaster. What would he say to that guy? He was Ash's "best friend." She cared about him, and Raiden had the sinking notion that the other man might not want Raiden tagging along, no matter what the duration.

Moth, bridge, whatever he was to Ash, it didn't matter. He was here now, and Stone would have to get used to his shadow—at least until Raiden moved on.

The next knock was insistent.

"Who is it?" Raiden's voice was gravelly. He coughed.

"Morgan-Roth."

"Hey." Raiden opened the door with a smooth sweep of his arm. Would the priest give them another lecture?

"Took you long enough." Morgan-Roth plowed past him and into the bathroom. Raiden grinned at the partly closed door. It sounded like someone turned on a fire hose. "Had to pee," Morgan-Roth called over the stream.

Right. First, he pissed, *then* he lectured them.

"Ash, Morgan-Roth is here. Again." Raiden used that fact to see if it would rouse the sleeping woman. She kept her head buried and pulled a blanket up to cover her body. She evidently didn't care about the priest's visit.

Morgan-Roth appeared out of the bathroom and glanced to Ash and then to him dressed in only his underwear.

"How'd things go?" Morgan-Roth leaned against his walking stick. His eyes swept Raiden's naked chest.

"Go?" Raiden cleared his throat again. Did the priest want to know about the sex? He pushed some of his hair back. "You want details?"

"Not that." Morgan-Roth took a quick step backward. "Did you talk? Get to know each other?"

"Ash and I still haven't gotten around to talking." Though they should have talked, not just fucked all night. "I want her to get up." He tapped her leg. Better late than never.

Morgan-Roth chuckled. "Best to find a way to keep yourself busy. She doesn't wake before noon, and even then, it's iffy."

Raiden glanced at the lump of comforters that had Ash hidden.

"Have you seen Stone?" Morgan-Roth asked as he headed for the door. "I was guarding Weaver's room, and I nodded off. I thought he might've come this way, and I missed him. I thought I'd talk to him first, about Ash. He knows I'm leaving when we get to Bosstown. I'm going to meet up with my brother."

"Felix?" Just saying his name made Raiden's hands twitch to punch a wall. If he ever saw the man, he would kill him.

"No, Silo." Morgan-Roth shrugged. "I have a few brothers." Morgan-Roth started for the door. "Anyway, if you see Stone, tell him I want to talk to him."

"What should I say to him about me and Ash?" That was a burning question in his head since last night, and he still didn't have a clue as to how to deal with Ash's shadow.

Morgan-Roth traced the cross on his walking stick. "I don't know that I can help you. I travel with Ash, and I keep her secret, but Stone and I haven't shared more than three words. There's a separation there, one I can't break through. The guy can't finish a sentence. He's always flustered, and he's not that bright. He's also always at Ash's beck and call. You'll figure out the best way to communicate with him. You're the bridge. I'm sure of it."

"Stone doesn't finish a sentence and he's dumb?" That wasn't how Raiden pictured the guy. He thought of him as the strong silent type. Good looking, and arrogant because he knew it. He didn't picture him as a bumbling idiot. "Is he stupid around Ash or everyone?" Raiden didn't picture Ash patient with a fool.

"He's always with Ash." Morgan-Roth looked thoughtful. "It's like he can't leave her alone. Kinda like how you couldn't leave her alone, only with fewer insults. A fellow moth."

None of that sounded quite right, but Raiden couldn't figure out why the explanation bothered him.

"Just talk to Ash about it." Morgan-Roth stopped at the exit.

"I will if she ever wakes up."

"Here's some advice. There's a side pocket on her bag with a can of instant coffee. Give her a few tablespoons of that, and she'll get up. Now, I have to get back to sitting in front of Weaver's room." Morgan-Roth held the door handle. "I'd prefer to be having a difficult conversation with Ash right now than sitting in the hall. That's how bored I am."

"Why don't you read a bible?" Raiden joked.

"I gave mine away." Morgan-Roth's expression turned earnest.

Raiden paused from heading over to Ash's pack and instead crossed to his bag on the floor. He pulled the puzzle cube with the different colors out of the side pocket.

"Here," he tossed the plastic toy to the priest, "try to get all the sides on the cube one color. It might help pass the time."

Morgan-Roth caught the cube then held it out. "Do what now?"

Raiden took a few steps closer and snatched the puzzle out of the other man's hand.

"Watch." Raiden twisted the sides until all of them were one solid color on each side. "This is what it looks like when you have it all figured out." After he held the cube up, he turned the sides again until every color was jumbled once more.

"That looks easy."

"I thought it was." Raiden shrugged. "But I've always been good at putting puzzles together."

Morgan-Roth pointed to Ash before he headed out the door. "Coffee might help you with the puzzle of Ash Winsor and Stone."

As soon as Morgan-Roth was gone, Raiden set about finding the coffee can. Coffee wasn't normally a food that harvesters carried. How did Ash get this?

After going over the directions, he got a cup of water from the bathroom and used his can heater to bring the water to a boil. He scooped the grounds into the cup as he watched the blankets move. Morgan-Roth was right. This was how to get Ash to awaken in the morning. He filed the information away for later. The piping hot liquid didn't seem that bad. He sniffed the colored water and then put his items away.

Standing at the foot of the cot, he tapped her leg.

"Ash. We should talk." They should've talked last night. Not just had mind-blowing sex. Just thinking about her screams made his cock stir. Years of not having a real lover had taken its toll on Raiden. Ash was the first person who could ease his joint pain and help him reach a happy ending. All it took was thinking about her, and his dick was ready for action. He wasn't sure if he should thank Weaver or beat him. Right now, he leaned more to thanking the man.

"Mmm?" Ash mumble as she sat up. Her hair stood up in all directions. It was a wild mass of fuzzy black curls. He'd never noticed that before. Maybe because the locks were always slicked back. He held his grin as she pried one eye open.

"Is that for me?"

"It's not for me."

She studied the cup. "What did you do to it?" She gripped the cup and her fingers wrapped around the sides. Raiden remembered the way those same fingers wrapped around his wrist last night. He still had scratches on his back and his wrists. *Helvete*, but he had to stop thinking about last night.

"I just followed the directions on the can. I'll give you a second."

She sniffed then sipped. A smile spread across her lips. He couldn't make her smile, but coffee could. Suddenly, Raiden pictured slapping the drink to the floor.

"I just eat a spoonful. I didn't know you could drink it. I thought it was food." She took another long draft and leaned back against the wall. "I'm up. What?" She gazed at him.

Raiden's mind went blank. When Ash looked at him with those big silver moons, his heart started to pound and there wasn't anything else in the world but her. She blinked. What were they talking about?

"We don't like each other. We just insult each other." That wasn't a good start.

"I know." She drank again, and her eyes dropped to the bottom to the now-empty cup. "And?"

"But we have to try for ten days. Moth to flame or bridge, or something." Raiden took the cup from her hand. Now that he put that out there, he felt stupid. Damn her. He didn't know what to say to her half the time. He kept waiting for the caustic Ash Winsor to return. The one he was used to who'd insult him with every breath she took. He didn't know how he felt when she just stared at him all wide-eyed, or when she admitted she hadn't had sex for the last two years. When Ash was vulnerable, he felt like he'd sunk in quicksand. He walked away from the bed and used the sink in the bathroom to rinse out his cup.

She still didn't speak. The silence ate away at him. Silence didn't usually bother him. He was used to traveling alone. What about Winsor drove him crazy? He slipped his cup back onto his pack.

"I won't insult you as much."

He smiled. Maybe she had no idea how to talk to him either. Raiden came to his full height while he watched her curl up on the cot. *Skit*, he didn't know what he wanted.

"How about you don't insult me at all?"

"You're pushing it, slush-head."

"Insult me less and," Raiden grinned, "I'll take some of your directions, but I won't be ordered around like a dog." He raised one eyebrow and waited for her to toss some weird mean insult that he wouldn't understand.

She didn't.

"You give all the direction in the bedroom." Her eyebrows rose.

"That's because the moth has hidden talents."

"We can make a deal." Ash pointed to the bed. "How about if I follow you in the bedroom and you follow me everywhere else?" She pointed to the door.

"Another deal?" Panic dug into his belly. Apparently, he liked her. That was an unfortunate turn of events. She would probably break his heart. A war raged within him. Weaver's tying his heartstrings bonded him to her. This wasn't real. To make this genuine, he would have to get to know her, just like Morgan-Roth said. Could they do that? Could they turn sex into love?

"I'm glad you're keeping track. I like deals." Ash's smile charmed him. Who knew? "Anything else?"

"I don't want you to call me Mutt." That was the best he could come up with for now. Everything else would just have to fall into place as they went along. He would have to be easygoing. Good thing being flexible and mellow was as natural to him as breathing.

"I can do that." Ash stood up. He wished she hadn't. She was still completely naked from last night. His eyes began at the top of her head and roamed down over her breasts to the slight flare of her hips. How the hell had he ever missed all this before? "Anything more, tough guy?"

"No. We're done now."

"We're not done." Her hand rose to pet his chest. She pinched his nipple, and he groaned. "Let's do something other than talk."

"I don't know." They were supposed to be talking not doing each other like rabbits.

"I'll give you a second."

"I might need more than that." He inhaled her scent, and Raiden nuzzled her neck as he pulled Ash into his arms.

"No, you don't." She laughed. "I think you know exactly what we should be doing."

Ash wiggled out of his arms and then bent down and grabbed his shirt. She pulled the top over her head as she hopped off the cot. There was something about her wearing his clothes that made his head swell with pride. He liked to see her in his shirt. It made her his.

"Where are you going?" He cleared his throat. "I thought the moth could get burnt." This wasn't real, he reminded himself again. They were stuck in some weird shit that his friend did to them.

"I'll just use the loo; then we can—"

There was a knock at the door. He should have expected it. Whenever he even thought about getting into an in-depth conversation with Ash, they were interrupted. It was probably Morgan-Roth again. This time he thanked the interruption. He shouldn't be screwing Ash every chance he got. He wasn't that kind of man. He wasn't a dog in heat.

The knock came again.

"Tell Morgan-Roth to wait." Ash dashed into the toilet room and closed the door.

"Better move, or he'll pee on you," Raiden called after her.

He heard her laugh on the other side of the door.

As he climbed onto the cot, he asked himself what he would do if it wasn't Morgan-Roth at the door. What would happen if it was Stone?

"Come in."

Chapter 6

The person who slid the door open wasn't Morgan-Roth. It was Nova, the red-eyed woman who was traveling with his old friend Weaver. She entered the room quickly with Weaver on her heels wincing like he was stepping on broken glass. Raiden was stunned. He assumed he would have to hunt the pair down if he wanted to talk to them. He didn't think they would show up in his room.

Nova's eyes swept over him making Raiden feel exposed. He scrambled to grab a shirt and his pants off the floor. His hand landed on his jacket, and he threw the fabric over his legs.

"I thought you were Morgan-Roth coming to use the toilet again." Raiden smoothed his hair down as he held the coat tighter to his body. What were they doing here? Would they untie them? Ash had said if they left them alone then Weaver would undo his voodoo. His joints started to throb like an icy wind sliced through his bones. So, this was over already?

He didn't want that.

"We didn't mean to interrupt you, but we have some questions. It's important."

Raiden's shoulders relaxed. This wasn't about them. For some reason, it made him feel better. He'd told the priest ten days. Raiden would honor that promise. Maybe Ash and her entourage would all learn to get along. He would never have to trek with Doug again. At night, he could sleep with Ash.

The bathroom door opened. Winsor stepped out and paused. Her eyes narrowed as she gazed into the room. She stopped in the doorway still dressed in Raiden's shirt. Hot. She tugged on the hem.

"I didn't want to bother you, but we've a few urgent questions for Raiden before the train pulls into Bosstown," Nova spoke in a rush.

Raiden sighed in relief. He didn't want Ash thinking he tried to bail already.

"Why should Raiden help you?" Winsor stepped further into the room toward him. He could see her putting her emotional armor back on. "You're a wanker. We've no reason to help either of you. You ruined decent HOCs," she stared at Nova, "and you tied us together." Her eyes flipped to Weaver. Did he see fear flash in her eyes before she glared?

Winsor crossed to the cot and then climbed up next to him. Raiden rolled his eyes at Ash's caustic tongue. She was scared. He could tell. Maybe she didn't want to be separated from him right now. He liked that. He threw part of his coat over her legs.

As he arranged the fabric, he noted that Weaver was eyeing Ash's chest where her breasts pushed outward. Was Weaver checking out his Ash Winsor? Anger shimmered in his belly. Weaver better knock it off before he got his face punched.

"Yeah, Weaver. I think after what you did, I don't owe you anything. Get out," Raiden snapped tersely. He wanted the man who could separate Ash and him as far away as possible. If Ash and he decided to end this, then he would find Weaver when he was good and ready.

His old friend's eyes dropped. Raiden still wanted to hit him.

"I can understand how you might be upset. Weaver came to say he was sorry and to separate you." Nova smiled, but Raiden didn't like the way she grinned at him.

"Separate us?" Raiden's eyes flipped around the room and then stopped on Weaver. So, just like that, he could change their lives yet again. What did Weaver think? That they were toys to be played with? *Helvete*.

"Right now?" Winsor frowned.

"We wanted to ask you some questions." Nova nodded. "I thought we could trade. Harvesters like to trade. You could tell me what I need to know, and after, Weaver could untie you. He'll make everything like it was before when you hated each other."

Raiden scowled. Weaver was still an asshole playing games with people. His old trekking-partner might go by the name "Arrow" now, and pretend to be a lost little boy, but Raiden knew Weaver all too well. He should have expected it.

"What questions?" Winsor asked.

"I was looking for a particular harvester train that has rooms like this train." Nova waved her hand around the room. "Except the space doesn't have a cot or any sort of bed," she paused, "right, Weaver?"

"Yea, it's a private room with no bed. And about the unbinding—"

"I can't answer that." Raiden cut him off. He had promised ten days, and he detested lying. He wasn't going to push for the unbinding until he gave Ash and himself a little more time. "I've never been in the private rooms until now. When you and I trekked together, we never needed one. Besides, it was too hard to find anyone with a key. But…" Raiden tried to recall what he knew about all the harvest trains. He paused. "I can tell you *Sloop* and *Catboat* don't have any private rooms at all. It's all cargo with a couple of passenger cars at the front."

"That's true." Winsor nodded. "Also, *Ketch* and *Clipper* have some, but they're new, so they don't have anything in them. No signs or fleam from the surface on the walls yet."

"I didn't know the trains were named." Nova rubbed her forehead. "What's the name of this train?"

"This is *Bilander*," Weaver spoke before Raiden could.

"That's some head injury." Raiden held his smile. What kind of weird game was Weaver playing with this woman he was traveling with? He wondered briefly what kind of money he was after.

"We can't help you," Winsor quickly spoke up. "The only other two trains you might be talking about are *Frigate* and *Windjammer*."

"Why don't you go look inside both of those trains when you get to Bosstown? They'll both be there." Raiden glanced to the exit. *Get out*, he silently added.

"They will?" Nova asked. "Why are those trains in Bosstown?"

"Most of the harvesters were heading to Bosstown in the first place." Raiden had been like everyone else. He'd hoped for some decent items to sell. "All the trains are either there or will be there. The above ground access there is nearest to the strip mall that popped above the ice enough for us to get in. I'm going with Ashley, I mean Winsor." Raiden and Ash hadn't talked about that yet, but then again, they hadn't spoken about anything significant. They needed to clear some things up and not just have sex. He pictured her naked and under him again. Maybe they could talk on the surface of the planet where it would be a death wish to get naked.

"We're not going to the strip mall." Winsor glanced at him, and Raiden wondered why. He thought everyone was heading to the dome. Everyone had talked about nothing but the strip mall for days.

"Why not?"

"Stone and I know where there's a whale mart. We're hunting it down. I got a hook in Water Base Azul for toothpaste. This is the mammoth haul. It's straight up glacial." Winsor smiled at him, and Raiden forgot Nova and Weaver were in the room. Ash was a thought thief.

"What does glacial mean?" Nova's question reminded him that they were still here.

"It's big." Ash's silver eyes stayed on his for a second before they dropped to his crotch. He grinned at her.

"Arrow could untie you, so you don't have to trek together." When Nova threw that at him, Raiden shot his eyes to Weaver.

Oh, so it was back to "Arrow" again? Why were they fucking with them? Raiden had helped them. Weaver was still a terrible person.

"We told you everything we know. We've nothing to trade with now." Winsor tipped her head at Raiden. Was that a question? Should they ask to be separated? They said ten days. Did she change her mind? "If we can't buy our way out of this, I guess we'll have to work it out. I mean, I'm skint."

Raiden sighed. So, she was still in. He didn't know what *skint* was, but he didn't care. His shoulders relaxed.

"I'm broke." Raiden didn't even have to lie. He had just sent every HOC he had to his dad. He couldn't even buy food if he wanted to, let alone a new pack. "You're right, Ashley. We'll have to stay this way for now." Raiden nodded slowly. "Tough break."

Winsor nodded and tossed him a sly smile. Okay. So, they were doing this. And if in ten days it went to hell, they would gather some cash and get separated. This wasn't a conversation, but at least Raiden felt more on solid ground.

"I'd only unbind you if you paid me," Weaver tossed out. Raiden expected that. Weaver hadn't changed. He was still looking for the money. Well, this time his crappy attitude was okay with Raiden.

"I'm broke," both Raiden and Winsor said in unison. He glanced at her as she pushed some of her hair behind her ear.

"We have to go." Nova headed for the door. "After you get your toothpaste, and if you find Weaver, then he can split you up. But I don't know where he'll be."

"It's a risk I'll have to take." Raiden would take it as it came. There wasn't anything more he could do at this point. He had given his word, and so far, Ash wasn't that bad. He smiled to himself. Who was he kidding? She wasn't bad at all. "Besides, by then I might be lost on the surface frozen to death. I figure I have a better chance of dying in a blizzard than I do of ever making money."

"I never get lost." Winsor glanced at him. "I can find my way through any storm or any amount of snow." Ash gave a quick frown and looked at Weaver. "But once I get all that money, I tend to blow it on," she paused, "the ivories. It might be awhile until we get enough money together."

"We can't help you then." Nova reached for the door. "Come on. These guys are stuck together. We have to go."

Chapter 7

As soon as the door closed behind Nova, Raiden looked to Ash. He wanted to gauge her reaction.

"They're leaving." It felt final to see Weaver walk out the door. His heart picked up. What if this thing between them crashed? What if she made him fall in love with her in ten days and then left? She'd destroy him. She couldn't do that, could she? Raiden wasn't like his dad. He would keep his heart and his mind. He was a tough guy just like Ash said.

"Yeah." She rose from the bed and didn't look at him. "You want to go after them? I got a gun."

Raiden thought about that and held his smile. "Yes and no."

She laughed. "You'll have to pay him," she grinned, "or we can shoot him."

"I truly am broke." Raiden shrugged. "I send every bit of money I can get my hands on back to my father. I can't even buy food. I even had to sell my gear. There's no way I could bribe Weaver." He wasn't sure if that was a truth or a lie. He might be able to get free of Ash without money or threatening Weaver with a weapon. He could leave Winsor and test the strength of the heartstrings Weaver had tied. He'd considered that as well, but at this point, he didn't want to do any of those things. What he wanted was a real relationship with Ash.

"What does your dad need all your money for? Can't he get his own?"

"He lost his mind. He's mentally unstable and can no longer think rationally. I pay someone to care for Dad on his water base." Raiden glanced at the door. "I remind him too much of my mother, and he becomes violent with me. I have to pay for a caregiver. He can't work, so I pay the water base boss to let him stay in his home, too."

"I didn't peg you as a good son." Ash came closer to him and wrapped her arms around his neck. "If you trek with me, we can make some serious money for your dad." She smiled. "And if we split up, we'd be missing out on some good sex." Her lips were so close he could feel them.

"Yeah, the sex is decent." That was an understatement. The sex was fan-fucking-tastic.

"Should we see if we can make it better? I should see if I can get you screaming."

They grinned at each other.

"Come on, big, bad Ash Winsor, king of the trains, make me scream."

She laughed and then snuggled further into his arms. Her ass peeked out below the bottom of his shirt, and he petted the lush curve. His dick hardened painfully in his underwear like he hadn't gotten off all night.

A knock roused him out of his fantasy. She froze in his arms.

"Your room is busier than a train platform."

"Who is it?" she called.

"Stone."

Ash became a flurry of activity. She scooped up her coat and her gun. Winsor then tossed everything bundled in her arms into the bathroom. Her pack went next; then she kicked her boots toward the sink. When her items were all in the other room, she turned to him.

"Don't tell him I'm a woman, or I'll cut off your dick," she hissed. "And don't tell him about us yet. Just shut your mush."

"My mush?"

"Your mouth."

"I don't lie, Ash. If he's your 'best friend,' you should tell him who you are."

"Stone is Ash Winsor's best friend, not mine, not Ashley's. Stone and I are just—" She faltered. "I don't know what we are, but he sticks around, and I like it that way. Don't muck it up, got that?"

"Are you going to tell him soon?" Raiden crossed his arms over his chest. He didn't like lying, and he wasn't comfortable with being dishonest to someone so close to Ash. Stone wasn't just anyone. The man had been with her for years.

"Gash, quit pestering me. I'm gonna tell Stone tomorrow." She tossed that out at him, and Raiden wasn't sure she was sincere.

This information gave Raiden the chills. A nagging idea clung to his brain. Maybe he'd made the wrong call getting rid of Weaver so fast. It wouldn't be the first time in his life he'd misjudged a situation. He'd made the wrong decision with Doug when he began to trek with him. He thought that at this point in his life he would be better at making choices in his relationships.

"Are you going to help me?" Her eyes grew huge.

"I don't lie, but I can keep my mouth shut. If he outright asks me, I'll tell the truth."

"I'm going to tell him. Tomorrow," she repeated. There was another knock. "Answer it, you dipso." Ash pointed to the door.

"So much for not insulting me."

"I said I'd do it less." Ash vanished into the toilet room. The door clicked close, and Raiden glanced around. He didn't have a shirt. Ash was wearing it. *Fanken*, he was answering the door half naked. He hated Ash's room.

With the sweep of his hand, he picked up his pants and pulled them on. As soon as they were buttoned, he opened the pocket door to Stone.

Stone was a head taller than him and incredibly handsome. The man fit his name. His chiseled good looks could be a white marble sculpture of art. His shoulder-length black hair was brushed back, and his pale-brown eyes burned with intensity. For a second, Raiden forgot what he was doing.

Stone's hand snapped out and grasped Raiden around the throat. Raiden instantly remembered he was half naked in Ash's room. Stone squeezed his neck just as those tingles shot down Raiden's spine. Clutching Stone's arm, he stumbled backward as Stone forced his way into the room. Even though the muscular, sexy harvester strangled him, Raiden noted his joint pain lessened. What was it about Ash and Stone that eased the constant ache in his body?

The smell of coconuts struck him when he gasped for air. Stone's hands were covered in the scent. As Raiden was forced toward the cot, he caught sight of a gun on Stone's hip. He didn't know what kind of gun that was. The weapon was bigger than Ash's. *Helvete*, Raiden's heart leapt to this throat. He was in for it.

Raiden wrestled the enormous muscular hand off his windpipe. Stone let go and drew his sidearm. The barrel was thrust into Raiden's stomach. Stone's handsome face could have been carved out of concrete. He kept up the intense stare-down. Raiden didn't want to fight Ash's best friend.

"Where's Ash? What did you do with him? What're you doing here? Where's Morgan-Roth?" Stone fired questions so fast Raiden couldn't have answered them even if he wanted to. What happened to the man who couldn't finish a sentence? Stone could certainly finish them as far as Raiden could tell. Ash's "best friend" shoved his pistol at him again, poking his middle. His deep-brown eyes bore into his.

"I'm—" Raiden began.

"What are you doing here?"

"I was—" Raiden didn't get any more words out. Stone barked at him again.

"What the hell is going on? Spill it," he snapped. "You're not saying much. Spit it out. Start talking, Mutt."

Raiden held his smile. Yes, he wasn't saying much.

"Ash and I—" he began again.

"Are you saying Ash asked you here? Are you saying he wouldn't tell me something like that? Are you saying I just left him when I should have stayed? Maybe I should've. What're you saying?"

"I'm not saying anything with a gun shoved into my bellybutton." His ass hit the back of the cot. Raiden sat down and then popped back up. He didn't want to fight, but if he had to defend himself, he would.

"Stone." Ash appeared in the bathroom doorway dressed perfectly. Her hair was slicked back stick-straight. Her huge coat was in place. The woman he'd had sex with was gone. In her place was every bit of the man Raiden was familiar with. "Lower the gun, cockroach."

"Ash, I just thought... I..." Stone waved his free hand around the room and then holstered his gun. "I should've…" When his jacket flipped back, Raiden could see a second weapon on his other hip and a cut set of abs under a lightweight cotton shirt. *Skit*, Stone was hot.

"It's a good thing you're pretty," Ash huffed. "Back up, ice-for-brains."

Stone took a step away from Raiden, but his eyes stayed glued to Ash.

"I was worried because…" Stone glared at Raiden. Once his hands were free, Stone fiddled with his shoulder-length hair. The strands curled at his nape, and a few locks slipped around his fingers. He didn't look at Raiden. As far as Raiden could tell, Stone was tongue-tied and forgot he existed. This must be what Morgan-Roth meant.

"Yeah, you seemed really worried. I haven't seen you all night." Ash lifted one smooth eyebrow. "What was it? Pussy or dick?"

"No, Ash… I didn't feel right after that shit went down in the hall, but I was…" He waved his arms around. "I thought…" Raiden had no idea what any of that even meant. Was that arm movement happy, sad, or confused?

The feeling of a storm skittered down Raiden's spine. He pushed the ache aside.

"I know what I'm doing," she said briskly. Apparently, she could understand Stone's lack of words. Raiden felt like he was getting a crash course in a foreign language, Stone-ease.

"What are you…" he waved his hand, "with..." His eyes raked Raiden's chest.

"I told Raiden he could trek with us. Morgan-Roth told us a few weeks ago that he would be leaving when he reached Bosstown. Morgan-Roth says Raiden will replace him. He's our bridge."

"Bridge? But we don't even like him." Stone still didn't look at Raiden.

"Raiden's staying. That's final."

"What happened to calling him Mutt?" Stone's eyes turned to stab at him. "And now…" He waved his arm.

Raiden sank down on the bed as Stone stared at his chest. Raiden crossed his arms over his nipples as the intense look gave him goose bumps.

"So what?" Ash asked.

"And is that all he's here for? To trek with… not?" Stone's eyes stabbed at Raiden's chest again. That look caused his skin to heat like he stood next to a fire. Raiden recognized the sexual desire he got with Ash. The sensation surged under his skin, but didn't he just promise to be faithful to Ash? He would never touch Stone even if he was the kind of man Raiden would normally bend over for.

"You're not shagging him," Ash snapped. "We aren't Doug."

Raiden glanced to the floor. Did everyone know about that? *Fanken.*

"I can explain about Doug," Raiden began.

"Don't worry about it, Raiden." Ash shook her head. "For once, Stone can just keep it in his pants." She gave a pointed look at Stone.

Ash must have noticed the heated way they looked at each other. Was there sexual desire there, or was that all in his head? Raiden dropped his eyes to the floor. He was with Ash, not Stone.

Raiden tried to remember what Morgan-Roth had said about how they interacted with each other. Maybe he could come up with the right thing to say. Raiden wasn't even sure he should talk to the other man until he knew what all the flustered arm-waving meant.

"I gotta keep it in my pants, but you can…?" Stone's eyes narrowed. "Mutt is your dog now?"

"I'm not a dog," Raiden bit out. He could dance naked right now, and he guessed neither one of them would notice. The way they looked at each other made his heart sink.

Helvete, it dawned on him. Raiden knew exactly what the flustered arm-waving meant. Why didn't he think of this before? He realized what was off about all this. His heart picked up. Stone was an idiot around Ashley. Her best friend was in love with her.

Raiden was tied to a woman who loved another man.

If Stone was in love with her, then he couldn't be with her, not even for ten days. He wasn't going to come between her and a man who loved her. That sounded like nothing but nonstop drama. He'd had enough pain when his mom had left his dad for another man. He wasn't going to be the "other" guy. Raiden refused to ruin lives. He would prefer to be alone.

He shouldn't have let Weaver leave. Could he get him back?

"I can do what I want, Stone. Same as you. You don't see me saying anything about the boys you bugger or the women you bang. I can do Mutt if I want."

"I'm right here. Stop calling me Mutt. It's Raiden. I'm right here." Raiden waved his hand at Ash. "I'm not a dog," he repeated. Raiden drew a hard line there. After what happened with Doug, he wouldn't go through that again. No one looked at him.

"You're…?" A muscle in Stone's jaw clenched so hard Raiden could see it move. "You fucked him?"

"No one is banging Mutt. We aren't going to force him to do anything, and either way, it's none of your business. It's not your snowstorm."

"You are my snowstorm," Stone snarled. "If you aren't doing him, then why…" he waved his hand to Raiden in only his pants, "and not calling him Mutt?"

"I made a deal. We're not calling him Mutt." Ash reached for her pack. Before she could lift the straps, Stone yanked the bag out of her hands and tossed it to the floor. He loomed over her.

"Fuck the deal." Stone spat, and his hands shook.

Ash didn't bat an eye. She lifted her chin and stared him down. "If you want to go over the plan for our next trek, fine. If you want to talk HOCs, fine. But talking about Raiden is finished now. He stays and he's free to do who or what he wants." Her tone was a royal decree.

Stone stepped back like she had slapped him. The harvester turned an unhealthy shade of white as the blood drained from his face.

"I'm getting dressed." Raiden was tired of this non-conversation, where he was passed over like old chicken. He wasn't "Mutt," and he didn't enjoy being talked about like an added item to hang off their packs.

Doug told him he wasn't worth the food he gave him for the blowjobs. He didn't believe that, and he never let Doug take away his self-worth. He refused to be nothing to Ash and Stone, either. He would simply leave if it came to that.

"You're choosing Mutt over me?" Stone took a second step back. In the small space, his move blocked Raiden from reaching his pack so he could dress and leave.

"What I choose isn't—"

"I waited. You said when you turned eighteen." Stone seethed.

Raiden coughed to cover his laugh. "Eighteen?"

"Shut your laughing gear." Ash glared at him.

"I get it." Stone spun on his heel and grabbed the door. "I'm not betting anymore, Ash. I can see when the odds are stacked against me. I don't have ice for brains. Two years…" He stormed out the door. It slid shut.

Raiden picked up his coat off the cot. What the hell was that all about? Ash told him she was eighteen? He scanned the woman next to him. Winsor was all woman's curves hidden under all that fabric. No way was she that young.

"Two years for what?" Raiden glanced at her.

"I promised Stone that we could have sex in two years. Once I turned eighteen." Ash's hands trembled when she reached for her pack. Raiden tossed his coat down and grabbed her hand before she could lift the massive bag onto her shoulders.

"And he believed that?"

"I don't have facial hair, and it was all I could think of to explain how I look. I don't grow a lot of hair." Tears welled in her eyes. "And I thought that by now I would've gotten the courage to tell him, but—" More tears gathered on her lashes, and Raiden pulled her into his arms. "He wants a man. He wants to fuck Ash Winsor, king of the trains, not me. He loves the idea of me, not me. Never me." Her harsh whisper was breathed into Raiden's chest. "I'm just a woman." In that moment, the dam of tears burst. She soaked his bare chest.

"It's okay, Ashley." She was far from *just* a woman. Ashley was his idea of perfection.

"It's not okay. You should've been dressed," she sobbed. "But I needed to wrap my boobs." She cried and gulped air. "He thinks I buggered you." She hiccupped. "I think it's over, and I didn't know what to do and," she hiccupped again, "I'm crying again."

"Yes, you're crying again." He held her as he rubbed the back of her neck.

"I never cry this much. Men don't cry, and now what am I supposed to do?"

"Men cry, Ash." Raiden thought about that. The urge to help Ash Winsor won out over every other idea he had. "We did have sex. He would've figured that out if we stayed together for ten days."

"But now he doesn't want to bet on me anymore." She cried harder. Raiden held her close and swayed to music that wasn't playing. As he hugged her, he thought hard about what had just happened. Ash cared for Stone more than the whole "best friend" garbage that she spewed. Did Stone love her? After what happened, he was fairly sure he did. And who was he in this mix?

No one.

He was here to break up the fragile relationship.

Long ago when Lowell rolled in and fell in love with his mom, Raiden always wondered how could this guy be okay with breaking up an existing relationship? And now he had done the same damn thing. He was Lowell. Stone was his dad, hurt and confused. Ash was his mom, who was about to kick Stone to the tracks because she wanted to be with him. Good sex and some voodoo Weaver had done didn't cut it. In the end, that's all this was. Good sex. *Helvete*, he didn't even know if she truly wanted to be with him. They simply wanted to screw because Weaver couldn't stay out of their business. Weaver was the problem here. Not him, not Ash, and not Stone. Fuck Weaver. What right did he have to mess with people's lives? Raiden was normally successful at solving puzzles. He would fix this, and Weaver could kiss his ass.

"Where did he go, Ash?" Raiden asked after her tears ebbed.

"I don't know. When I first met him, he would drink himself stupid, and I would find him. When life gets hard for him, he tends to run away. But he hasn't done that in a long time. He has grown up a lot being with me."

"So, you have no idea?"

"Sometimes he picks up an easy lay and goes back to his room, especially when I want to go out." Her voice became bitter as she explained. "I think he sucks guys off like he's trying to win the first prize for having the best head bob." Ash paused. "I'm not sure where he is. We could ask Morgan-Roth."

"We'll go talk to Morgan-Roth and find Stone. We can explain to Stone about what Weaver did." Raiden squeezed her shoulder and then pulled out of her embrace. Good sex wasn't enough. The most fan-fucking-tastic sex in the world couldn't keep Raiden in the middle of two people in love. If she wanted Stone, then he wouldn't be her second choice. He needed to get out of this combination. "After we see Stone, we will find Weaver, and money or no money, we'll have him separate us. Everything can be like it was before."

"I thought we'd give this a try. Ten days. I made a deal." Her large silver eyes drilled into his. "You made a deal too, tough guy." Her hand stole around his neck.

Yeah, for a second there, he wanted to give this a try too, but not at the price of Stone and Ash's heartache. He may not like the other man, but he wasn't a home-wrecker, and he wasn't willing to be Ash's "Stone fill-in." That would be the last thing he would be.

"That was before I found out that you're in love with another man, a man who is probably in love with you. I'll tell Morgan-Roth that the bridge is out."

"It's not that I love him. It's complicated." Ash swiped at her tears. He could see her putting on her "king" armor.

She was in love and not willing to get hurt. He understood that, but that was for her to figure out. What he could do was get out of the middle of the two lovebirds.

"I'm going to uncomplicate it." He tugged out of her embrace. "We'll see Stone, then Weaver. All deals are off, Ash Winsor."

Raiden gathered up his clothes and his pack with Ash's eyes on him. After he disappeared into the bathroom to get dressed, he slapped his hands down on either side of the sink. He concentrated on the sting of his palms and the renewed twinge in his joints. He had the distinct impression that Stone might love Ash Winsor as much as she cared for him. He probably should've never gotten involved with her to begin with. He needed a second to solve this dilemma. Good thing he was skillful when it came to puzzles.

Chapter 8

After Raiden and Ash finished dressing, they shouldered their bags and made their way off the train. Just as they hit the platform, Raiden spotted Morgan-Roth near a stall selling freshly skinned fish. The huge man leaned next to one of the big tanks with live fish waiting for their death.

"Stone's drinking hard, and he went to the dome," Morgan-Roth said as soon as they walked up. "Are you going, or am I?"

"We're going." Ash gave a brief nod but didn't show any emotions. "We'll head there now."

"You sure you don't need me to talk to him?" Morgan-Roth studied Raiden.

"I'm going." Raiden jerked his head toward the hall to the dome. "I'm the bridge," he added sarcastically.

"Did Ash and Stone get into a fight?" Morgan-Roth asked.

"It wasn't a fight." Ash shrugged. "Stone's a twit."

Raiden's eyebrows rose. Apparently, the name-calling wasn't exclusive to him. She hid her sorrow and torment over Stone well. If Raiden hadn't witnessed her tears before, he would think she couldn't care less about Stone. Ash was a decent liar. Too bad, he knew that she was torn up inside. She couldn't hide her true emotions from him.

"Did Stone say anything about winning?" Morgan-Roth looked thoughtful.

"Winning?" Raiden shook his head. "I don't think so."

"Then it's still okay. When he starts with the winning and the betting, and the taking-a-chance stuff, then he's distraught. If not, he's still in."

"Still in what?"

"He's still invested in their relationship. Stone needs Ash for direction. You can help them figure out their puzzle."

The priest didn't say anything more. Ash's world was more involved than Raiden had thought. Morgan-Roth's directions didn't even make sense. Morgan-Roth seemed uncertain. He'd never seen either Morgan-Roth or Ash unsure about anything before.

Maybe Ash didn't hide her problems as well as he thought. Morgan-Roth knew something he wasn't saying.

"I need you to keep an eye out for Weaver." Ash glanced back at the trains parked along the tracks. People meandered all over the platform. "We're gonna ask him to divide us. We're going back to the way we were before. This was a bad idea."

"Hold up." Morgan-Roth's eyes jumped back and forth between the two of them. "We made a deal. Ten days."

"No deal." Raiden cut in. Like hell would he let Ash discuss their problems with Morgan-Roth like he wasn't even there. He'd had enough of that with Ash and Stone this morning. "That was before I found out Stone is in love with Ash. I'm not getting between them."

"But love is—" Morgan-Roth started. Ash cut him off.

"You can give me a speech later, Priest." Ash adjusted her sturdy pack, spun on her heel, and marched away. "Follow me, Raiden."

Raiden strode after her. As they wove through the other harvesters, she glanced behind her at him. They made their way down a long, narrow hall away from the train platform. The room emptied as the temperature began to drop. A few harvesters leaned against the cement pillars that took up both sides. Some smoked, others drank. Everyone talked in low tones since the echo bounced off the cement walls.

At the end of the long corridor, the hall opened to sharp, steep stairs. Together they climbed, and bit by bit, the air became even colder until Raiden could see his breath. At the top of the stairs, there was a wide door with a heavy plastic curtain covering the entrance. A handful of harvesters, who lounged against the wall, glanced at them as they walked. The small group parted so Ash could pass, and one of the men even opened the plastic drape for her. As soon as the massive doorway was thrown open, the dome came into view with an icy gust of air.

Raiden had been in a few domes around the NEDs. They generally looked the same, but this one was bigger than the last one he had been in. Domes were created from old football stadiums or concert halls. If the structure was sturdy and if it could be covered, harvesters used the spot as a staging area before they started a trek. Raiden followed Ash past a sign that read "Gill Stadium" hung off a bench. This area was as close to the surface as you could get. The colossal enclosure housed the snowmobiles, sleds, and sled dogs. The turf was a mix of snow, mud, and fake grass. Overhead, a partial plastic and metal patched ceiling towered above them. Raiden grimaced at the smell of dirty men and wet dogs.

Directly from where they entered, Ash and he zigzagged around stacked containers and multiple styles of snowmobiles. Men, mostly, and a handful of women grabbed extra gear to prepare for the surface. A few harvesters sold newer snow pants and hats.

Raiden patted a few of the huskies as they passed them in their dog houses. He followed Ash as she headed toward a beat-up RV near the furthest wall of the stadium.

"Do you know where Stone is?" Raiden didn't have to ask if Ash was worried. Her quick march and icy glare spoke volumes. Raiden didn't add that he was concerned for Stone. He wasn't worried about the fact that Stone thought Ash and he were having sex. No, that was an issue they could all work out. What bothered Raiden was Stone might be drinking and trekking… alone.

"I'm going to find out."

Raiden nodded. They would find Stone and tell him they wouldn't stay together. Stone would get over his jealousy, and then Ash would simply have to admit she was a woman. Morgan-Roth would have to tell God to find another bridge for the two of them. It was a workable puzzle as far as Raiden was concerned.

As they reached a set of red snowmobiles, he spotted Doug and two of his harvester friends. The man was insane. Raiden didn't want to face him again, but Doug couldn't seem to let him go. The obsession was borderline psychotic. He'd never felt anything for Doug, and whether the man wanted him or not, it didn't matter. Raiden realized he'd used Doug just like the harvester had used him. Sure, Raiden had blown him, but it was for the money. Doug wanted his devotion. The harvester would never have his loyalty.

"You done fucking Mutt yet?" Doug called to Ash as they passed. "I'm ready to get my dick wet."

Ash stopped so abruptly that Raiden bumped into her pack. Raiden didn't give Doug any sort of reaction. Doug would just love if he got under Raiden's skin.

"Walk away, Ash." Raiden set his hand on her elbow. Raiden generally liked to walk away. He'd finish a fight if there was no other way, but he preferred tact and negotiation first.

"When you don't have a dick, you have to toss the dice a little harder," Ash whispered to him before she turned to face Doug. Her hand went to her gun.

"I'm gonna rip out your intestines and feed them to you," she called to the men.

Doug threw his hands up. "That's a no." His friends laughed, and he chuckled.

"Tosser," Ash snapped. "I'm going to shoot him one of these days."

They reached the old RV shoved near the wall of the dome next to a set of broken bleachers. The wind whipped at Raiden's hair, and he pulled his long brown leather coat tighter around his shoulders. Glancing around, Raiden noted a shed and a neat line of shiny blue-and-white snowmobiles. The chain of vehicles had a spot where it appeared like a snowmobile was missing from the row. Tracks in the mud-snow mixture on the ground headed toward the exit.

"I'm going to check in with my guards and see if they've seen Stone."

Of course, Ash Winsor had guards.

Ash gave a low whistle. The door to the RV opened and rattled. Raiden expected more hefty men like Morgan-Roth and Stone. Out popped a little boy. The child couldn't have been more than eight or nine.

The boy wore a puffy coat covered in fur like Ash's. Pulled down to his eyes was a gray knitted hat with a pom-

pom dangling by a thread. His pale-blond hair was uneven like it had been cut with dull scissors.

"Ford, have you seen Stone?"

The little child's eyes misted with tears as he studied Raiden.

"Stone said you weren't with him anymore." The child pointed accusingly at Raiden. "You broke them up." The boy's voice was a whisper of anguish. His bottom lip trembled.

Raiden closed his eyes. Even if the boy wasn't a biological child of Ash and Stone, he still felt like he'd broken up a family. Raiden's mind flashed to the day his dad told him his mother was leaving with her boyfriend. Raiden felt like he had ruined everything in the world for this kid.

"We aren't together," Raiden said quickly. "Ash and Stone love each other."

"Stop saying I love him," she whispered to Raiden. Ash turned to the boy. "Tell me where Stone went, and I can go explain it to him."

"Chevy knows. He's inside."

"Wait here with Raiden." Ash turned to the RV. "If Humper shows up, don't move. I'll be right back." Ash disappeared into the vehicle leaving Raiden with the boy staring at him.

"Humper?" Ash must not have heard him, but the boy did. As the door banged shut behind Ash, the child answered his question.

"Humper guards the snowmobiles. Chevy and I take care of all of Stone and Ash's gear. We recharge the batteries in the snowsuits." The boy spoke with pride, but then he paused. "Unless Stone doesn't come back." His little face scrunched up as he held back tears.

"I'm going to get Stone back." Raiden paused. "Who's Chevy?"

"Chevy is his brother," Ash answered as she came out of the RV. She carried what looked like a large black blanket slung over her arm. "They aren't blood brothers, but I've been keeping them since I found them. They have been together for years." She tossed the blanket to Raiden, and he caught it. "Stone and I agreed that they would be safe here."

"Found them?"

"Sure. Kids are abandoned all the time. If their parents die of Snow Flu, sometimes their just on their own. I found Ford in a beat-up Ford pickup near the underground farms. There was hot trading going on for the truck, and Ford hid in it looking for food." Ash tugged on the boy's pom-pom as he smiled up at her. The kid looked at Ash Winsor like she could make the snow melt with a smile.

"And Chevy?" Raiden held out the blanket when Ash pointed to the fabric. It wasn't a blanket but a thick black insulated bodysuit. A control box was sewn into the sleeve.

"I discovered Chevy much the same way. That was back when I was on the Equator with Morgan-Roth. Mo-gee is looking for his kid. We found Chevy in a Chevy Malibu."

Raiden quickly slipped off his jacket, and his nipples hardened into points as the cold air cut through him.

"Wait, I thought Morgan-Roth was a priest. How did he have a kid?" He immediately pulled the snowsuit over his pants and shirt and attached the rope loops on the front.

"When he was young, Mo-gee was a bit wild. He had a kid the usual way, slush-head." As Ash handed him a hat and glove set, he pondered the fact that she had apparently traveled all over the C.T.O.N.A. He'd never been out of the NEDs. There were days when Raiden thought about leaving the Northern Earth Dens, but then the idea of deserting his dad would drive guilt into his heart. He couldn't abandon his dad like his mom had. If he didn't send money to their water base, he wasn't sure what would happen to his father. His dad couldn't work. The poor man was so broken he could barely get out of bed.

After he was covered head to toe in some of the most expensive gear he'd ever worn, Raiden fiddled with the buttons on his cuff as his bones started their normal dull ache.

"Don't turn on the heat until we're outside." Ash waylaid his hand, and he followed her to a dark-blue machine with a massive sled secured on the back.

"I gotta get my ax. Wait here." Ash threw her pack next to the sled and then disappeared into the shed.

Just as Raiden had tossed his pack next to hers, an enormous white dog came barreling around the RV. The animal spotted Raiden and headed straight for him. Raiden dropped to his knees as the dog approached and held out his hand. The white beast stopped right in front of Raiden and tipped its head to the side.

Raiden had never seen a dog that big. He continued to hold out his hand, and after a second, the dog trotted up to him. He slipped off his gloves to pat the fluffy head.

"Humper." Ash's sharp command made both Raiden and the dog jump. The dog sat.

"What's wrong?"

"Humper is normally—" Ash began, but the dog's shrill bark cut her off. In the next second, the animal shot toward Doug and his buddies who walked by. They made a wide berth around the dog. Raiden thought it looked like the men were walking along an invisible fence. The dog didn't stop barking until the harvesters were out of sight.

"Humper is trained to kill if you get close to any of my equipment. I'm surprised he didn't rip you apart," Ash said as soon as the pet was at her side. "I trained him from a puppy to protect Ford and Chevy and Honda."

"Honda?"

"Honda stole my motorcycle. It's how he got his name. He refused to tell me his real name when I met him. Sorta stubborn." Ash nodded toward the RV. "He's inside. He's got his dander up because he thinks Stone and I aren't together anymore. We're the only family those boys have. I have to take care of them."

Raiden studied Ash.

"You have a soft heart, big, bad Ash Winsor." Ash was looking after a priest, a man-child, three boys, and a dog. He wondered who cared for her. Maybe Morgan-Roth had a point. Well, as soon as Ash told Stone she wanted to be with him, it would all get better. Stone would have to man up and care for her properly. Ash needed someone. Raiden would make sure Ash told Stone she was a woman. That was the simplest solution.

"Go fuck your mom," she grumbled.

Raiden laughed. "Anyone else I should know about that you're looking after?"

Her eyes met his. "Maybe you a little."

"Me?"

"I took issue with Doug when you started to suck his dick in exchange for someone to trek with."

"Does everyone know about that?" Raiden was happy he had his facemask covering everything but his eyes. His cheeks burned.

"Not everyone." Ash tightened straps around her bag. "I'm king, so I know things."

"I needed the food." He lifted his pack onto the back of her Polaris. "I was starving."

"I get that. It's only that I have a thing for consent, and the deal was bloody monkeyshines." She didn't look at him while she spoke but talked to her bag as she used straps to mount his sack next to hers. "Your bag is torn. I can replace this. And you don't have the proper gear to be on the surface. I'll have to outfit you when we have more time."

Raiden placed his hand over hers and wished they weren't wearing gloves. "We weren't together, Ash. You can't blame me for being with Doug. Would it make you feel better if I told you I hated what we did together?"

"No!" Ash's head snapped up. "That's worse."

"It is?"

"I'm not busted up because you've been with some guys, Raiden. You're a harvester. Stone sleeps with anything that moves around here." She shook her head at him. "I don't blame you. I know you were doing what you had to do after Weaver left you blizzard and broke." She looked up, and her eyes bore into his. They were like silver globes. He could stare at them for hours. "I blame Doug for taking advantage of you. If you'd liked him, that would've been alright with me. But you didn't want him. He enjoyed treating you like a dog."

"You treated me like a dog."

"I was trying not to have sex with you. That's different. You and I were—" She paused as her brow crinkled. "I don't know what we were doing, but I never wanted to hurt you, Raiden. If I had wanted to hurt you, I would've just shot you and been done with it."

"Thanks for not doing that."

"You're a slush-head." Ash grinned. "You know, I always looked forward to seeing you on the train. I liked how you would try to insult me."

"I didn't try. I did insult you."

"I'll let you think that." Ash laughed. "I might like you one day. I get a kick out of you."

Raiden couldn't help the warmth that filled his chest. Ash had been trying to look after him. She was the most complex woman he'd ever met, but he liked it. Winsor was like an ever-changing brainteaser. She wasn't boring.

"I might, one day, like you too." He dropped his chin to her shoulder and nuzzled her scarf. "I like what we do together."

"I know." She smiled at him and then pulled on her facemask. "I wanted to tell you that you could trek with me for nothing, but we never got along, and I didn't know how to say that to you."

"No one takes advantage of me, Ash. I could fight him if I wanted. Doug and I used each other, and now it's over." A smile hung on his lips. "You've been paying attention to what I've been doing for how long?"

Ash shrugged. "Don't be a prat." She pointed to his bag, and he checked the straps on the sled. "I just kept an eye on you after Weaver left. Not that I was worried or anything like that."

Raiden chuckled at the lie. He decided not to ask her much more right now. She still couldn't look at him.

"I take it you're driving?" He pulled his goggles down, and the view became a yellow tint.

She exhaled a deep, husky sound. "You know it. Get on, Mutt."

"Fine," he paused, "Ashley."

She glared. "Don't call me that around here." She glanced around like someone might have heard them. Only Humper was around. The dog still sat waiting for a new command.

"I'll call you Ashley in the bedroom and Ash out here if you call me Raiden. Not Mutt."

"Deal." She pulled on her goggles. "I just forgot." Ash turned around and tapped the back of the seat.

"I think I've lost count at what deal that is." He smiled. At least, that was one item they had worked out. He climbed on behind her and hugged her to his chest. His arms slipped around her waist.

"I like making deals. I wouldn't keep count if I were you."

Slowly, through the mud and slush, Ash maneuvered toward the door of the dome that let out into the wide world of ice. The wind made the snow swirl and dance, and he could barely see in front of them. Raiden tapped the button on his sleeve. A dry heat immediately started in his thighs and began to spread.

Ash paused at the doorway and turned around to face him.

"Even after we're not connected in any way, I want you to know that you can always trek with me. You don't have to make a deal or suck my dick. You can just travel with me and Stone. The same goes for Stone. He'd never force you to do anything. You can hang with us."

"Deal." When she said things like that, he wanted to keep his ties to Ash Winsor.

Damn, maybe it was complicated.

Raiden didn't speak as she kicked the vehicle into high speed and zoomed out of the open door into the blinding white light of day. They hit the first drift, and his arms around her waist gripped tightly.

"Do you know where you're going?' Raiden yelled over the engine as they began to twist around snow mounds. Ash hadn't asked anyone other than the boys about Stone. Raiden hoped she knew where she would find him because Raiden had no clue.

"I never get lost. It's a gift. It's one of the main reasons my uncle said it would be okay for me to harvest with him. He needed me, and we always made good HOCs for my cousins," Ash called over her shoulder as they skipped across the ice like a disk. "And I've been trekking with Stone for a long time. I'm titanium. Don't get your panties in a twist."

"I thought when you said you never get lost it was just an empty boast. More of you being... King Winsor."

"I've a few of my own hidden talents other than being good at pretending to be a man."

Raiden laughed as his ass started to go numb. The vibration under his butt rumbled through his thick outer snow pants. His toes were the first thing to get cold as the bodysuit fought to keep the freezing temperatures at bay. The rest of his body thrilled at where he was pressed close to Ash. His chest was warm, but he didn't think that had to do with the suit. He buried his head against her neck. His goggles fogged up.

Up ahead, he spotted a handful of sleds in the snow. As they plowed through another bank of fresh powder over ice, he noted the snowmobiles were piled high with spools of wire. Two men were tightening straps on a few boxes they had stacked.

"You see Stone? Boys said he's here. He owes me a pound of flesh," Ash barked out above the rumble of the snowmobile as they slowed down closer to the other harvesters.

Both men glanced up. They exchanged looks. Raiden couldn't see their eyes since their goggles were tinted black.

"Last I saw him, he was over on the other side." One of the harvesters waved toward an iced-over roof peeking above a massive snow drift.

"Next to the mermaid sign," the second guy added. "The green one."

Ash scarcely waited for the other man to finish his directions. She tore off, and he had to quickly wrap his arms around her waist again so he wouldn't be thrown. He wasn't prepared for the speed or the rapid acceleration of a pissed-off woman.

They raced around the area where the roof sloped, and he spotted the broken sign.

As they zoomed closer, Raiden spotted Stone. The large man was half in a drive-through window and half out of it. He looked wedged in, and a bottle of liquor was clutched in one of his gloves.

Raiden couldn't tell if he was alive, but he figured that once Ash was through with him, Stone would wish he were dead.

Chapter 9

Raiden stood back as Ash bent over an intoxicated Stone. He hung out the drive-through window, and when he saw her coming, he tried to wiggle his hips. He didn't get free, but only fell further toward the snow. Icicles spiraled down his chin, and snowflakes were caked to his facemask, giving Raiden the impression that Stone had already fallen face-first multiple times.

"What the fuck, you bloody lug?" Ash grabbed Stone's shoulder, and then Raiden heard her grunt. Straightening, she leaned back and kicked Stone square in the stomach. Raiden grimaced. Even with all the layers on, those boots in the belly would still hurt.

"Knock it off, you squall." Stone swiped at her boot when she would've kicked him again. "I'm trying to serve coffee." The last word was slurred as Stone tried to drink out of his bottle—unsuccessfully. Stone's scarf was knotted around his neck. He shoved at the fabric and spilled alcohol over his facemask and then down the front of his snowsuit. After yanking at the fabric a second time, he wiggled his hips again. Ash kicked him again, and he lost the bottle. The glass clanked on the ice as it rolled away.

"Stone! Get your ass up." Ash's bark was furious, but Stone didn't seem to notice. He tried again to fit through the little window, and he hung a tad further toward the ground.

"Fuck off, Torch." Stone lifted his head. His goggles were tinted a pale yellow, just like Ash's. Stone glared at Raiden. If Raiden thought he had a chance of getting back alive, he would have left them both there. The way Stone looked at him, freezing to death might be an acceptable option.

Stone finally wiggled the rest of the way through the window and then crumpled onto the ice. He rolled over and came to his knees. He paused and wobbled. Raiden leaned down and wrapped his arm around the other man's shoulders to steady him. He expected Stone to shake him off, but he didn't. With legs like a year-old baby, Stone finally rose to his feet.

"I can't, Ash." Stone's voice was whisper-soft, and Raiden wasn't sure if she could even hear the comment over the wind. Raiden felt his words. Stone's declaration reverberated in Raiden's chest. His joints, his bones screamed, making him stiffen. The spasm was just like the sensation he felt when he knew a snowstorm was about to descend. Raiden couldn't get a read if this was a fight pending or just another storm on the surface somewhere.

He paused and held Stone firmly while he hunted through his emotions. When he knew a storm was on its way, he felt the warning in his shoulders and knees, like his bones alerted him. This pain was different. His heart was advising him of a storm of a different kind. Yes, in two seconds, all hell would break loose between Ash and Stone. The argument was brewing, and Raiden wasn't sure he could stop it.

"You can't what? Can't get up? Can't get your head out of your ass?" Ash's body language screamed for a fight. "What can't you do?"

"I can't be with you and him. I can't bet on you. I'm never going to win." Stone sagged against Raiden. Defeat crystallized in the air. Morgan-Roth's cautionary directions were now lit up like neon. Stone had used the word "win" and even Morgan-Roth knew that meant trouble.

"Brace for impact," Raiden mumbled to himself. He felt helpless.

"Why the hell not? We've been together for years, and Morgan-Roth was around. Why can't we have Raiden?"

"Have him?" Stone shoved away from Raiden and stalked toward his snowmobile parked a few feet away. "*We* don't get Woofer. *You* get him." Stone stumbled over nothing and then bent toward the vehicle. "Don't you get it? There is no *us* or *we* or anything." He dropped to his knees. "You weren't fucking Morgan-Roth." He yelled over his shoulder. "This is polar-bear-shit, and you know it."

"You've been plowing your way through trains of harvesters for years, and that wasn't a problem. I've never said anything while you got it up for whatever man or woman you fancy." There was misery behind Ash's words. Stone's more promiscuous sexual adventures were clearly a huge problem that maybe they had never talked about.

Raiden took a deep breath. How much of this was his issue to deal with? He supposed all of it was since he was tied to Winsor. He wanted to fix things for her. He would try to solve this puzzle partly for himself as well. As a child, he'd wished someone would've shown up and helped his mom and dad figure things out.

He just had to take a second and think.

"Who I screw isn't your snowstorm," Stone fired back at her just as he finally hauled himself up onto his vehicle. "You want me to live like the priest?" He swayed. "Like…?" He waved his hand.

"Like hell. You are my snowstorm." Ash hurried to Stone on his snowmobile and Raiden followed.

Raiden had the urge to point out that Stone had said the exact same thing to her this morning, but at the last second, he changed his mind. Did the two of them know that they were so in love that they'd crossed into Crazy-ville? He didn't think so.

"It's different, and you know it." Stone sat hard on the seat with an audible *oomph*.

"How is it different?" Ash crossed her arms over her chest as much as she could with her snowsuit restricting her movements. She came around to stand directly in front of Stone, so he couldn't move without running her over.

"Because I was just waiting around for you to finally realize you wanted to have sex with me. That was the deal." Stone started up his snowmobile, and the machine rumbled in the silence that followed his words. Ash wouldn't look at him. Raiden took a deep breath. Now would be a good time for her to admit she was a woman.

"I can't fuck you. I thought you understood how it was with us." Ash's voice held tears. "I never made that deal." Raiden could hear her sniff even over the engine. What the hell was wrong with her? Why wouldn't she just tell the truth?

"I once thought it was that you couldn't have sex at all. Now I get that you can't have it with me. You don't want me."

"I can't do this with you," Ash whispered. Fear rolled off her in waves. "It's too hard."

What was too hard was facing Stone and telling him the truth. Raiden got that, but he didn't think Stone would take her words that way.

The two of them stared at each other in silence for so long that Raiden thought they all might die from hypothermia. He stopped himself from rolling his eyes. There had to be a way for these two to get together.

"I don't love you, Ash Winsor." Stone looked down at his gloved hands. "I'm not betting on you anymore." Raiden had the feeling that was the biggest lie he'd ever heard.

It was good Ash was wearing goggles. Otherwise, the tears would be icicles on her cheeks.

She turned away from them both and headed back to her vehicle. She acted like the statement didn't even bother her. Raiden knew better.

"I don't love you, either," Ash threw out. Raiden changed his mind. *That* was the biggest lie he'd ever heard. "And sometimes you bet, and you lose," she called over her shoulder. Her chin rose.

One thing Raiden was sure of at this moment. They both loved each other something stupid, and he was in the middle of it. Was this how his dad had felt? Maybe that's why his dad asked his mom to leave when he did. His father had to get out from between his wife and her lover before he lost his mind. Well, Raiden always thought his dad just gave up. He wasn't going to do the same thing. He'd stay and help them get their heads out of their butts, while he somehow kept his sanity. He didn't know why he had the urge to help these two; it was probably what Weaver did to him, but Raiden would stay, and he would puzzle this out.

"Ash and I aren't staying together, Stone. Ash wants to be with you," Raiden said as he reached her vehicle. He explained quickly before she could start her engine.

Ash threw her leg over the seat and glared at him. "Shut your laughing gear."

Stone stared at them. Raiden stood between the two of them, waiting to see if that sentence would ease the tension. Stone turned to face him. Raiden's muscles cramped, maybe with the cold, maybe not.

"Is that true?" Stone studied them both.

"I came to tell you that we're gonna find Weaver and have him divide us." Ash shrugged. "This was a mistake. This thing with Raiden is just Weaver's binding. We're tied up for now."

The word "mistake" made Raiden's stomach drop. Loving Ash didn't feel like a mistake. It felt right, even being in the middle of her screwed-up love life. He couldn't say that.

"You were gonna…?" Stone tossed his arm out and swung it between the two of them. Stone glared. "Right now?" He appeared skeptical. Raiden couldn't blame him.

"Yeah, ice-for-brains. We were gonna talk with Morgan-Roth about it until we found out your stupid ass came out here on a bender."

Stone kicked his snowmobile into gear and drove until he was parked directly next to Raiden.

"And then you and I…?" Again, he waved his hand back and forth. Stone's eyes studied him. Raiden wasn't sure what that meant or how to answer that if it was a question.

"You know, you shouldn't drink and trek." Raiden raised an eyebrow as Stone pulled up even closer next to him. Several feelings rose within him. He liked it when Stone stared at him like he was doing now. He felt inclined to say anything to Stone just to get the other harvester to notice him. Raiden liked the attention, but when Stone stared at him, he also forgot everything in his head. If he wasn't careful, Stone would steal all his words, and he would be left waving his arms like a spastic. The harvester would probably be able to relate.

Stone shoved him. He slipped on the ice but caught himself before he fell.

"I know the basic trekking rules, Blue's Clues. Thanks for the tip. I just decided I didn't care what happens to me if Ash and I were over."

Raiden's held in his grin. If this was Stone not loving her, then he didn't know what love looked like.

The throbbing in his joints didn't go away as Raiden stamped his foot and shifted. He shifted his leg as the insistent feeling crept up to his knees. For a moment, he forgot about Ash and Stone. This twinge was the sign of a real storm. He wasn't always a hundred percent accurate, but this time he felt sure. As he sniffed the air, he glanced at the gray clouds. Snow was on the wind. Raiden knew that smell. The blizzard was closing in.

"What the hell are you doing, Toto? You want to get back to Kansas?"

"You gotta pee?" Ash asked him. "Morgan-Roth always got out here and had to piss."

Raiden couldn't decide how much to explain about his life. Usually, the harvesters he trekked with didn't believe him when he said he knew a storm was coming. Doug never listened to him. He would make fun of him and keep him in the snow for hours watching him wriggle in agony.

"What's the problem?" Ash set her hand gently on his arm. He looked down at the thick gloves covering her hands. The urge to protect her, to love her, was ever-present. No matter what his head said, his heart had its own ideas. He sighed. Weaver did this, but he couldn't change the connection now. He had to look after her as long as they were bound. He would warn her of the change in weather.

"A storm is coming. It's pretty big." He closed his eyes to read the discomfort. "In twenty minutes, forty-eight seconds. Snow, ice, the whole works. I'm almost sure this time."

Both Ash and Stone glanced up at the clouds first.

"Almost sure?" Ash asked.

"It hurts in my joints." He nodded. "Like arthritis. Sometimes I get it wrong, but this time I think it's going to hit."

"It's your gift?" Stone asked.

"If you want to call it a gift. I call it torture." Raiden looked at Stone. "If we stay out here the pain will get more and more acute." If Stone wanted to take his anger out on Raiden for stealing Ash, here was his chance. Stone might enjoy watching the man who stole his love scream in pain. Raiden decided to leave the choice wide open. "Do you want to stay?"

The harvester shrugged.

"Red-rover, red-rover, let's get the hell out of here." Stone revved his snowmobile.

Chapter 10

The dome was bustling when they entered. Ash and Stone crisscrossed around men, dogs, and equipment as they headed toward the RV. They parked their sleds side by side, then in unison whistled for the boys. A few men looked at them as soon as the engines died. Stone swung off his snowmobile with ease. Raiden found himself enjoying the way the other man shed his snow pants and top. He pictured him stripping for him.

Just as the boys appeared, Raiden remembered that he shouldn't be staring at Stone like a lust-filled teenager. He hopped off the vehicle. His legs still vibrated due to the powerful engine, and his joints hurt due to the storm. He leaned against the seat as he adjusted to the solid ground, and he tried to stretch. Ash drove the snowmobile like she had stolen the damn thing, and Raiden figured it might take him a lifetime to get used to the way she steered. Of course, he wouldn't get a lifetime with her.

When the door to the RV opened this time, both Chevy and Ford came out of the trailer. Ford, he had met before. The boy was wearing the same hat with the pom-poms. He threw a look Raiden's way that shrieked interloper. Chevy was a few inches taller than Ford and maybe a year older. His brown hair stuck out around a baseball cap. He didn't look at Raiden at all.

"If you wanna win?" Chevy asked Stone as he picked up the man's suit.

"You gotta bet, little man," Ash stated as she tapped on the bill of Chevy's baseball cap.

"Betting a long shot." Stone pulled his coat back on over his shirt. He handed his heavy gloves to Ford.

The boys smiled. Raiden had no clue why those statements seemed to calm the children, but for whatever reason, they did, and he was happy the kids were no longer worried about their quasi-parents.

Raiden and Ash followed Stone's lead. They began to strip out of their outer gear, and the boys gathered up the equipment as the items hit the ground. Raiden shoved some of his personal things into his pack and then unrolled the long, heavy leather coat he preferred to wear in the tunnels.

Stone yanked on a sizeable black duster trimmed in bear fur, as he followed Raiden's movements. Stone hovered next to Winsor as she shimmied out of her outfit. Raiden pulled off his goggles and began to shake the extra snow from his hair. He had just handed Ford the goggles when he saw Doug approach.

Ash and Stone were punching each other in the arm, but they glanced up when Raiden quickly pulled on his bag. He jiggled his pack and hoped that Doug wasn't heading for them. It was a wish in vain.

Doug and three of his friends stopped next to the vehicles. To Ash's credit, she didn't act alarmed. In fact, Raiden thought Ash appeared like no one approached her at all. She just folded her snowsuit and didn't react to the other harvester. Stone leaned against his snowmobile and didn't even turn around. The lack of acknowledgment angered Doug in no time.

"Are you done with Mutt yet?' Doug slithered closer to him. "I've about eight inches that need to be licked, dog." He slapped Raiden on the ass. Raiden wished Humper was around.

"Try four," Raiden scoffed.

Doug reached out and grabbed the back of Raiden's neck. Raiden shoved off his hand and shifted away. They both turned when they heard the click of a gun.

"I said he's mine," Ash snarled. Her gun was leveled at Doug's crotch. "We can make that two inches."

"You got Stone to suck you off. What do you need Mutt for?"

"Maybe I like the way he tastes," Stone stated flatly. He produced the same gun that had been aimed at Raiden earlier. He didn't envy Doug.

Raiden eyes widened when he realized what Stone said. Was Stone protecting him?

"Walk away before you get all of my eight inches." Stone held up the gleaming barrel. The weapon was huge. Raiden decided he would have to ask him what kind of gun he carried when they were on friendlier terms. That was *if* they were ever on friendlier terms.

"When you're done using him, just give me a shout," Doug muttered as he walked away. "I'll be waiting."

"What a piss-slit." Ash sighed as Doug headed to the far side of the stadium. She started toward to exit on the opposite end of the field. Raiden and Stone followed behind her. Raiden walked in a fog as he thought about what had just happened. Why did Stone defend him? He kept asking that question repeatedly. In addition, if Ash planned to get rid of him, then why was she acting like they were staying together? He wondered if they could actually trek together after they were no longer bound. She'd offered, but he didn't think they could do that. Stone would hate it.

"Are you guys going to tell Doug when I'm not tied to Winsor anymore?"

"Hell no," Stone spoke first. "That guy would rip you apart."

"You're protecting me?" Raiden stopped walking. Stone spun around and glared at him. Ash halted as well.

"No, it's just..." Stone waved his hand. "You know." He tossed his hand out again. Raiden had no idea what any of that arm-waving meant.

"Thank you," Raiden said quietly.

"Don't fucking say thank you." Stone tugged a new bottle of Harvester Whisky out of his pack. "If you want to thank me, just don't be with my Winsor." Stone pushed past Ash and stomped toward the doorway of the dome. When he reached the stairs that headed down into the underground tunnels, he turned around. "I'll be in my room on *Clipper*." Stone disappeared into the dark stairway.

"I should go talk to him," Ash grumbled. She didn't seem pleased with the prospect. She turned to the stairs and took the first step. Just as her foot hit the cement, a young man that Raiden had seen around once or twice collided with Ash. They both stumbled and sidestepped.

"Gash, Essie. What're you doing?" Ash put her arms out, and the other man steadied her from falling down the stairs.

"I was looking for you." Essie pulled a stocking cap from his pocket and yanked it over his black curly hair. "*Follar invierno.*"

"Why?"

"Morgan-Roth said he needed to see you right way. I've been looking for you, but I didn't know you were on the surface. I'm heading back to H.S.P.C. HQ, so I don't have a lot of time. I've gotta catch my train."

Ash glanced back at Raiden. "You go and talk to Stone for me. Tell him that we're being separated. Explain that Morgan-Roth wanted us to try for ten days, but that we're not doing it. Just stay with him until I get there."

Raiden shook his head. He had already tried to explain, and Stone had been nothing but distrustful of him. Besides, he hated it when she ordered him around. He wasn't going. The idea of talking to Stone was about as appealing as licking old cheese off a muddy floor.

"Stone might play nice when you're around, but I'd bet my last HOC that he'd shoot me just for fun." Raiden shook his head again. "No dice." Alone with Stone? What if he embarrassed himself, like if he stared at Stone's handsome face too long? Ash's friend might figure out that Raiden had a thing for him. He closed his eyes briefly. It wasn't a "thing." Raiden just thought Stone was sexy. That's all. No one could blame Raiden for appreciating an attractive face and intense brown eyes.

"Raiden, will you do this for me?" Ash's voice dropped. "Please." The seductive quality of the tone made his blood heat. She warmed him as his brains turned into a puddle. Yeah, he was going to keep an eye on her "best friend," and they both knew it.

"I'll explain what I can, but I'm not staying if he's hammered. And you should tell him the truth."

"I'll tell him tomorrow." Ash nodded.

"Where's his room?"

A smiled brightened her face. She was lovely when she smiled. He gazed into her silver eyes and forgot that anyone was around. She leaned toward his ear. Her warm mouth tugged on the silver spike that ran through his lobe. He shivered with pleasure.

"*Clipper*, room fourteen." Her warm breath tickled a few of his hairs, and he gulped. "I'll thank you for talking to him."

"Yeah, you will." Raiden adjusted his pants and then remembered his audience. He glanced behind him. Other people around the dome were looking. Essie smoked his blue pipe and watched them. Raiden could hear everyone's silent speculation on what Ash and he were up to.

"Push me away, big, bad Ash Winsor," he whispered in her ear.

She shoved him hard. Raiden stumbled to the wall and then righted himself. Behind him, a few people laughed.

"Get going, tough guy," she barked.

Raiden hid his smile. He could already picture all the ways she would thank him. Her silver eyes flashed. He would talk to Stone and then meet up with her later.

Chapter 11

After shoving and pushing through the harvesters lounging and jaw-jacking on *Clipper*, Raiden finally reached room fourteen. The door was locked. No one was around the train car, and the surrounding rooms were empty. He knocked a few times but got no answer. He had no idea where Stone was, but he figured if he started at the front of the train and moved to the back, he would find Ash's drunken best friend sooner or later.

Three train cars in, he spotted Stone loafing in a circle with five other harvesters in the center of broken plastic bathtubs. Stone threw back shots of a drink from a tiny glass being passed from man to man. Raiden assumed the drink was Harvester Whiskey since that's all he'd seen him consume so far. A game of Boxcar Dice was in full progress. Small stacks of money were in piles in front of everyone with a growing heap in the middle.

Stone threw down his carved ivory dice. They rolled to a stop next to the wad of HOCs.

"I call."

"Full house."

Money exchanged hands. At no time did Stone stutter or stammer. He made a full sentence and didn't stare or play with his hair. The arm-waving he'd witnessed around Ash was gone. Stone was a grim, hardened, cutthroat harvester. Right now, Ash's best friend looked more like what Raiden had pictured before he'd met him. He shook his head as he pushed closer to the group.

As he got nearer, Raiden realized he hadn't made up his mind on what he wanted to say to the other man yet. He paused at the edge of the betting circle and stared at Ash's love interest. Yeah, he could see it. Stone had the kind of rugged good looks that would dole out wet dreams. Stone looked up, and his intense brown eyes had Raiden losing his mind.

Skit, it was time to think fast.

"Ash said to talk to you." He sounded like he begged. That wasn't going to work.

"You can suck my dick." Stone threw down more money and scooped up his dice.

"I'll admit I've thought about it, but I don't think this is the time or place," Raiden murmured. Sucking Stone's dick wasn't the worst idea. He found the man attractive, except he was supposed to talk to him with his pants closed. This was about Ash. Raiden was supposed to be loyal. He had promised a priest, and for however long this lasted, he would be faithful. Good thing Stone was just being caustic.

Folding his arms across his chest, Raiden noted the way Stone slurred his words during the next set of betting. He drank again and swayed. The harvesters would take all Stone's money if he kept playing juiced-up.

Stone threw bad dice. The loss was heavy. Raiden sidled closer to Stone until he stood directly behind him. The scent of coconuts wafted. He leaned closer and inhaled.

"Are you sniffing me?" Stone tipped his head back, and his eyes caught Raiden's. "I thought the name Mutt was because of your last name. You want me to rub your belly too? Maybe scratch behind your ear?"

"I'm not sniffing you." Raiden had to stop doing that around Ash and Stone. The thing was, why did Stone smell like coconuts? He hoped his mind was simply playing tricks on him. He liked the smell. That couldn't be good.

"Whatever." Stone dug out a hefty wad of HOCs from his pack and threw it down.

"Come on, Stone. We're going to your room." Raiden grabbed Stone's bicep when he reached for his dice again. The muscles felt like granite. His fingers tingled. Not this again. He would just ignore the sensation.

Raiden snatched his hand away before he acted stupid. He wanted to rub Stone's arm. He breathed in Stone's coconut scent again. When the other man noted the inhale, he glared at him and then threw his dice down. Snake eyes. Stone handed his money to the winner.

"Fuck off, Snoopy," Stone slurred. "I'm not your snowstorm."

Unfortunately, right now, Stone was his snowstorm. Shaking his head, Raiden grasped Stone's arm a second time. This might end up in a fight, but he wasn't going to let Stone lose all his HOCs because he was sauced and angry. Stone needed to sleep it off. He pulled but trying to move the muscled harvester was like trying to push a cement pillar.

"Don't make me fight you." Raiden snatched the dice from the air right as Stone threw the cubes toward the center of the players. The dice was in his pocket before Stone even noticed.

"Like you could fight me, Fifi." Stone laughed as he looked around. "Where's my...?" Stone's brow wrinkled in confusion, and then his black eyebrows drew down over his eyes. Raiden took his bewilderment as an excellent time to get him moving.

"We're heading to your room." Raiden scooped up Stone's money and pocketed the HOCs. "Follow me."

One of the dice-playing harvesters laughed. "You got a new boss?"

"I've got no one." The sadness behind those words sliced through Raiden. Stone pushed Raiden away and awkwardly got to his feet. He wobbled and then shoved Raiden when he tried to steady the harvester.

"That's not true." Raiden kept his voice low. "I told you, Ash and I are splitting up." He didn't want to get into this in front of all the men sitting in the circle.

"I'm going to my room," Stone remarked to no one in particular before he stormed toward the exit. Raiden chased after him but stayed a few feet away, so Stone didn't turn around and swing at him. As he walked down the hallway, Stone bounced off the walls. Ash's friend looked like a human game of ping-pong.

As soon as Stone reached a sleeping car in the back, he didn't go into room fourteen but kept on until he was at the end of the line. When Stone finally halted before a door, it took him a few seconds to get the entrance open. Just when Raiden thought Stone wasn't sober enough to get into his room, the door slid open with a swish.

For a split second, Raiden toyed with staying in the hall. At the last second, Raiden slipped inside the room. From his own experience, Raiden knew that drinking alone never made anyone feel better. After he entered behind Stone, the door closed.

Stone spun around when the lock clicked.

"Will you just leave me alone?" Stone threw down his pack and pulled out a dark glass bottle from a side pocket on his bag. "I don't want you around." Using his teeth, he yanked out the stopper while he shoved off his coat. "Leave." Red wine spilled to the floor.

"I'd like to." Raiden had about a hundred activities that would be better than dealing with a drunk.

Stone glared at him and then pulled off his shirt and his heavy sweater in one smooth move.

The half-naked burly harvester had Raiden forgetting his name. He forgot why he had followed Stone to this room. Hell, he forgot about Ash Winsor. Stone had chiseled pecs and washboard abs that made a perfect "V" toward his pants. His skin was blindingly white like the snow, but the black hair that was sprinkled from his chest down toward his pants contrasted in an erotic way. Raiden's fingers itched to slide along that fuzzy trail.

For the first time ever, Raiden thanked the pain in his shoulders. He concentrated on that to keep his pants on.

Stone wasn't looking at him. He unbuckled his gun belt and tossed the weapons toward the bathroom. Wobbling, he then pulled open the button on his pants. Stone jerked so hard that the first fastener popped off. The plastic disk bounced off the wall and then clattered to the floor.

"So, what did Ash tell you to do? Come here and fuck me? Is that going to make it all better? Isn't that what you do, Kibbles? Exchange sexual favors for things you want?"

Raiden winced at the reference to his previous relationship and then considered the name. Kibbles wasn't a step up from Mutt, but it was an improvement over Fifi. Stone was obeying Ash. She told him not to call him Mutt. He supposed this was as good as it was going to get.

"I needed the money for my dad. I made a deal with Doug because I had nothing left to sell. I was starving. I ran out of gear, and then I ran out of food."

"Fuck." Stone wagged his head back and forth as if trying not to let those words into his ears.

"Ash had to talk to Morgan-Roth, but then he's going to find Weaver."

"He didn't send you, Lassie?" Stone guffawed at his own joke and then stared him down. The urge to run started to build. Not from the budding fight, but from the erection burning in his pants. *Skit*. When had that shown up?

"I'm here to talk to you. Everything will go back to the way it was." Raiden took a deep breath and then regretted it when Stone's coconut smell filled his nostrils.

"Maybe I don't want everything to go back to the way it was." Stone untied his boots and then kicked them off. He leaned heavily on the cot. "Ash is a snow licker who just wants to keep me following him around like a dog. You're probably used to that."

"Ash cares about you." Raiden stepped forward to steady the harvester. He spread his hands over the other man's chest. His skin was soft and oiled. Electricity made Raiden's palms tingle, and he yanked his hands away. He shouldn't have touched him. Raiden gulped. What the hell was he doing? Stone's eyes with that same intense quality to them bore into Raiden's. He wanted to look away. He couldn't.

"Maybe…" Stone wrapped one arm around Raiden's waist and leaned closer to him. "I should see why Ash picked you over me. What do you do that's so spectacular in the bedroom?"

"Spectacular?" He couldn't move, couldn't jump away. His feet had grown roots. Stone leaned in, and he was hypnotized. The smell of coconuts and hot male drenched him. His mind took a vacation.

Before he could say anything more, Stone kissed him.

The brawny harvester pulled on Raiden's coat lapels as his lips crushed against Raiden's mouth. Stone tasted like wine, male, and a little like Ash's sunshine. With his mouth still firmly attached, Stone yanked Raiden toward the cot with his hands dug into Raiden's shoulders. Bringing up his hands, Raiden planned to push Stone off, but instead, his unruly fingers slipped to the other man's neck.

No. He had to let go, but he had the strangest feeling Stone needed him now more than ever. Stone shoved Raiden's coat off his shoulders before his mouth lifted.

"You're so hot," Stone panted. Raiden had never been more shocked, muddled, and turned on. He wanted to get down on his knees and open his mouth. He slapped his hand on Stone's bare chest when the harvester would've kissed him again.

"What about Ash?" he breathed as he tilted his head out of Stone's reach. One of them had to sober up, and since he hadn't been drinking, he supposed that "someone" should be him.

"Forget Ash Winsor. Be with me."

"I can't."

"I can't either, but I can try. I can try tasting you and holding you. I just have to touch you." Stone grabbed both sides of Raiden's buttoned-up shirt. "You can try out white meat instead of dark."

The sound of ripping cloth and fasteners hitting the tiles distracted Raiden just long enough. Stone's mouth captured his lips again, and his tongue speared in to take over. Stone licked and sucked until Raiden couldn't recall anything he would've said. Raiden's brain was now firmly nestled in his underwear. *Helvete.*

"All good dogs know the command *come*, right?" Stone placed Raiden firmly between his thighs and grabbed

Raiden's dick through his pants. He squeezed the growing erection as he groaned.

"Stop it, Stone. Don't do that." Raiden didn't want Stone to sound like Doug. He wouldn't sit, stay, come, like someone's trained poodle.

"Don't you get that I want to stop it? I do. I want to, but I can't. I have to touch you. I have to feel you." Stone's other hand gripped him around the neck. His fingers rubbed over Raiden's lips as he studied his face. The way Stone looked with all that concentration had Raiden's head swimming. His tongue licked at Stone's fingertips when they brushed his mouth as if testing the smoothness. The salty taste of the other man's skin went straight to his head like a stiff drink. He wanted to suck, any part of Stone's body.

"Stone, please," Raiden began.

"Was Ash gentle with you?" Stone's fingers traveled a path to the edge of Raiden's thick cotton undershirt. With another yank, Stone had the top over his head and onto the floor.

"No." For a second, Raiden tried to think about Ash. Her curves and the way she rode him had his cock twitching. Ash gentle? He wouldn't consider their sex that mellow.

"I'm not gentle." Stone's eyes darkened with need. "I'll try to be. I'll try to make this good for you." Raiden's cock grew and filled out his jeans. The head was becoming painful as the rim pressed against the zipper.

Shifting to the side, Stone shoved one of the many pillows off the cot as he set his hand down next to Raiden's hip. The twinge in Raiden's shoulder was a welcome feeling. He tried to use the pain to clear his head. Again, he leaned back, which only exposed his neck and chest like an invitation. He was fooling around with Stone and not stopping. What the hell? He'd promised the priest ten days of honoring Ash. Maybe he *was* a dog.

"Stone…" He tried to come up with all the reasons that they couldn't do any of this. All that came out was a sensual rumble from deep in his chest. It didn't matter what sounds he made, Stone ignored him. The other man seemed lost in the moment. Stone's mouth went to his neck, and his tongue snaked up to the spike in Raiden's earlobe. *Fanken*, how did both Stone and Ash know he liked that? He moaned involuntarily.

"Say my name again." Stone's other hand went to the front of Raiden's jeans. The sexy harvester had the buttons undone before anyone said anything more.

Stone jerked the jeans down, and they caught on Raiden's boots. Neither one of them paid attention to the fabric. Stone's eyes widened as he stared down at Raiden's cock where the distinct outline was visible in his underwear. Stone grinned before he leaned down to lick at Raiden's nipple.

"Stone, don't…" Raiden bowed his back as Stone sucked the small point. He felt his teeth graze his skin.

"Did Ash bend you over?" Stone's words slurred right before he brought his mouth in for another dizzying kiss. Raiden couldn't answer. Stone's lips smashed hard until Raiden thought he could taste blood. The smell of the coconuts and the taste of this delicious man made him delirious.

"No," he moaned in between kisses. Raiden felt the sharp nip, and then the suction. He couldn't help it. He drew on Stone's tongue and drank in the other man until a whirling sensation started to steal his equilibrium. His hips rocked against the cot making a banging squeak against the wall. Never in his life had he been this excited. Ash was the only person he could think of who had ever made him lose his mind like this. Every inch of his skin was on fire. The pain in his shoulder and his knees vanished. Ash had done this to him when he'd touched her. Automatically, his fingers went to his underwear. His hands stilled. What was he doing?

"Did Ash strip you naked?"

Raiden tried to think. That wasn't how it went. "No."

"I want to see you naked. I want to lick you." Squeezing his shoulder, Stone then shoved Raiden's briefs into his tangled jeans. Raiden lost his balance. He clutched at Stone's biceps. *Skit*, he had to stop this before he went any further. He should've left ten minutes ago. Back when he still had his brain in his head instead of his dick.

"Did Ash tell you that he loves you?" Stone's zipper went south.

"No." Raiden thought about the bitterness he heard. Stone was using him to feel better about Ash. He was an "Ash Winsor" substitute. In another time or place, Raiden might've been pleased by that. He had always thought of Ash Winsor as an amazing man, and if someone wanted to pretend he was that amazing, then he would find it amusing. The problem was, none of this was about him. If Raiden didn't know Ash Winsor or if he didn't understand the two-year achingly painful love that Stone was obviously carrying around, then he would just get some sex and walk away. He couldn't do that. Raiden struggled with what to say to explain that he and Ash would be over as soon as they found Weaver. Stone needed to be patient and to stop kissing him long enough to listen. "He—"

Stone's pants slid to his ankles. All the words were forgotten.

Ash's best friend had the type of dick that made Raiden's mouth go dry. Stone's erection was encased in tight black briefs exactly like the ones Ash had worn. The monster peeked over the edge of the fabric as if to get a better look at Raiden. Stone grabbed the mass and squeezed. A spot of pre-cum darkened his gray elastic band.

Raiden looked up into Stone's eyes, hoping for a minute of clarity. He didn't even need a full minute, just time enough to pull his pants up and walk out. He didn't even get a second.

"Did you say you loved him?" Stone's eyes were bloodshot. Maybe alcohol was the reason, or perhaps restless nights thinking about Ash Winsor did that to him. Raiden's heart squeezed painfully.

"No."

"I don't love him either."

What a lie.

Stone steered Raiden to the center of the cot. Tripping, Raiden struggled with his twisted pants. Stone pulled Raiden up and positioned him on the bed.

"Did Ash suck you off?"

"No, I—" Stone's mouth captured Raiden's lips again. The harvester drew on Raiden's lips until they were both out of breath.

"I'm going to." When Stone yanked Raiden's boxers down, Raiden barely noticed with Stone's tongue caressing his mouth. However, he did notice when the other man's hand skimmed his erection. Stone began to tease the head with his thumb. Around and around, his fingers spun.

Raiden threw his head back and panted when Stone dropped his mouth down on his cock. Stone started to suck his shaft with the kind of intensity that matched his eyes. Raiden didn't even know this sort of passion with a man existed up until now. The number of blowjobs he'd received in his life he could count on one hand. None of them were any good. They couldn't even distract him from the acute pain in his limbs. Stone, on the other hand, wasn't just good, he was fan-fucking-tastic. That amazing wet tongue rubbed Raiden's slit as pre-cum gathered and dripped. His eyes rolled back in his head.

When Raiden tried to slow Stone, so he wouldn't orgasm in his mouth, the tugging on Stone's hair didn't seem to make any difference.

"Stone, stop it, please," he begged. He'd never exploded in someone's mouth, and he was positive Stone wouldn't appreciate the action. "Please, Stone. Stop," Raiden pleaded, but the suction became unbearable. Raiden's dick hit the back of the other man's throat. Stone's mouth ran ripples up and down Raiden's shaft. When Stone's tongue rapidly flicked the head, Raiden's sensitive cock pulsated.

Bucking his hips, Raiden came hard, unable to stop the bombardment to his senses. Raiden threw back his hand while he tried not to tumble backward onto the cot. His seed was vigorously drawn from his body as Stone ruthlessly drained him, not letting one drop go. Raiden groaned as his head sagged to the side. He'd give Stone an award for that.

When Stone let Raiden's cock slip from his lips, Raiden tried to stand. His head spun. He'd never felt anything like that before. Stone grabbed his wrist and stared down at him.

Raiden wasn't sure if he should run or fight. His stomach clenched with disappointment at himself. He had no idea what to say to Ash when she found out what he had done. Why couldn't he stop? The desire for Stone tied him up in knots.

Licking his lips, Stone ran his fingers along his underwear.

"Did Ash fuck you so hard you shouted his name? I bet that was hot."

Yes, Ash Winsor. That's who they should be talking about. That's why he was here, not to get sucked. He was here because Ash loved Stone, and vice versa. He wasn't anyone, and he had to get out from between the two of them.

"No." Raiden took a deep breath. "Stone, don't—" He was going to say, "Don't keep doing this to yourself," but that never came out.

Stone jerked his underwear down.

Stone's cock sprung free as if the shaft just waited for the green light. His massive hard-on dripped. Stone's dick was as white as the rest of him, and maybe if Raiden wasn't so turned on, the harvester's white marble cock would be slightly funny. That was a very big *maybe*. It was hard to make fun of a cock that large. Raiden couldn't take his eyes from the blue veins under the pale skin. His erection pointed directly at Raiden as if picking him out of a crowd.

"Did Doug fuck you?" Stone kicked off his underwear and stood there in only his socks.

"No." Doug had made him get down on his knees in exchange for trekking on the surface, but Raiden had refused to give up his ass. Doug would've hurt him just for his own entertainment. The psycho harvester had tried to choke Raiden on a few occasions, but his dick was simply too small.

"I'm going to." Stone peeled off his socks. "I'm going to be deep inside of you." The articles were tossed toward the other scattered clothing. Stone paid little attention to the fact that he was now naked, but it was the only thought in Raiden's head. As Stone dug in his pack, Raiden reached for his pants. His hands trembled. Was he trying to take them off or pull them up? After a few seconds, Stone produced a white plastic tube.

"I..." Raiden licked his lips as he searched for an explanation.

"I use coconut oil. I like it for my hands but..." Stone tossed the item on the cot before he pressed his naked chest to Raiden's pecs. "The oil will make it better when I'm filling you. It'll be so smooth." Stone rubbed back and forth. "You'll feel every inch of me."

Helvete, Stone's description made all his skin tingle. His chest grew warm with that buzzing right under his skin. He felt no pain, just pleasure saturating every corner of his body.

"I don't—" he groaned into Stone's neck. He tried to say he didn't think this was a good idea. Again, it was as if Stone didn't hear him. His teeth nipped at Raiden's lower lip. Chills ran down Raiden's spine.

"Bend over, Spike. I'm going to pleasure you until I'm all you think about. I'm going to be all you dream about." Stone's soft hands pressed on the small of Raiden's back as he spun him around. Stone shoved Raiden on his belly over the cot.

"Stone, wait." Raiden wanted to adjust his position. Pulling at one of the fleece blankets, he tried to tuck it under his body. Raiden decided he was a down and dirty dog. He was trying to make himself comfortable, so Stone could fuck him, and he'd enjoy it more. He'd never thought of himself as a shit harvester with no morals or loyalty, but it appeared that's exactly what he was.

Raiden's heart beat out of his chest when Stone's hand started to rub up and down his back. His cock began to harden and swell all over again. Was it possible that Stone could make him climax again? He didn't think that was doable, but then again, passion and heat like this had never happened to him before. Only Ash had been able to make him fuck all night. She had chased away the ache in his bones—and Stone had the same power.

Stone pushed until Raiden was face down into the sea of blankets. Raiden's boots were still on the floor, and he tried to widen his stance by kicking at the fabric. His jeans prevented his legs from spreading. Excitement uncoiled in his stomach. Raiden's breathing picked up when Stone's hand roamed over his ass.

"You smell like fruit," Stone murmured to his skin as he kissed Raiden's neck and shoulders. Pausing, Stone leaned over and picked up the bottle. The other man nibbled on Raiden's neck and the spike in his earlobe. Raiden heard the pop sound of the cap being removed. The smell of coconuts got stronger. Stone stepped closer, and his cock brushed Raiden's ass.

Trying to get a better stance, Raiden kicked to open his legs wider. His boots made a squeak against the tiles as he shuffled his feet.

"Stone, wait. Please." He wanted to take off his boots and strip naked. If he was about to make a horrible life choice, he might as well do it all the way. "Stop." He wiggled, and his underwear fell deeper into his jeans.

"God, I wish I could stop." Stone kissed down his spine. When Stone lifted his head, Raiden glanced over his shoulder. Stone's brow was furrowed in preoccupation as he scooped out a glob of white goo onto his fingers. A drop of cold coconut oil hit his cleft.

"Stone…" Raiden shifted his hips as goose bumps rose. Stone's warm hand pursued the oil that traveled down his balls.

"Do you want to know what I'm thinking?" Stone asked him.

He didn't want to know what Stone thought while they did this. Stone was probably thinking about Ash Winsor. For a heartbeat, Raiden wanted to pretend that Stone liked him, that this handsome man wanted Raiden.

"No."

His fingers slipped between Raiden's ass cheeks. His palm then dropped lower to cup Raiden's sack and slide back and forth. Stone's hands stroked everywhere. Raiden's eyes rolled back into his head.

He gasped out when Stone tugged and played with his dick before moving over his pouch again.

"This could've been different." Stone's finger probed his hole. He added more oil. "You're hot. You could've wanted me. Winsor could've wanted... I don't know."

Raiden pressed his forehead into a soft blanket on the cot. A hiss escaped his lips when Stone's finger slipped into his ass and surged forward. The sexy harvester proceeded to glide the thick digit back and forth. Raiden's cock swelled unbearably. *Helvete*, that felt incredible. He didn't care how big Stone was. He wanted to be filled. Raiden wanted to be taken.

Maybe he could come again. He shivered at the thought.

"I want Ash to look at me the way you look at me," Stone continued. "You stare at me like you want me inside of you. I can see it in your eyes." Stone added a second finger and stretched the tight fissure wider. "When you look at me, I can't stop wanting you."

"Stone, please." Raiden bucked his hips. The pressure was precisely what he liked, slow, smooth, and insistent.

"I'm going to fuck you, and we're going to forget about Ash Winsor. You're going to think about me."

Raiden couldn't think at all. Stone was right. He was no longer thinking about Ash Winsor or promises. He wanted to be fucked by Stone. Raiden might even think about Stone long after he, Ash, and Stone went their separate ways.

The slow sliding in and out movement continued. More oil was added to Stone's fingers. The wet sound of the other man's digits slipping in his backside filled Raiden's ears. The strong smell of coconuts intensified.

"*Helvete*." Raiden wanted Stone inside of him now. "Stone, please," he begged. The wait made him light-headed. He tried again to pull his legs further apart. "Give me a second."

Stone removed his hand from Raiden's cleft. The abrupt loss made Raiden tremble. He took a deep breath. Good. Now he could take his pants off completely. Raiden's hand released the side of the cot. Quickly, he moved to grab his shoes. He unlaced one boot. The other tie was a tangled knot. Raiden swore under his breath as he yanked on his pants. His jeans came up to his knees instead of off. Stone stopped his awkward tugging by pushing his arm away. Shoving him back over the cot again, Stone pressed Raiden's hands flat next to his head. Stone pinned him, and Raiden let him do it.

"You got your second. I can't wait anymore. I have to have you." Stone lightly fluttered over Raiden's hole again while running his fingertips down over his taint to palm his balls. "Are you ready?"

"No." Raiden wanted his pants off, but he wanted Stone inside of him even more. "Please," he whispered to the cot. Raiden wasn't even sure what he was asking for now. Sex? To take his pants off? Both?

It didn't matter. He just wanted Stone.

Stone set both his large hands on either side of Raiden's ass. Pulling his cheeks apart, Raiden could feel the tip of Stone's erection at his puckered entrance. The sexy harvester used his thumbs to gradually spread him farther, and then Stone surged forward against the opening.

Raiden moaned into the blankets. Stone stilled. Just the tip of his cock was pressed inside of Raiden's body.

"You hate me, don't you?" Stone asked.

Raiden couldn't answer. His tongue was stuck to the roof of his mouth. He couldn't even breathe right now, let alone talk.

"Gur," he groaned. That wasn't even a word. He closed his eyes as embarrassment made him want to yank a blanket over his head. He reached for a pillow to put over his face. Stone would think Raiden was an inept bedmate if he didn't start to have a little finesse. Honestly, he did have a few talents in the bedroom, but at this rate, Stone would never find that out. He didn't want to let Stone down. The same inclination to impress Ash Winsor had risen to the surface. He wanted to dazzle Stone, and he was far from dazzling anyone.

"Do you hate me, Spike?" Stone yanked the pillow out of his hand and exposed Raiden's flushed face. His tongue ran over the piercing in his earlobe and then down toward his neck. Raiden shivered.

"No," Raiden finally growled out and then threw his hands back to clutch at Stone's thighs.

He heard Stone exhale right before he inched forward. Stone grabbed Raiden's hands and placed them on the cot once more. After caressing Raiden's back and shoulders, Stone slid his palms down to squeeze his ass. Stone's hands returned to Raiden's thighs digging his fingers into the flesh. When Stone moved his cheeks apart again, he set his thumbs on either side of his dick and added more oil. Raiden could feel the cold coconut grease and then Stone's thumbs rubbing the lubricant into his skin.

Flexing his hips slightly, Stone's erection settled further into Raiden's waiting hole. The pressure was exactly what Raiden needed to make his entire core shudder. He buried his face in a pillow near his head and moaned like a bitch in heat. Stone would make fun of him later, but right now, he couldn't seem to care.

Raiden's dick swung under the cot, and he tried again to get his boot off. The shoe that he'd loosened the laces of finally came off his foot. He kicked his pant leg off and opened his legs. His right hand went to his cock. Raiden wanted to touch the sensitive head and stroke to completion. Stone moved just the tiniest tip upward of his hips. The head of the other man's shaft was now fully stretching Raiden's body. The stinging fullness made him euphoric. This was so much better than any man Raiden had ever been with.

His breath heaved out as Raiden lifted his head and pushed back on Stone's shaft. The action embedded Stone deeper, and Raiden quivered when Stone's cock slipped past his prostate. He heard Stone growl and then grunt. Raiden fondled the head of his own erection and squirmed with Stone inside of him.

"I'm a horrible—"

"Stop it, Stone." Raiden didn't want to hear any more poor-me-I-don't-have-Ash whining from Stone. He wanted to be fucked, and Stone should get started. Raiden couldn't find the words to explain that he wanted this. He moved his hips, and Stone's cock slipped out part way hitting that bundle of nerves again. Raiden closed his eyes.

Thrusting forward, Stone shoved his cock all the way to his balls. Raiden screamed into the blankets and buried his face. Stone was much longer than he had thought. Raiden caught his breath and relaxed.

"Snowballs." Stone slapped his hands down on Raiden's lower back. For a second, he went still. "You feel... I... love..." Stone sputtered and then bent forward to Raiden's shoulder. "It's crazy to..." He kissed the skin before dropping his forehead into Raiden's neck.

"Please." Raiden flexed his hole in a silent command for Stone to move.

"Damn, Spike," Stone slurred. "You're tight. Ash and Doug didn't fuck you, did they? It's just me. Only me."

"No." Raiden looked over his shoulder. Stone was flushed. His glaringly white skin had a light stain of pink that traveled up his neck and into his cheeks.

Stone moaned, and Raiden thought that sound might be the most erotic sound he'd ever heard a man make. He could feel Stone shake.

"I think I'm going to come."

"Stone, don't—"

This couldn't be over so soon. Raiden didn't get the chance to tell Stone to not come yet. Stone withdrew part way and then drove into him. The friction forced Raiden's eyes to close and a silent scream of pleasure to whistle past his lips. The feel of Stone's smooth dick gliding in and out of his body prevented Raiden from thinking about anything else. He needed this to get the man out of his system so he could get his head on right. Raiden's hands snapped to the edge of the cot. He fumbled with a fluffy blanket until he found the metal bar. He gripped the iron rod that held the bed up until his knuckles turned white.

"Has anyone man ever fucked you like this?" Stone pistoned his hips harder. The cot rocked against the wall.

"No," he gasped. "God, no."

When Stone shoved forward again, this time Raiden planted his legs, and let his ass take the deep penetration. He swore Stone's shaft would be imprinted in his body until the day he died. Every time Stone's cock hit that perfect spot inside of him, he couldn't help but whimper. Gliding in and out, Stone built more speed. Somewhere along the way, Raiden lost his mind.

"I'm going to come inside of you," Stone whispered to the spike in Raiden's earlobe before he licked the silver piercing and dropped his forehead to his shoulder. Under the cot, Stone reached for Raiden's cock. He gripped Raiden's hard shaft. "I have to—"

Raiden's groan was loud enough to hear from the hall. Stone's palm was covered in melted coconut oil, and his soft hand skimmed over Raiden's ultra-sensitive head. The action made Raiden buck. Stone's dick pounded in and out of his ass as Stone's hand pumped over Raiden's cock harder and faster to coordinate with every deep thrust.

His balls felt full and his cock was eager. Raiden would explode if Stone kept this up. He would climax again for Stone just like a trained animal, and he couldn't stop it. He didn't want to stop. A tingling sensation spiraled down his spine. The feeling rocketed around his entire being. The pain in his body was long gone. All he could feel was a pure, undiluted pleasure. A dizzy exhilarated feeling took over just like when he was with Ash. He couldn't think. He could only feel.

"I'm going to come in your ass, Spike." Stone shuddered and then penetrated him at a new angle.

Raiden unraveled.

Stone's cock struck the perfect spot inside of Raiden's body with new force. The man massaged his prostate like he had a detailed map of Raiden's body. There was nothing more but Stone's cock, hand, and driving hips. His body had a new owner.

As he rose up on his toes, Raiden shouted his release into the blankets next to his head. Ropes of white semen spurted out of his body just as Stone's cock swelled and then filled his back passage with hot seed. The sensation was an entirely different feeling than anything ever before. Ecstasy threw a warm blanket over him.

They didn't move. Little sweet aftershocks went up and down Raiden's spine as he felt Stone finally stir. They both groaned as Stone's softening penis slipped from Raiden's body.

"I'm sorry, buddy," Stone's voice rasped. "I mean that." He crawled up on the cot, and to Raiden's shock, he grabbed his arm. Clumsily, Raiden followed Stone up onto the bed with one pant leg still hung around his booted foot. He collapsed next to Ash's best friend. A part of him waited for Stone to tell him to get out. Most men on the harvester trains didn't sleep together.

When Stone didn't tell him to leave, Raiden unlaced his boot and kicked off his jeans. He relaxed on one of the satin pillows next to Stone and sighed. After a few moments, he turned on his side.

"About Ash and everything," Raiden began. He placed his hand on Stone's shoulder. Stone rolled toward him and threw his arm around Raiden's waist. The man was totally out. His deep breathing fanned Raiden's face. Stone nuzzled into his side and began to snore.

Raiden sighed again. He didn't want to have a conversation anyway. Actually, he never wanted to talk about what just happened. He was a dog who at the first scent of action dropped his pants. Stone made him feel like a horny teen. How would he explain to Ash what he'd just done? What would he say when Stone woke up?

He needed a second to clear his head. He'd talk to them tomorrow.

Chapter 12

A hard, rough mystery item hit Raiden in the gut. His eyes popped open. Staring down at him was a man he'd never seen before. Confusion streaked through his brain. Where was he?

Raiden looked at his naked frame. His boot had been dropped on his pecs. He clutched the leather sole to his chest as he tried to clear the fog draped over his brain.

Two things struck him at once. One, he had sex with Stone. Two, his shoulders and knees didn't ache. He could barely process either one of those things.

"What the hell?" He glanced around as he sat up. There were two strangers staring at him. Raiden didn't know the harvesters. He was still in Stone's room on *Clipper*, and the deep snore that came from next to him signified that Stone was out for the count.

"What're you doing in my room?" Another boot was tossed at Raiden. This time, he caught the flying footwear before it hit him. Raiden held the laces and rolled off the cot and onto his feet. His ass objected to the quick rise, and he groaned, but still, he felt better than he had in ages.

"I thought this was Stone's room." Raiden picked up his clothes. He yanked on his underwear and pants, and then hunted for his shirt.

"Stone asked to borrow my key so he could piss." The harvester who had thrown Raiden's boot added a dirty look as if Raiden didn't comprehend that he was unhappy. His scowl followed Raiden around the room as he dressed.

"Did you fuck in here?" the second man said. His face scrunched.

Raiden got on his shirt and socks. He didn't answer. He couldn't believe that indeed he had gotten fucked in here. Every time he moved, the sting from Stone's penetration reminded him of what a terrible person he was. He'd judged Weaver for years as being one of the most immoral human beings he'd ever met, and now look at him. He could give Weaver a run for his money.

"Stone." One of the strangers shoved at Stone's shoulder. Raiden winced. He didn't want to face Stone. What would he say?

"Get out," Stone growled.

Raiden took that as his cue to get the hell out of the room. He had to talk to Ash. He would explain what he did, and then they would get untied. They were going to do that anyway. Raiden briefly considered how hurt she would be, as he yanked on his leather coat. He couldn't be the one to make her cry. Everyone else simply thought of her as titanium. With everyone else, she had to be big, bad Ash Winsor, but with him, he was the one who was supposed to let her be soft, be vulnerable. He was supposed to be her help, her bridge. Raiden had failed. And not just a little failure, a big, colossal, avalanche-sized disaster.

Raiden slipped his pack onto his shoulders just as Stone opened his eyes. The handsome harvester's hair was half over his face, and he stared at him through the black tangled strands. *Fanken*, he looked even better this morning than he did last night.

"Scruffy, don't go." Stone's eyes captured Raiden's, and for a second, he considered staying.

Raiden pulled his hair into a ponytail and looked away. No, he had to leave and now.

With a jiggle to his backpack, Raiden hauled his ass out of the room and away from Stone. He hit the train hallway and glanced around.

Stopping before the first door, Raiden played out what he would tell Ash. He had to come clean. They would split up, and he would never see either one of them again. Stone and Ash would get together like they were supposed to, and Raiden would… he didn't know what he would do, but he wouldn't be the man who would ruin their relationship. Raiden could make all this better. He just didn't know *how* exactly.

After throwing open the door, Raiden headed back to room fourteen. That's where he was supposed to be. Jogging through the halls, he stopped at Stone's real quarters and knocked. No one answered, and Raiden sagged against the door. Where was Ash? Did she come looking for them and they were in the wrong room? He wondered if she finished her business with Morgan-Roth. *Skit*, last night he should have been with her. He thought about Stone's smooth hands and his rough thrusts. He closed his eyes as his cock twitched along to the replay. What now?

"You look like a lost dog."

Raiden lifted his head from the door and regarded Doug. Fan-fucking-tastic. This was just perfect. Just when he thought this moment of inner turmoil couldn't get any darker, Doug shows up.

"Just leave me alone." Raiden spun on his heel and stomped toward the opposite direction of the insane harvester. He didn't know where he would head next, but anyplace other than here sounded excellent to him.

"Were you looking for Winsor?" Doug asked him just as he reached the door to the next train car. "Because he was looking for you last night." Doug paused. "I know where he is."

Raiden turned around as his eyes slanted into a glare. Doug never helped him unless there was sex involved. *Helvete.*

"What's the deal?" he asked skeptically.

"Not what you're thinking. Ash has money. I take you to him and Ash tosses some HOCs my way." Doug shrugged. He pulled out a bag of dried banana chips and popped some into his mouth. "Just thought you could use some help," Doug spoke as he chewed. "Since you lost your new owner."

The sound of his teeth crushing the fruit was the only sound between them.

Raiden finally headed back over to where Doug stood. He eyed him.

"Where's Ash?"

"He headed out on the surface about an hour ago. I saw him in the dome geared up and gone."

Raiden's confused frown switched to a scowl. Why did she go back out? Was she looking for him and Stone? Maybe she was helping Morgan-Roth. Raiden jiggled his pack out of habit, and Doug held out the bag of fruit.

"Want some?"

Raiden again gaped at Doug, bewildered. Why was he kind to him?

"What do you want, Doug? I told you I'm not sucking you off anymore. I'm with Ash now." Raiden had to force the words out. He was supposed to be with Ash, yet he had fooled around with the man she loved. Raiden still couldn't believe how easily he had just bent over, literally.

For years, Raiden hadn't been with anyone, and then due to the loss of Weaver and his poor trekking skills, he had accepted Doug's offer. Raiden had been happy to keep his own company other than what Doug forced on him. He was less likely to get hurt that way. Now after Ash, Raiden felt like his libido had taken over. He went from not interested in sex to spreading his legs after one kiss. He would prefer to turn off the lust.

Raiden scanned Doug. Well… he still didn't want him, so that was a comfort.

"I don't want anything, Mutt." Doug crushed a few more chips from the sack in his hand. "I just told you. Pitch a few bills my way and we'll be even. I just thought I'd help you out." Doug turned to walk out the door of the train car.

"Wait. You'll tell me where Ash went?"

"Better. I can take you."

Raiden's heart beat a little too hard, but he wasn't sure if that was because he was scared to ride with Doug on the surface, or if he was scared to see Ash and tell her he had slept with the man she loved. It was probably the second thing.

Back when Stone had just sucked him off, he thought that would be a hellish conversation, but now he would have to tell her he had the other man inside of him. He groaned.

"If you don't want to go, fine with me." Doug started for the exit again.

"No, I want to go. And what do I have to do to get a ride to see Ash?" Raiden still had a hard time believing Doug had even one altruistic bone in his body.

"Nothing." Doug chewed. "I told you. When we see Ash, just have him pay me a few bills." He shrugged and then pointed to the door. "Are you coming with me to the dome or not?"

Raiden stared at Doug's back for a second. He wanted to put this off, maybe forever, but he knew he couldn't. There was no "tomorrow" to push this aside.

"Fine, let's go, but no sex or blowjobs or anything. I just need a ride."

"Sure, Mutt."

Raiden winced. He wished Doug wouldn't have been so helpful; then he could indeed say he would tell Ash tomorrow.

Chapter 13

The snowsuit Raiden wore wasn't anywhere near as insulated as the one Ash had lent him. His old suit had lost its ability to protect from the bitter cold months ago, but this outfit was all he had left of his gear. The biting wind forced Raiden to press as close to Doug's back as he could get. They zipped along on Doug's high-powered snowmobile across the snow dunes, as they hunted for Ash. Doug navigated the ice and snow with ease, as they zoomed toward wherever Ash was trekking.

At first, Raiden tried to follow where they headed, but after the third or fourth sharp turn and the fifth ice tunnel, he gave up. He held on to Doug's barrel chest, and soon, his concern for what he would say to Ash distracted him from his surroundings. Raiden stopped paying attention to the snow lashing against his goggles and started to rehearse the speech he would give Winsor. He would tell her he had made a mistake. Would she believe it was an accident? Raiden could add that he was out of his mind. He would say to her that Stone was loaded.

The minute he recalled how drunk Stone had been, Raiden dropped his head onto Doug's shoulder. Why didn't he walk away? After that first fantastic kiss, Raiden should have run like a polar bear was after him. Stone didn't even know what he was doing. The more Raiden replayed the night in his head, the more he recalled how Stone had spent the whole time talking about Ash. Raiden cringed and then considered if he should tell her that part. Maybe if she understood that Stone had been upset and wanted comfort from Raiden, then she might not be as furious. Raiden shrugged that off. She was going to be livid no matter how he explained it.

Raiden's head flipped up as the machine slowed. They advanced toward a building that looked like the walls had sunk into the snow. Part of the roof was missing, and the words "Best B" was all that was left of an ice-covered sign.

Under the yellow letters, he spotted a set of broken glass doors that were partway covered in ice and frost. An enormous snow mound blocked the majority of the entrance. Ash was here? Why?

Normally, he didn't trust Doug, but he couldn't use his wariness of the harvester to get out of this uncomfortable upcoming confrontation. Plus, Doug had always been safe on the surface. No, he wouldn't dodge the ass-chewing. Raiden would face Winsor. If she was here, he would tell her what he had done.

As Doug slowed to a crawl, Raiden stared at the building as he readied himself for Ash's anger or tears. He hoped for anger. The tears cut him up inside. Whatever her reaction, he would stay and take it. He deserved to hear whatever she had to say. He would remind her they were splitting up, and soon, she and Stone could be together just like she wanted.

Doug slowed his Ski-Doo to a stop, but he didn't kill the engine. He used his thumb to point at the structure.

"Get off, Mutt."

Raiden automatically climbed off the sled and unstrapped his pack. He'd trekked with Doug so many times that he acted out of habit. He pulled on his pack and turned to examine the dark doorway peeking over the mini ice mountain.

"Ash is inside?"

When Raiden turned around, he noted that Doug hadn't killed the engine of the snowmobile and gotten off yet. Doug pulled the sled further away. The harvester started to circle Raiden. He drove slowly around and around. Doug was easily already six feet away from him. Raiden's brow wrinkled as this situation became more and more frighteningly clear.

"I don't have any idea where Ash is." As Doug spoke, he made a slow circle around Raiden. "I can't believe you came with me." Doug chuckled. He was just out of Raiden's reach, and the ring widened with every pass.

"What the fuck, Doug? You said you'd take me to see him."

"I lied. What else did you expect?" Another rumble of the machine and another pass. "Here's how this is going to go. You'll come back and suck my dick and let me fuck that tight ass of yours whenever and wherever I want, and I won't leave you out here to die."

Raiden took a few steps closer to see if there was any way he could get onto the machine. Doug maneuvered the sled further away, and muffled laughter could be heard under his mask.

Scanning the frozen collapsing building and then the landscape of ice, Raiden had no idea where he was. Even if he had paid attention, he wouldn't know. Even if he knew, he couldn't walk back. He was a human-popsicle if left here, and they both knew it.

"Fine." Raiden tried to see Doug's eyes through his dark goggles. Doug didn't stop moving but kept rotating. Raiden tried to keep down the growing panic. "I said yes."

"I think you don't mean it."

Raiden clenched his fist. Of course, he didn't mean it. He wondered what he would have to say to get out of the ice and back on the machine and into the dome.

"I mean it. I was going to tell Ash it's over." Raiden gagged on the words. The sad fact was that wasn't a lie. The little bit of time they had in the sun was now finished. The sex with Stone marked the end of whatever weird relationship Ash and he had built, and no amount of Weaver's voodoo would keep them together. Raiden was sure of that if nothing else.

"You can stay out here and think about your loyalty to me. Maybe if you freeze off your toes, you'll remember who you belong to, dog."

"What?" Doug wouldn't really leave him out here. Would he? Raiden had already lost the side of his foot to the ice when he and Weaver nearly died in that snowstorm. The idea of going through that pain again scared him to his core. "Doug, please don't do this, man."

"I like it when you beg." Doug laughed. "I can't wait to hear what you'll say when I get back."

Before Raiden could say anything more, Doug revved the machine into high gear and sped away. After only a few moments, Raiden was left in the snow in the middle of nowhere.

What the hell was he going to do?

Looking to the sky, he closed his eyes and felt for a storm. A storm was his first concern. His joints didn't hurt. Ever since he started to have sex with Ash, the pain had been ever so slightly easing. Last night with Stone, the throbbing had stopped all altogether. Now he didn't know what that meant. Did the lack of pain mean he couldn't tell anymore if a storm was coming?

Raiden found himself shrugging as he started toward the frozen construction. Even if he knew when the snow was on top of him, it wasn't like he could do anything. So, what if Ash and Stone had fucked his gift right out of him? He didn't care. He wouldn't have changed what he did.

Alone in the snow, hiking toward the "Best B," Raiden had to admit the truth. If he could go back in time, he wouldn't change anything with either Stone or Ash. They had been amazing. They would be a fond memory as he got older. When he died alone, he'd think about them. They would be great together. They'd be happy.

Fuck. He wanted them to be happy.

Reaching the snow that blocked the entrance, Raiden paused to watch a few snowflakes dance in the cold air. The wind was successfully infiltrating his suit. He'd go inside and stay out of the blustery weather until Doug came back for him. Raiden climbed over the immense, hardened snowbank and then skidded to a stop in front of the glass doors. He used his boot to break up the ice enough to enter the shop.

Inside the "Best B" were counters on the left. Broken electronics littered rows of frosted-over plastic shelving. The store was stripped bare of all wiring and any items that were salvageable. Damaged light fixtures hung from wires where the ceiling was still stable. Raiden was reasonably sure that harvesters had done over the place. That's probably why Doug knew about it and wasn't concerned Raiden would be found.

Raiden got his footing on the snow and ice that had poured in through the broken roof. He clambered over a busted cash register frozen to the blue carpet. When he reached the front counters, he contemplated taking off his pack and looking for extra clothing to keep him warm. He'd sold just about everything. The amount of gear he owned was appalling, but maybe he'd be lucky, and there would be an item or two left.

He dug out a threadbare scarf and hat that no one wanted. The added articles didn't keep the chill out, but he put them on anyway.

Stomping his foot, Raiden felt the cold eat at him. He tapped his foot and then dug for starter kindling, Harvester Whiskey, and matches. Walking around the shelving near the exit, Raiden looked for items to burn. Starting a fire was the only thing he could think of to stay warm until Doug returned. Fear made his stomach churn. His eyes flipped to the glass doors. What if Doug didn't come back? No. The harvester was mean, but Doug wouldn't kill him. Would he?

Just as Raiden turned around to explore the rest of the room, a faint scratching sound at the back of the building caught his attention. He paused and listened. What was that? More snow coming in? Ice cracking? He headed back over to the counter and scanned the area.

The bellow of a polar bear momentarily paralyzed Raiden on the spot. He didn't even look to where the animal might be. Raiden dashed for the exit and squeezed back through the door.

Raiden looked backward. Movement of white flashed next to the glass doors. Terror fueled him. The cold became a forgotten memory. He started up the hill of ice. Slipping and skidding, he tried to climb the pile of snow, but it was difficult without his ice cleats. His leg caught on an ice rock, and his ankle twisted painfully. Another roar broke the air.

Raiden flipped his head back as he crawled over the ice dune. A huge polar bear came out of the building. The animal spotted him and headed his way. Throwing his body off the mini-mountain, he rolled down the other side and landed with an audible crunch. He scrambled to his feet and started a dead run.

Up ahead, Raiden thought he saw the glimpse of a snowmobile on the ice. He said a prayer of thanks to whoever was trekking this way.

Raiden had just stopped to wave and holler for whoever was on the ice when a cramp seized his joints. He hit the ground as his knees and shoulders spasmed. A storm was here. His eyes misted with tears as the familiar soreness dug its claws into his bones. Raiden cried out, but the exclamation was only a muffled scream. The storm would be here in four minutes and thirty-two seconds.

The sound of an engine broke into his daze of agony. Just then, another bellow of the polar bear had him spinning backward. The bear was at the top of the ice hill. The animal climbed slowly down the incline toward Raiden. He turned around and leaped to his feet. Out of the corner of his eye, he thought he saw a snowmobile to his left. He began to sprint toward what he hoped was help. Another mini-mountain of snow rose like a blockade ahead of him. Shoving aside a second spasm of joint pain, he dashed toward the pile of ice. Maybe he could hide behind the snow mound until the person on the snowmobile showed up. Perhaps Doug had returned.

Raiden's ankle hurt, but the sting was no worse than in his knees and shoulders. His empty pack felt like the straps alone weighed about two hundred pounds. The canvas strap that had ripped on the train began to give out.

He hit the ice mountain and started to pull himself over the top. This ice was smoother, and it was harder to get solid footing. He slipped at the top where an area was particularly flattened and fell onto his belly. He held onto the one band of material that still held his bag onto his back.

Just as he was about to throw his legs over, he heard another roar. The bear had caught up with him. Raiden flipped on his back and gaped in horror. The beast rose on its hind legs and stared into his eyes. For a moment, Raiden was petrified. He couldn't think or move. This was how he would die? Mauled to death?

Raiden turned over onto his stomach and threw his body over the snow in a scramble. The bear swiped at him. Searing pain stabbed through him, causing a bloodcurdling scream. The bear's claws slashed across the back of his knee down to his calf. Raiden tumbled over the ice and rolled down the bank. He fumbled onto his hands and knees and refused to look at the lacerations.

Again, the sound of the snowmobile was on the wind. *Doug? Please, anyone?*

Raiden stumbled to his feet. He swayed and then dropped to his knees. His whole body throbbed, and his leg warmed from the blood. He clutched the ground to steady himself. Snow began to fall. Slowly at first, the snowflakes fluttered, but then more and more of the landscape started to look like a white sheet had been yanked over the sky. The clouds crowded overhead, and huge flakes launched their descent. The storm was here. His whole body shrieked that the storm would kill him. A grim smile stretched across his face. He wasn't going to die in the snow; a polar bear would eat him.

Raiden tried again to get to his feet when he heard a shout

"Get down on the ground, Porkchop," Stone's yell cut through the air. Raiden glanced up. Never had he been so happy to hear someone insult him.

Stone hollered as he rode his Arctic Cat straight for him. At the last second, Stone turned sharply and then bounded off his vehicle while the machine still moved. He drew the pistols on his hips like a gunfighter Raiden had seen in an old movie.

"Kiss the ice, you fuck-knuckle," Ash commanded. She appeared out of the snow like magic at Stone's side. Her weapon was drawn just like Stone's, and they started for him.

Raiden wasn't sure what to make of the directions or the insults. His head was so crammed with pain that he couldn't make sense of anything anymore. He glanced behind him and saw nothing but a swirl of snow. Raiden followed the dictate just as his legs gave out. He dropped to the ice. When their shots split the air, he glanced up. Ash and Stone walked calmly through a blizzard, shooting. Neither one even looked at him. What were they doing?

His whole body hurt, his blood soaked his bodysuit, and he was dizzy and afraid. But in his head, all he could think about was the fact that the two people he cared about ignored him. He laughed. There was probably something seriously wrong with him.

Raiden looked over his shoulder. The outline of the polar bear was fuzzy in the wind and snow. In the whirling storm, he couldn't even tell if Stone and Ash hit the bear or not.

When Stone's and Ash's boots were at his shoulder, they stopped firing their weapons. Raiden looked up at Ash as she slipped her pistol into her holster.

"Thank you." They had saved his life.

"Fuck your thank you, you dink." Ash kicked his arm. Raiden groaned. "You like to trek in toilet paper?" She shook her head. "Unarmed? Alone? No gear?"

"I—" Raiden began, but she cut him off.

"I should let you bleed to death for being a dough-head. You deserve this, you daft cow." She kicked him again. It wasn't hard, but he rolled over on his back to get away from her.

"The ice plays for keeps." Stone holstered his guns as Ash crouched next to Raiden's leg. "Can it, Ash. You can punch him later. We have to get out of this storm." Stone pulled an item from a small backpack on his shoulders. He handed what looked like a huge fabric bandage to Ash. Raiden sensed Ash's hands on his leg, but the skin had gone numb. Raiden wasn't even sure if that was the cold or the fear.

"The storm will last two hours and forty-one seconds." Raiden closed his eyes as his teeth began to chatter. This time he was sure it was a storm, not a fight between Ash and Stone.

They nodded at him.

"Ash, you know where to go?" Stone picked up Raiden like a child, and he wanted to complain about being carried like a weakling, but right now he couldn't argue. He just shivered in the other man's arms.

"I always know where to go." Ash gave a muffled laugh from inside her facemask. "Ice-for-brains."

Raiden closed his eyes again and listened to their boots crunch on the snow as they swiftly marched toward their machines. All he could see, when he opened his eyes, was a wall of white. How they even knew where they had parked was beyond him. As they walked, he wondered how they knew to come to this spot at all. Why were they trekking this way? That store was stripped.

"Did Doug tell you he left me out here?"

"Doug left you here?" Stone and Ash said in unison.

"You sold all your gear." Stone spat. "That guy…"

"I'm gonna shoot him." Ash turned away from them and disappeared into the storm.

"If Ash doesn't, I will." Stone reached his Arctic Cat and threw his leg over the seat. Raiden snuggled further into Stone's arms. Neither one of them had answered his question.

"How did you find me?" he asked after Stone had settled him in front of his chest on the snowmobile. The other man wrapped his arms around his body from behind.

"I'm gifted." Stone tightened his arms around Raiden's stomach and pressed his chest against Raiden's back. "If I hold an item in my hand, I can find either a copy of the thing or that exact object if I have a piece of the original. I must have a piece of the original though. That's important. The only side effect is that I have a compulsive need to have two of everything."

"You had a part of me? Like what?" Raiden's teeth chattered as he looked up into Stone's face covered by his mask. He wished he could read Stone. Even without a cover, Raiden didn't know what to make of the other man.

"Forget about it. Don't ask." Stone turned on the engine. "Just warm up on me as best you can. We'll follow Ash. He always knows the way."

"I'll just ask you later."

"Just relax. I got you." Stone dropped his chin to Raiden's shoulder and leaned into his ear. Stone's warmth seeped into Raiden's back, and he closed his eyes as he tried to push the pain away.

Raiden sighed. "I'm not going to forget."

"You orgasmed. I held your come that sprayed under the cot," Stone whispered.

When the words registered, Raiden was speechless, disgusted, and oddly charmed. Stone was as complicated a puzzle as Ash Winsor. Had Stone really gone out of his way to help Raiden? Raiden didn't know what to make of that.

"Yuck."

"I told you not to ask."

"Thank you. That's gross, but I'm glad you and Ash saved me."

"I'll make you a deal. If you want to thank me, just don't mention it." Stone threw the machine into high gear, and they sped off before Raiden could say anything more.

Chapter 14

The ride back was a blur of white and burning agony in his leg. Raiden slumped against Stone and tried to suck the warmth from the other man's suit. If he thought about Ash and Stone, the throbbing in his body ebbed. He concentrated on the man with his arms wrapped around him.

When they reached the dome, he never thought he would be so happy to see dirty harvesters and melted snirt.

Ash and Stone pulled their machines next to their shed, then whistled. The boys peeked out of the door to the RV.

"Get me the med-pack," Ash barked at Chevy as soon as he appeared in the doorway of his home. Chevy ran to do her bidding. Just as the boy returned, Raiden spotted Doug strolling next to his snowmobile on the far side of the dome. His muscles involuntarily tightened. The stiffness of his joints made him groan.

Stone reacted to the sound. He swung off the snowmobile with Raiden cradled in his arms. Raiden squirmed, but Stone held fast.

"Put me down." Raiden wiggled again. "I'm fine."

"You're a total fucking marshmallow." Stone laughed.

"Marshmallow?" Raiden pushed up his goggles and looked at Ash.

"Squishy and soft, and would melt," Ash called from her sled. "Just add a little heat and you'd be white goo."

"Do you want to face-plant?" Stone asked him. "I know you hate me, but I'm not letting go."

He didn't hate Stone, far from it. He opened his mouth to ask him about that decree when Stone turned to Ash. He adjusted Raiden in his arms making Raiden groan a second time.

"You got this?" Stone's eyes narrowed at Doug next to his snowmobile, laughing with two of his friends. Stone's glare was so hot the look could've singed off Doug's eyebrows.

"You'll protect Raiden?" Ash asked Stone. Her eyes shot to Doug and then flipped back to Stone.

"He's ours." Stone gave a quick nod. She did the same thing.

"Stay in the house with Ford." Ash gave a quick instruction to the boys and then started across the dome without looking back.

"No, Ash." Raiden tried again to get out of Stone's arms. "Leave Doug."

"Like hell I will," Ash called over her shoulder as she headed straight for the harvester. Stone eased Raiden to the ground but didn't fully let him go.

"Stone, go after Ash. Help him." Raiden clutched at Stone's arm and captured his eyes. He couldn't explain to the other man how much the urge to protect Ash tormented him. Ever since he'd been inside of her, the need to guard her had escalated. The pain in his body, when he was worried about her, had increased tenfold as well.

Raiden glanced at Ash's back as she strode toward Doug and his group. A bone-chilling shudder raced down his spine. If anyone could understand the need to care for her, Stone should be able to. Stone loved her, even if he denied it.

"What for?" Stone rolled out a clean blanket and moved Raiden onto the center of the cloth. He opened the med-pack that Chevy had brought. "Ash is King Winsor. He's titanium. It's only Doug."

"But you love Ash." Raiden stilled Stone's hand when he tried to unzip Raiden's snowsuit. Ash wasn't king. She wasn't titanium. Ashley was soft and sweet, and she was theirs to love and protect.

"I never said that."

"You don't have to say it. I know it."

"He doesn't want my..." Stone reached for Raiden's suit again and began to take off the top. Stone had just gotten the top half off Raiden's suit down when he stopped to glance at Ash.

Stone and Raiden were too far away to hear the conversation, but Raiden saw Doug's head snap up when Ash approached him. She walked up to Doug and immediately threw the first punch. Raiden winced when Doug hit her in the face. She blocked the second hit and kicked him in the stomach. Doug lunged at her.

Raiden tried to rise when Doug pinned Ash, but Stone held him down. He was in so much pain he wasn't sure if he could go to Ash's defense, but he had to try.

"Stop moving. I gotta look at your leg. You're losing blood. We need to clean and wrap this."

"Ash is down." Raiden struggled to rise. "We have to help." Stone held him by the shoulders. He gripped him tightly, but finally he looked over his shoulder to the fight. Ash was up, and she punched Doug again. A group of men had made a circle around the pair. The harvesters blocked Raiden's view. "Help him," he pleaded with Stone.

A shot sounded. Raiden's heart jumped into his throat. He prayed Ash wasn't the one who got hurt.

"Is Ash okay?" Raiden rolled onto his knees before Stone dragged him back down to the blanket.

"Ash probably shot Doug. He said he was gonna." Stone shrugged casually like it was an everyday occurrence for Ash to kill someone.

Raiden panicked. Men shouldn't hit women, let alone try to beat the crap out of them. Plus, being tied to her, he had the urge to fight for her, to safeguard her. A dark thought struck him. What if someone spoke up about her having a gun, and the H.S.P.C. came to arrest her? Could that happen? Raiden could deal with their splitting up, especially if she had Stone to watch over her, but he couldn't have her off in the world alone. He would never let her be taken by the H.S.P.C. Raiden would kill anyone who touched her.

He glanced at Stone. Stone could touch her, but he was the only one. Raiden needed Stone to understand. He would have to teach Stone how to take better care of her before he went away.

"Stone, I have to help Ash. We're united." He glanced at the other man. "Weaver tied us together. This connection is killing me. When you get hooked to Winsor, you'll understand."

"I get it now, Scrappy." Stone leaned back on his heels but didn't let go of his shoulders. "I used to dive in and save him all the time. I couldn't help myself. It killed me too when he'd go off and fight. I worry about him if I don't know where he is all the time. I pretend to bring people back to my room just so he gets furious and hangs around. I swear it feels like I have to guard him or something, but he hates if you get directly in his way. You gotta let him be. If you get in his way too much, he becomes a real squall. We follow him."

Ash appeared out of the crowd. She holstered her gun as she approached them. Blood streaked down her face, and she swiped at the stream impatiently as she marched.

"Fuck you, Ash Winsor." Doug appeared behind her limping. "One day, you won't be armed." Blood gushed from his leg.

"Doubt it." She spun around and stood a few feet away from Doug. He held his calf as a red stain on his pants grew. "Now you're even with Raiden." She faced the crowd. "If anyone messes with Raiden or Stone, I'm gonna shoot you."

The harvesters around the dome nodded. Money exchanged hands. If Raiden had been up for a bet, he'd have said the odds were good that wasn't an empty threat.

Doug took a few steps toward Ash as she started for them again.

"Walk away, Doug," she said without turning around. "You have four limbs, and I've got a lot of bullets. Be happy you can still walk."

Doug leaned on one of his friends and then cursed under his breath as he hobbled away.

"Why isn't he patched up yet?" Ash asked when she reached Raiden's side. She grabbed a clean white cloth from the bag and placed the fabric under her nose. "You two twat-waffles think now is a good time to chew the fat?" She pushed his shoulder. "Turn over onto your belly."

"He wouldn't let me work on him until you were safe," Stone explained.

"Aww." Ash grinned at Raiden. "Being a twelve-year-old girl again? You're cute, tough guy. Did you want to fight for me?"

"Hell, yes, I wanted to fight for you." Raiden gritted his teeth at her snide remark. "I care about you. That's what people do, especially men who are tied to you." Raiden glanced at Stone. "Men who love you."

Ash's eye's jumped to Stone. They stared at each other for a few seconds.

She shrugged. "Stone wasn't worried."

"Maybe I was." Stone shoved her shoulder. "Are you okay? I know you're a good fighter, but he hits pretty hard."

"You taught Stone some ear-banging?" Ash smirked from Stone to Raiden, then back again. She dropped to her knees next to Raiden's leg and pulled the cloth from her face.

"Ear-banging?" Raiden asked.

"Empty flattery," Stone supplied.

"It would take me years to understand all your insults." Raiden chuckled. "It's not empty flattery. I want to help you. I'm tied to you." He looked to Stone. "Maybe I don't dislike either of you as much as I thought."

"Me too." Stone shrugged.

"You two crack me up." She started to remove Raiden's boots. "I'm fine. Doug punches like a senile squirrel."

"Squirrels don't punch." Stone shoved Ash's leg.

She laughed and then sobered. "Enough fucking around. We have to stop the bleeding, and we'd better get a move on. We're hopping the next train." Ash whistled for the boys again.

"What's the rush?" Stone asked.

"Morgan-Roth told me that Weaver was taken to H.S.P.C. HQ in Dallas by some agents. We'll get Raiden cleaned up. Then we're heading there." Ash buried her head in the med-bag, and then her head popped up. "Ford, get me scissors." She began to study Raiden's leg. "I'm gonna have to cut the fabric." Raiden's pants stuck to his skin, and the melting snow had made everything wet. "You still want to separate, right?"

Ash didn't look at either of them. The soft way Ash asked Raiden that question had both Stone and him staring at her.

"We agreed that—" Before Raiden could finish his sentence, Ash spoke with a bitter chuckle.

"Of course, you want to separate. You just went out to the surface with Doug to get away from me."

"He was trying to get away from me," Stone whispered to himself as he grabbed Raiden's leg and rolled him to the side. He groaned when his leg was jostled. The sound was from pain, but also, they were ignoring him again. He sighed.

"I was looking for you." He grabbed Ash's hand when she started to yank off his wet sock. "I wanted to talk to you."

"Doubt it." Ash rolled her eyes. "You were looking for me in an abandoned building because you know that Ash Winsor just *loves* fleam." After her sarcastic comment, she turned to Chevy. "Unload the bear."

"The bear?" Raiden glanced around, and his eyes settled on the carcass of the polar bear on the back of Ash's sled. The animal had been gutted. Raiden closed his eyes at the gruesome picture of the mangled animal. He took a deep breath. If Ash could do that to a bear, he wondered what she would do to him when he told her why he had been searching for her on the surface. Well, he wasn't a coward, and he hated lying. He gulped. "I was hunting for you. I wanted to tell you that Stone fucked—"

"We need alcohol." Stone cut him off. He gave Raiden an imploring look. Raiden scrubbed his hand over his face. Fine. He'd tell her tomorrow.

Skit, he sounded like Ash.

"I'd prefer to drink water," Raiden said through clenched teeth, as the movement of his leg started to chase the blessed numbness away. "I like being sober."

"Here." Ash handed him her canteen. He took a sip as Stone handed her another bottle from his pack. "The alcohol is for your leg. We have to clean it as best we can." She paused. "What did Stone fuck?"

"Stone fucked up. I was on the surface to tell you that." Raiden took another sip of water as Stone's shoulders sagged with relief. "He was gambling, and he was drunk."

"That twelve-year-old girl in you really takes over, doesn't it? I didn't peg you as a nark."

"In about a minute, you'll wish you were drunk." Stone took the bottle from Ash. "You ready?"

"No." Raiden looked from Stone to Winsor. "What am I ready for?"

Neither harvester looked at him.

"I'll give you a second." Ash took the canteen and then pulled his torn pants away from his shredded calf. Raiden couldn't bring himself to look at the damage.

"I need more than a second." He flinched when Ash moved his leg again.

They wouldn't pour that liquor on him, would they?

"Sorry, tough guy." Ash pulled another piece of cloth from his leg just as Stone poured the alcohol on the open wound. The shock and excruciating pain robbed him of thought. Everything went black.

Chapter 15

Heat surrounded him, bathed him, and hugged him. Raiden thought at first that the warmth was pleasant. Soon, he changed his mind. His stomach rolled, and he started to feel like he was cooking. Sweat gathered between his shoulder blades. The whole world swayed. He rocked back and forth, and he couldn't get the swaying to stop. He reached for full consciousness. Why was he so hot?

Raiden thrashed and pushed at whatever heavy thing pinned him down.

"Hey, Puddles. Stop moving like that. Keep your leg still."

Stone.

Raiden opened his eyes and looked up into Stone's brown eyes staring down at him. That bastard had poured alcohol on his leg. Ash had helped.

"That fucking stung. You and Ash are sadistic."

"Down, Barky." Stone grinned at him.

Raiden felt a hand running through his hair. Stone was petting him? That seemed a little too soft for Stone. Glancing around, Raiden looked up to his left. Ash was next to him stroking his hair back. Stone sat leaning back against the wall.

"We needed to clean it. Don't be a twelve-year-old girl." She chuckled. He licked his lips. She felt nice. He didn't want her touch to stop.

"I'm a tough guy."

She laughed. "Doubt it."

"How do you feel?" Stone held his hand. The other man's warm, steady palm pressed against his fingers. They kept the ache in his knees and shoulders away, but his leg and ankle throbbed. He shifted and clung to Stone's hand.

"I'm okay." Raiden took a second-deep breath, but he couldn't seem to still the rocking motion. Were they on a train? "What's going on?"

"You were cold, so we set up this heated blanket." Ash motioned to the blanket covering his body. They were back on a train. He tried to remember leaving the dome, but the travel was a hazy memory at best. Stone had carried him again. That part he recalled.

"You passed out," Stone leaned back, "like a drunk opossum."

Raiden nodded. The pain had been unbearable. He wasn't surprised.

"I thought you were gonna scream. I'm impressed you didn't." Ash smiled. "You're tougher than you look."

Raiden sat up slowly. He was on the floor of a private room on a train. The room was empty except for Stone's pack near the toilet room and the bed they had made.

The train was the movement that had been making his stomach tumble. As he sat up, he placed his hand on the wall, and the blanket slipped down. The walls were empty of fleam.

"Are we on *Bilander*?"

"We hopped on *Ketch*," Ash supplied.

The sound of the air rushing past the train was all he heard other than the rustle of the blanket. Even outside the door, the hall wasn't noisy. Raiden figured it must be late.

"Were you two sleeping?"

"No." Stone settled himself on the floor next to Ash.

"We were looking after you. The moth had his wings ripped off." Ash leaned on her pack and eyed him. She pushed Stone's shoulder. He punched her back. Their attempts at showing affection were severely lacking. Raiden made a mental note that he would have to teach Stone and Ash kissing before he left them.

Raiden glanced at Ash when she scooted closer to Stone. She didn't touch him, but he noted her attempt to get nearer to the other man. He did a double take when Raiden realized she had a black eye.

"What the hell happened to you?" Raiden reached out and tipped her chin up so he could better see the shiner. She smiled at him as she tipped her head first one way then the other.

"Doug and I disagreed on leaving people in abandoned buildings. Don't you remember?" Ash showed off her black eye like Raiden's mom used to show off her new lipstick.

"Disagree? That's funny." Stone laughed. "Ash tried to kill him."

"He's the worst kind of hitch-sucker," Ash groused.

"You can't go around shooting people. Aren't you worried about the H.S.P.C. coming after you one of these days?" Raiden gathered his hair into a ponytail and then realized he had nothing to secure the strands. "It's illegal to have guns." He let his hands fall.

Ash and Stone ignored him. He smiled. They wouldn't be them if they didn't stare at each other all goofy.

"I didn't try to kill Doug. If I had wanted to kill him, I would have." She stopped gawking at Stone for a second and looked at Raiden. "I just maimed him. I left him hurting. That's how he left you." Ash produced a small black hair band from her pocket and handed the tie to Raiden. "I have my gun for the surface. The H.S.P.C. can suck my dick." She winked at him before she leaned back next to Stone. They touched shoulder to shoulder.

Raiden pulled his hair up. Maybe she paid more attention to him than he thought.

"You should've killed him." Stone studied Ash. "Or I should've." Ash shoved him and he shoved her back.

"You shouldn't have let Doug hit Ash." Raiden came to his knees. He remembered the fight now. He also recalled with vivid clarity the pain of Ash and Stone cleaning his leg. The pouring of the liquor had been agonizing. He moved slowly. Every adjustment of his calf made his eyes water.

"Ash can handle himself. He's King Winsor." Stone's voice held pride.

"I'm alright, Raiden. Better than you." Ash pointed to his leg.

As the blanket slipped further off his body, Raiden realized he was naked. His eyes flipped from Ash to Stone. They both just grinned at him.

"Did you strip me?" He searched the sleeping quarters for his bag. It was nowhere around the room. Panic had him clutching the blanket. "Where's my pack?"

"It's right there." Ash pointed to Stone's bag next to the door.

"That's Stone's." Raiden scanned the room again. Did they strip him naked and toss out his backpack? They wouldn't do that, would they?

"Stay calm, Ruff." Stone put his hands up in a peace gesture. "I have two backpacks. I gave one to you. I put your stuff in it."

"You have two?" Raiden asked, and then he remembered what he said about the side effect of his gift.

"It's just this thing I've done since I was a kid. I have to have two of things as long as one is a little different from the other." Stone pulled the blanket from his white knuckles. "Your bag was dead."

Heaving a sigh, Raiden stared at his new sack. He'd never owned anything so sturdy and well made. Why would Stone give him this?

"You didn't have to do that." Raiden gulped back the surge of emotion.

"Yeah, I did." Stone's eyes skidded away from his.

"Don't worry about it, Raiden. Stone always has two of everything. If he can't get an item on the surface, he'll steal it underground." Her eyes danced, and then she glanced at her friend. "Stone, remember that one time you wanted a green apple and a red apple?" She grinned. "We went through hell to get those, and after Stone had them, he didn't even want to eat them. I ate them."

Stone studied his boots. "I get hung up."

"Hung up?" Ash laughed. "He's neurotic." She glanced at Raiden's new sack. "Your bag has extra pockets on the outside and is dark green. Stone tells me his isn't so bulky and isn't dark green but *olive* green." Ash was clearly teasing the other man.

Stone shoved her shoulder, and she shoved him back. Raiden smiled at their inside jokes and then pushed off the electric blanket and stood.

"I'm getting dressed." When he wobbled, Ash stood up and wrapped her arms around him.

"We had to rip your pants to clean your leg. They're trash now, too."

"When we got on here, we just took them off and tossed them." Stone nodded. "I put a new pair in your bag and some shirts."

"You didn't need to take off everything else I had on."

"That was just for fun." Ash snickered. Stone grinned at him.

Raiden looked down at his leg, half afraid of what he would see. He had never gone head-to-head with a polar bear before. So far, he had been lucky. He studied the bandage just under his knee. The white cloth had spots of blood bleeding through. The crisscrossed dressing didn't look that bad.

"Thank you." Raiden was more than lucky. He was blessed to have Ash and Stone. Losing them was going to be harder than he had thought. He owed them his life.

"Don't mention it." Stone got up to grab Raiden's new pack. He slid the sack closer to the three of them. "Just get dressed and stay off your leg."

"Is it bad?" Raiden asked when he realized the two of them scrutinized his leg. Gingerly, he put some weight on his foot, and his ankle bitched at him to sit back down. He forgot he had twisted it. Reaching for the wall, he leaned hard on his uninjured leg.

"No." Ash shrugged. "It's bad but…" She let go of him and sat back down. "It's not as bad as what happened to Stone."

As Raiden yanked the bag closer to him, Stone watched him. When the other man's eyes traveled down Raiden's naked body, his skin heated on its own. Raiden gulped and told his cock sex wasn't going to happen again. He tried to remember what they were talking about.

"What happened to Stone?"

"The first time I met Ash, I was drunk on the surface of the planet. I couldn't get my act together." Stone picked up the blanket and knotted the fabric around Raiden's waist. "I used to be a shit harvester. I got loaded and thought trekking was a good idea. I wanted something stupid that I'd gotten hung up on. I ran into a polar bear who decided I was dinner." Stone turned his back to both Ash and Raiden. He slipped off his black fur-covered coat and then pulled up his sweater and undershirt.

Stone had four long, distinct scars from his spine toward his hip. The mended flesh was dark pink furrows on his pale skin. Raiden could easily see where the bear had sunk its claws into Stone.

"You killed the bear?" Raiden reached out and traced the puckered flesh. He ran his finger down Stone's skin before he realized he had caressed Stone and the touch had nothing to do with the marks. Raiden dropped his arm to his side. "It's hardcore." He glanced at Ash to see if she had noticed how he admired her friend.

"Ash killed the bear, not me. It's how we met." Stone dropped his shirt and turned around. He shrugged at her. "He saved my life in a few ways."

Ash acted like she wasn't listening. She pulled out Raiden's puzzle cube from her bag and started to flip the mismatched colored sides in her hands.

"What do you mean 'back when you were a shit harvester'? You still are a shit harvester, turd-wad." She didn't look up but smiled at the puzzle.

"Suck my dick." Stone kicked her leg, but she kept her eyes on the toy. "Don't listen to him. I'm better now." Stone glanced at Raiden.

"Better now?" Raiden took Stone's hand when the other man offered it. "Because you healed up after the bear got you?"

"Not just the bear. My whole life got better after I met Winsor. I was trekking to begin with because my mom kicked me out of the house. She told me that I'd never find what I was looking for there. She's kind of a hard-ass, and at first, I blamed her for ruining my life, but then I decided she was right. It had come to the point where I was compulsively stealing from everyone I knew. I had to have two of everything, and I couldn't stop pocketing everything I saw. I was arrested repeatedly. I was lying about it, and after a while, my entire family got sick of the stress. I was lost after I left home. I didn't know what I'd do with my life. I didn't plan to be a harvester, but I ran out of money and places to stay. I started trekking with no idea what the hell I was doing. I met the bear, then I met Ash." Stone gingerly wrapped his arm around Raiden's waist. "Ash shot the bear and carried me to his snowmobile. He brought me back to the dome and patched me up. He sat with me for days while I mended. I've been with him ever since. He's a jerk, but I'd follow him anywhere."

"Ash, I thought you trekked with Morgan-Roth after—" Raiden realized what he would have said and stopped abruptly.

"I did normally travel with Morgan-Roth." Ash flipped her eyes to him and set the cube down. "My uncle had just headed home to England with my little cousins. Morgan-Roth was helping them get ready for the trip." Ash shrugged. "That day, I was doing my own thing. I missed them and needed some cold air to clear my head. I wasn't looking for anything particular." She glanced at Stone. "Then I came across this dingle-cone, and I just thought he'd be worth betting on." Ash pointed to Raiden's pack. "Get dressed, tough guy."

"Why didn't you go home to England with them? Why did you stay with Morgan-Roth?" Raiden pulled out what he could find in his bag to stay warm. There were extra clothes and items Stone and Ash must have added. He noticed his soap was missing, but he thought he would look for it later.

As he pulled on his undershirt, he considered that if Felix had hurt Ash, then it would have made sense for her to leave. She could've had a whole new life with her family far from the trains.

A chill ran down his spine from the cold, but the shudder was accompanied with a strange emptiness. If she had left that day, he would've never known her. Even if they weren't meant to be together forever, he was glad he got to be with her this short amount of time. He was happy he got to be with Stone as well, even if that had been so very wrong.

As he pulled on his jeans, Raiden realized he wanted Ash again. He wanted to feel her before she would be with Stone and no longer his. Being inside of her also drowned out the ache in his bones. The way she erased his aching pain was addictive, and he would have a hard time letting that go.

"I had my reasons."

Raiden buttoned his pants and then pulled on heavy socks that seemed brand new. He could barely remember what they were talking about. All he was thinking about was the idea of being inside of her once more before Weaver split them and she went with Stone.

"Besides," Stone added, dragging Raiden out of his thoughts, "you're a good harvester, Ash. You didn't need to leave like your cousins did. They were girls."

"They needed to leave because they were girls?" Raiden didn't think this conversation was heading in a safe direction. His lower back hurt.

"Yeah." Stone handed him Raiden's boots. "Women can't live this kind of life. It's too dangerous for them. Snow Flu and trekking. Ash's uncle thought he'd get his girls a better home. It was good that those little ones got a solid home. This is no life for women. There is a reason you don't meet a lot of ladies on the trains and why all of them have about twenty guys buzzing around."

Raiden winced as his head flipped up to look at Ash.

"Women can harvest, ice-for-brains," Ash snapped.

Raiden's joints ached. *Fanken*, another quarrel. He stretched his shoulders. He wasn't feeling up to this.

"Yes. Women can be harvesters." Raiden glared at Stone. Raiden hoped the other man would shut his mouth.

"Yeah, they *can*..." Stone shrugged. "All I'm saying is that if a girl harvester got pregnant, then what's she gonna do? This is a hard life and babies are important."

Ash and he stared at each other. Both their eyes widened at the same time. They had never talked about that. They'd had sex all night. She could be carrying his baby now. What if Doug hit her and she was pregnant? Raiden's head filled with all the things he would have to worry about if she had his baby. Stone would have to help him.

Raiden's eyes flipped to Stone. Why did he think he would need Stone's help? Would Stone stay if Ash carried Raiden's child? Would that change things? Would they stay together if they had a kid?

A smile kicked up one side of his mouth as he thought about holding their baby.

Ash shook her head at him as if she could read his thought.

"What's so funny?" Stone asked him. "What's the joke?"

"A woman harvester could give her boyfriend the baby," Raiden said. "He might be helpful with kids. He might like kids." Raiden raised an eyebrow at Ash. "I like kids."

"You like kids?" Ash crossed her arms over her chest. "You would stay home with a baby? I didn't peg you as a nanny."

"That's me." Raiden grinned. "Moth, bridge, nanny."

"Don't forget slush-head." Ash guffawed.

"I guess, the guy could keep the baby." Stone sank to a spot next to Ash. "That could happen. It wouldn't happen to me since I meet women so rarely, but..." He waved his hand toward the door like all the people outside of this room could have babies but not him.

The pain in Raiden's limbs melted away. Stone had no idea he could totally have a kid. If he and Ash had sex, Stone could be a father. The thought of Stone as a flustered arm-waving parent kept the grin on Raiden's face. Stone would need his help with a baby.

"After she had the baby, she could go back to trekking and make some serious money." Raiden smiled. He didn't know why the idea of a child pleased him so much. He never planned to have kids. He figured he would always be alone. His smile melted away. That's where they were heading. Raiden would soon be alone.

Ash kicked Stone. "You don't know anything about making money. You only know how to blow it."

Raiden laughed.

"That would only work if her boyfriend knew something about babies and she knew something about trekking." Stone laughed and pushed Ash. "Doubt it."

She pushed him back. Raiden smiled. It wasn't kissing, but the batting at each other did make him feel like part of their group. His chest warmed when Stone punched his shoulder.

Ash and Stone took up places next to each other in the room. They chatted and smacked each other while Raiden took a deep breath and tried to settle his still-upset stomach. Raiden could always feel the sexual tension between Ash and Stone, but currently, it didn't take shape in the form of insults and anger. The pair played, and he enjoyed watching them. He tried to relax. It wasn't working.

After he cleaned up in the toilet room, he sat down searching for a way to ease his joints. Stone moved closer to him and wrapped the blanket around his shoulders. Raiden leaned on his shoulder. Ash used her pack as a pillow and picked up the toy cube. He exhaled heavily.

"You don't look good," Stone observed.

"How good should he look after a polar bear sunk its claws in, ice-for-brains?" Ash fiddled with the puzzle cube. "He'll be fine. He just needs to rest."

Raiden didn't bother to comment since they had their own discussion. He let them chat. He still felt off. Raiden wondered if the rolling feeling in his belly was because of the lie he carried. When Stone and Ash were giggling with each other, he couldn't bring himself to start spitting the truth. He knew he should, but he liked seeing them happy.

Ash curled up closer to Stone. She scooted her pack near him and then placed her head on one of the pockets while she watched him. Raiden stared down at her mouth which was in a pout as she tried to solve the puzzle. He wanted to kiss her and not have Stone hate him for it. He wanted more from Stone too. Raiden tipped up his head. He wanted a few seconds of closeness. They had shared something special when Stone was inside of him, but whatever the feelings had been, it had vanished. In fact, all the connections were off, and his stomach hurt. Maybe he was a twelve-year-old girl just like Ash said.

Deep down, he knew everything was off because he had slept with Stone and he shouldn't have. The way they lounged together felt like lies. There were lots of secrets in the room. This wasn't about Ash being a woman anymore. It wasn't about how they loved each other and wouldn't admit it. That was still out there, but none of those things were his lie. Having sex was his lie. He would have to tell her about what he had done, and the sooner the better. Raiden had to stop waiting for tomorrow.

"Ash, I need to talk to you," Raiden began.

Chapter 16

Stone didn't let him start his confessional. "Are you hungry?"

"I guess." Raiden wouldn't be surprised if Stone didn't slap his hand over Raiden's mouth. The thought of food made his stomach sway like he was being swung around the room.

"Here." Ash tossed him a small plastic container and her canteen. "Stone and I were just talking about how you're too skinny."

"Hang with us, and you'll be as fat as Winsor in no time."

"Call me fat again, and I'll castrate you while you sleep." Ash hit Stone in the arm and got up. "I'm gonna check on Raiden's coat."

"My coat?"

"Ash skinned the bear and took its hide. He's adding the fur to your jacket." Stone opened the plastic container and held up dried meat. "This is your bear."

"I'm going to wear the fur of the bear that almost killed me?" Raiden leaned away from the meat hanging out of Stone's mouth.

"Don't be such a wimp. The bear didn't *almost* kill you. It got a piece of you, and now you have a piece of it." Ash pushed Stone. "Besides, Stone does it."

Stone petted the fur on the collar of his coat draped in his lap.

Raiden's face wrinkled as he pictured Ash peeling a bear. She was intelligent and skilled. And he was going to lose her as soon as she found out what he'd done.

"I guess, if Stone can wear a bear, so can I." Raiden also supposed he could wait a few more minutes to tell her the truth. Besides, he would need his coat for when she kicked him off the train. If he was lucky, the train would be parked.

"I'll be right back." Ash pulled on her coat. "Stay out of trouble." She nodded to them. Raiden wasn't sure which one of them those directions were for. If he was honest with himself, they both needed a chaperone. Even knowing that Ash would be crushed finding out that they had screwed, he still couldn't stop himself from thinking about doing it again.

Raiden scooted to the far side of the room as soon as Ash vanished out the door. He had better not push his libido to the limit by Stone's touch and smell. Raiden would cave like a rotten pillar if Stone kissed him again.

As soon as the door closed behind Ash, Stone came to his knees next to him.

"Benji, you gotta help me out here." Stone tugged on his hair like he wanted to rip out the strands. He pressed his fingers to his forehead. "Do you want me to beg? Is that it? I will."

Raiden stared. "What?"

"I know shooting the polar bear won't make up for what I did, and I know there is probably nothing that I can do to make it up to you, but please don't tell Winsor what

I did." Stone reached for Raiden's shoulders, and then his arms dropped. "Oh, God." Stone's head slumped into his hands. "I know you hate me. I get it. I hate myself, but I couldn't stand it if Ash hated me too." Stone's eyes pleaded. "I didn't realize how bad I needed Winsor until I thought about how he'll leave me when he finds out. I lied when I said I don't love him. I love him, and if he hates me, I'm not sure what I'll do."

"I don't hate you, why do you keep saying… wait… you love him?" Raiden was pleased that finally one of them had admitted it.

Stone's head snapped up.

"After I was kicked off my home water base, I couldn't get my shit together. I couldn't hold a job, I kept stealing, and everything I touched, I made a mess of. My brothers are perfect, and I'm a fuck-up." Stone paused. "I was couch surfing, and I stole my brother's guitar and sold it. I straight up took money from my other brother, and he beat the shit out of me." Stone captured Raiden's eyes. His intense stare immobilized Raiden. "I didn't have any direction until I met Ash. When I'm with Winsor, I can control the urge better. Ash is my torch. When I follow him, I know where I'm heading. What can I do?" Stone gave furtive glances to the door.

He had used full sentences, but Stone might as well have waved his arms and done that gap-talking Raiden was getting used to. Raiden had no idea what he was saying.

"What you can do is start by telling me what you're talking about."

"You want me to say it?" Stone's troubled eyes were back on him for a minute. His whisper was full of anguish. Raiden thought about telling him he didn't have to say it, but then he realized he still wasn't sure what this was about.

"You're going to have to say it."

"I raped you." He breathed before he looked at the floor. "I know it was wrong. I don't know what got into me. I touched you, and I made a mess out of my life again." The muscle in Stone's cheek ticked. "I know Ash has a hard-on for consent. He doesn't talk about it, but I know someone raped him once. Please don't tell him what I did to you. I'll make it up to you. Please."

Raiden's brain overflowed with information. He went still as he tried to process. Did Stone know Ash was a woman this whole time? Who told him about Felix? What else did the man know?

Stone didn't take his silence well.

"You can fuck me. I'll bend over, and I won't move. We can make it even, or if you want, you can do it until I bleed. I've never had…" Stone rubbed his temples. "…inside, just I've given… blowjobs, and this one woman a long time ago… I wanted Ash to be my first for anal…"

"You what?" Raiden was disturbed at the thought. "I'm not going to make you bleed."

"I'll suck you off. I'll do anything."

"Just stop talking. I need a second." Raiden held up his hand. "You know about Ash being raped?" He focused on that first. "Did Ash tell you about Felix? Do you know about anything else?"

"You know about Fletcher? Did Morgan-Roth tell you?" Stone looked as surprised as Raiden felt.

"Ash told me. How do you know?"

"Ash didn't tell me; I just pay attention. I don't have ice for brains." Stone rose and checked the hall before he sat back down next to Raiden. "I know Morgan-Roth patched him up after his brother assaulted Winsor." Stone drew his legs up and wrapped his arms around his knees. "I met Ash right after it happened. I didn't buy his bullshit story about falling on the ice, and it took a while for two black eyes and a broken nose to heal." Stone paused and studied the ceiling. "I also know that Morgan-Roth and Ash are hunting for some type of valuables. They talk about the temperature that the item is kept at. Kelvin, Celsius, Fahrenheit, that sort of thing. Felix took the treasure."

That answered one question. Stone knew about Felix, but he had no idea about Ash's gender. This treasure Morgan-Roth and Ash were looking for—that was odd. Raiden still had to figure out why Stone thought had he raped Raiden. Raiden had been into it. Was Stone that drunk he didn't remember?

"You think you raped me?"

"Don't fuck with me." Stone's eyes turned into a glare, and then he sighed. "I said I was sorry. What should I do?"

"Answer my question. Why do you think you forced me?" Raiden asked. "You were hammered." Maybe Stone didn't remember what happened.

"I wasn't that drunk. I was on my way to sloshed, but I remember everything. Shit." He shook his head. "All you did was say 'no' over and over again and struggled. You said 'don't' and 'please.' I remember that you tried to grab your pants to pull them up. I know what I did. I thought I wasn't that kind of man. I swear, I'm not like that. That night, it was like I couldn't stop. You got under my skin, like a compulsion. I did try to fight it. I just… I'm sorry. I'll make it up to you."

Stone was clearly disturbed. He genuinely thought he had forced him. Raiden needed to set him straight.

"I said 'no' because I was answering your persistent questions the whole time."

"I didn't ask a question."

"I mean it. You didn't make me do anything. If I didn't want to have sex, I would've fought you."

"Fought me?" Stone gave a grim laugh. "I'm five inches taller than you are. I outweigh you and," he paused, "I have a gun. Two of them."

"The guns were on the floor, and I could fight you and win," Raiden insisted. "Even armed."

"Are you trying to make yourself feel better or me?" Stone didn't wait for an answer. "I know what happened. I said I was sorry. Now just tell me what to do to make this right. I'll do whatever you want if you promise to never tell Ash. We can make a deal."

The door slid open. Ash entered holding Raiden's coat. She tossed the jacket to him, and he caught it. She sat next to him on the floor.

"It's not as disturbing as I thought it would be." Raiden patted the fur.

"It'll keep you warm." Stone captured his eyes. "And I'll get you a better body suit than that dishrag you're using. I have two. You can have one of my snowmobiles also. Whatever you want."

"Gash, Stone. Feeling generous?" Ash tipped her head to the side and then looked at Raiden. "If you trek with us, you'll have the best gear. Stone can hold an item in his hand and find us another one on the surface. It's true, moth. We'll get you anything you want." She smiled. "No dick sucking in exchange." Ash offered Raiden her canteen, and he took a long drink.

"Yeah, I won't touch you." Stone gave another pleading stare before he dropped his eyes to the floor. "I promise."

Raiden's stomach rolled again. His joints didn't hurt, but his stomach started to feel like he'd gulped down a hot iron. At some point, he would have to finish his conversation with Stone. He hated that idea. It was probably the reason his stomach hurt. He pushed away the plastic container of bear meat. Was he honestly considering never telling Ash in exchange for Stone's equipment? Raiden wasn't a whore.

"Are you okay?" Ash watched him. "What were you talking about?" She glanced at Stone.

"Just twelve-year-old-girl gossip." Stone hunched his shoulders.

Raiden pressed his lips together as he set his coat aside. Suddenly, his stomach lurched painfully. He dove for the bathroom. Raiden reached the toilet just as he threw up. He heaved over the dirty porcelain until he thought he might die with his head hung near the water. He sagged when his stomach finally relaxed.

"It's just dried bear meat," he heard Ash say from the doorway. "I've been eating it."

"He didn't eat any. He just drank water." Stone touched his shoulders and then pushed Raiden's hair back. "Infection? Maybe we didn't clean the wound enough?"

"This train has a stop," Ash murmured. "Water Base Cure."

There was an uncomfortable silence in the bathroom. Raiden gulped air, then dry-heaved into the toilet.

"We'll get off at the hospital. It might be an infection." Stone sounded pained like stopping at Water Base Cure would kill him.

"We're gonna get separated," Ash murmured. "Nothing has changed, Stone." She petted some of Raiden's hair back. "We just have to make one stop on the way."

Chapter 17

Raiden dozed in Stone's arms. He awoke when they hopped off the train. Someone jarred his leg as Stone carried him through the busy water base platform. He held in the scream, partly so people wouldn't look at him and partly so Stone and Ash wouldn't call him a baby, or some insult to that effect. Instead, he buried his face in the other man's neck.

They followed Ash away from where the primary water base gate guard checked people into the entrance. As Stone zigzagged through the crowd, Raiden used his breathing to keep his gag reflex repressed. Raiden couldn't gather enough energy to ask where they were headed.

On one end of the platform, the swarm of people finally thinned out. Up ahead, Raiden noted two wide glass doors with two armed men in plastic suits and sealed masks protecting the entrance. To the left of the doors, a singular rectangular window waited.

Stone and Ash marched up to the glass without giving the guards a second look. Inside, a plump woman sat eating an apple and reading a stack of papers piled in front of her.

She glanced up when they approached. After scanning them, she went back to eating and shuffling paper.

Crunch, crunch, crunch. Half the apple was gone, and still she didn't speak. Ash gave an irritated huff.

"We want admittance to the hospital." Ash's demand broke the silence first. She stared stormily at the apple eating woman as she crossed her arms over her chest. Ash's whole demeanor signified that Ash was in charge and wouldn't take "no" for an answer.

The plump lady righted her sweater and then glanced up. Her drowsy eyes skimmed over Stone holding him. She shrugged.

"Name?" The chubby woman puckered her lips.

"Ash Winsor."

"Problem?"

"My friend is sick." Ash motioned to Raiden as her brow crinkled. "Can't you see that?" Ash sounded exasperated.

Raiden gulped down air and closed his eyes willing his stomach to settle.

"Stone, set me down." Raiden took another deep breath.

"Is your friend vomiting?" The receptionist went back to eating her apple as if they weren't even in front of her.

"Yes." Ash glanced at him and then back at the apple-eater. "I said he's sick." Her voice grew a tad bit louder.

"Ash, hey, it's okay," Raiden began, but his stomach rolled. He gulped air. He would tell her to cool off, but first he would not spew.

The woman flipped some of the papers in front of her.

"If the patient is vomiting, you cannot enter the hospital for twenty-four hours. Come back when he's better." Her monotone voice bled apathy.

"When he's better?" She glanced at Stone. "This is a hospital! You're supposed to make people better."

The woman shrugged. "It's the rule."

"Fuck the rule," Ash barked as she slammed her palm against the cement next to the window. The guards near the doors turned to face her after her outburst. Their eyes followed her through their masks.

"Hospital admittance policy states that the client needs to be vomit-free for twenty-four hours to know he doesn't have Snow Flu." She took another bite of the apple. "Come back later."

"Raiden needs help now." Ash's voice held barely leashed fury. "Not later."

"He doesn't have Snow Flu," Stone growled. "We've been with him nonstop. We would have it by now if that was the problem. I think it's an infection."

"Rules are rules." The lady went back to her apple.

Ash prowled near the window and then moved closer to the door. Raiden sighed. He would just have to wait until his stomach settled.

"It's fine, Ash." Raiden reached out for her arm and brushed her coat. "Stone, stop her."

Just as Stone set him on the cement next to the glass doors, Ash reached for her gun. Stone saw her go for her holster, and he had his arms wrapped around her body before she could draw the weapon. The big harvester threw his arms around Ash's shoulder and anchored her to him.

"Let go, you dick-weed." She tried to shove off Stone's arms. Both guards raised their weapons.

"Move on, harvester," the guard to Raiden's right shouted.

"It's a free platform," Ash bit out.

Stone pushed her back away from the guards and kept his hands on her gun.

"Let go, you overland trout." She jerked away from him.

"What's an overland trout?" Raiden began to rise, but his stomach protested. He gulped and forced himself not to go through another bout of tossing stomach acid. At this point, he had nothing left inside of him, so he didn't even know what was coming out.

His question was ignored, so Raiden slumped back against the wall. He shivered on the cold cement.

"Ash, let's leave and come back later." Stone bent down and wrapped his arms around Raiden.

"Let's go," Raiden croaked. "I'll probably be fine."

"No fucking way. You're gonna see a doctor."

Just as Ash reached for her gun again, two doctors in scrubs walked by the glass doors. One of them had dark hair and a handsome face. He drank out of a pink plastic cup as he glanced at them. The man next to him was a tall, well-built blond. Both men were attractive and young. When Stone saw them, he clutched at Raiden's hand.

"Raiden's right." Stone yanked him to his feet. "Let's go. He'll probably be fine." Stone bent down and scooped him up like he didn't weigh anything. The movement brought Raiden to the brink of hurling again. He just scarcely held himself together.

"I hope you fall off a train," Ash said to the woman behind the glass. She began to follow Stone toward the end of the platform.

They were about to start twisting their way through the masses when the hospital doors opened with a silent swish. The two doctors stepped out past the guards.

"Stone, wait," Raiden murmured, but that was the last of his energy, and he dropped his head to Stone's chest.

Stone kept walking.

"Marion Stone," the dark-haired doctor shouted. "Wait up."

Stone froze.

Ash spun around with her hand on her gun.

Raiden picked up his head and peeked over Stone's shoulder. The dark-haired man in the light-gray scrubs handed his cup to the blond next to him. No one moved. Stone didn't turn around. Raiden felt the muscles in Stone's shoulder stiffen. The doctor stepped toward them.

"Marion," the doctor repeated. "Come on."

Stone's shoulders dropped as he spun around to face the two men.

"Mather." Stone sighed.

The dark-haired doctor glanced at Ash's hand on her weapon, across Raiden, and then to Stone. "What're you doing here?"

Stone took a few steps back toward the glass doors, but he walked like he was moving through quicksand the entire way. Ash stayed at his side, but her hand came off her gun. Her lack of gripping the pistol made Raiden feel better.

"Doctor Mather." Stone sounded resigned like talking to the doctor was forced. "Did you get the HOCs I sent you? And the other stuff?"

"I got everything." As he spoke, the doctor grabbed Raiden's hand from Stone's shoulder. He placed his fingers on his pulse. "What's wrong with your boyfriend?"

"Your name is really Marion?" Ash asked. "I kept thinking this guy was a ding-a-ling."

"That's my name, but don't call me that," Stone grumbled. "And Fluffy here isn't my boyfriend or..." Stone tossed his head back and forth. He looked at Ash. "I'm not..." He trailed off and then looked at Raiden. "He and I are not like Ash and I, but Ash is..." The doctor raised an eyebrow when Stone glanced around again. "I knew we shouldn't have come here," he finished as his cheeks flushed.

"Is your boyfriend sick?" Doctor Mather asked.

"Raiden is sick." Ash paused. "And," she grinned, "Marion has been looking after him."

"Knock it off, Ash. I mean it."

"Got it, Marion." Ash chuckled.

"It's too late. We know," Raiden whispered.

"Moths can get flattened," Stone whispered back.

"Yeah? Bridges are sturdy."

"Sick with what?" the blond doctor interjected.

Before Raiden could give an answer, he began to gag. Raiden threw his hand over his mouth to stop the stomach acid, but the bile spilled between his fingers. The fluid splashed the front of Stone's shirt.

"*Helvete*," Raiden groaned. "Put me down."

"No point now." Stone stared at his shirt.

"Mather." The blond appeared to have not noticed that Raiden had just retched. He peered at Raiden while he talked. "You know that patient who came in with the funny hat?" The strange doctor's eyes were glazed over like he was lost in thought. He stepped closer to Raiden and Stone. His head tipped back and forth. Stone took a quick step backward.

"The 'tickle my pickle' hat?" Mather took his cup back and sipped.

"Please put me down, Stone." Raiden was uncomfortable with the gaping from the stranger.

"You were shivering." Stone shook his head. "The cement is too cold."

Fan-fucking-tastic, now Stone picked this time to stop ignoring him and pay attention to everything he did. Raiden groaned.

"Are you two *doctors* going to help us, or are you just going to stare?" Ash produced a plastic bag from her pack and handed the sack to Raiden. "Raiden's not that handsome."

"I wish you'd given me this before." Raiden stared at the sack.

"So, do I," Stone agreed.

"No, not that hat." The blond doctor stepped closer suddenly. "Do you remember the older man who had the hat shaped like a penis?"

"I remember." Mather stared at Raiden. "Marion's boyfriend looks like that?"

"I look like a penis?" he asked Stone. "I think I liked moth better."

"He's not my…" Stone stammered

"Who the hell is this guy?" Ash used her thumb to point at the stranger staring at Raiden.

"This is Baron. He can see cells inside your body," Stone answered. "He's saying the sickness in Raiden's body matches another person that Mather and Baron have helped here at the hospital. Mather is a surgeon. Baron's his assistant."

Ash's eyes flipped to a glare. She probably picked up what Raiden figured out. Stone knew these men well.

"Is it an infection?" Ash asked. "Is it Snow Flu?"

"Bad water." Mather sipped out of his cup. "Bring him inside and I'll fix it." He motioned to the guards as he headed toward the door. "Marion, tell your other boyfriend to keep his gun in his holster."

"You heard him, Ash." Stone glanced at her.

"I'm not Stone's boyfriend," she sputtered. Winsor looked momentarily taken aback by the reference. She glanced at Raiden. "I'm just with the one. The three of us aren't like that."

"Sure." The doctor chuckled. "This way."

They all followed Mather and Baron into the busy main waiting room of the hospital. As they passed the mixture of individuals sitting and sleeping on plastic chairs, Raiden wiped his hand on his pants. He glanced at the vomit on Stone's shirt.

"Could we make a deal? Can we just never mention that I threw up on you?" Raiden asked as they started down one of the long, tiled halls.

"I'll never mention it if you promise to never mention that my name is Marion."

Raiden smiled. "Sorry, no deal."

Chapter 18

The inside of the hospital smelled like antiseptic. Raiden could smell his sweat, the stink of the train, and his vomit. He wished he could use his soap, and he wanted to apologize to Stone, but he didn't get the chance to do either.

As soon as Stone set him down on an exam table in a quiet private room, Doctor Mather gave the harvester directions for getting cleaned up in the doctor's lounge. Baron, the blond, told Stone he would show him where the room was located.

After they left, Ash sat next to Raiden, while Mather slipped a needle into his arm. The doctor added a tube and hooked him to an IV bag. Ash adjusted her pack and tapped her foot. Soon she leaned forward and then back in the chair. She became more and more fidgety while the other man worked.

"I'd like to look at your leg. Baron commented that it looked wrong." Mather filled a syringe and then held it up to the light. "Take off your pants."

"He was attacked by a polar bear. We bandaged his leg." Ash stood up and began to pace restlessly next to the door. The doctor watched her for a moment before he looked back at him.

"Stone is decent with caring for wounds, but I just want to look." Mather studied Ash as she peeked out into the hall.

"Fine." Raiden nodded.

"I'll help you." Ash came back over to the table and unlaced Raiden's boots. He kicked them off before he dropped his jeans to the floor. As soon as his pants were gone, Mather unceremoniously stuck the needle in this thigh.

"*Helvete*," Raiden swore.

"I'd also like to take blood samples and check you for sexually transmitted diseases and infections." He began to unwrap Stone and Ash's handiwork. "You as well, Ash. Just a sample."

"Why?" Ash's eyes widened.

"Because if you guys are having sexual intercourse with Marion, I want to make sure you're healthy."

"We're not," Ash insisted. Her eyes dropped to the floor.

"You're not healthy?"

"We aren't banging Stone." Ash exhaled and glared at Raiden like he should speak up. Now would be a good time to say he'd let Stone do him, but when Mather poked at his injury, he clamped his mouth shut so he didn't swear again.

"You don't need to lie to me." Mather lifted his leg. "I can tell Marion is in love. He likes you both. I'm not actually surprised. He always liked pairs. Two hats, two pens, two pieces of fruit. He wanted two, but one had to be noticeably distinct from the other. I used to hate that about him."

The doctor was right. Stone was in love with Ash. Even if Mather had the situation wrong and it was Raiden who'd fucked him, it didn't matter. Safety for everyone was important.

"But he doesn't love—" Ash began.

Raiden cut her off. "Take the samples." Raiden clenched his teeth when Mather rolled him over. "Do whatever."

"How long have the three of you been together?" The doctor asked, while he busied himself with Raiden. He attached a tube into the IV in Raiden's arm, and Raiden noted that his stomach started to settle. Whatever the medication was, Raiden felt relaxed, and the pain floated away. When he flipped over again, he stared up at the light above him as Mather took Ash's blood sample.

"Ash and Stone have been together for a couple of years," Raiden answered. "I'm new, but I don't belong with them. I'm going to split and be on my own." For a moment, his heart hurt. If only this had been different. If he could have met Ash first, then she could be his. If Stone and he had met under different circumstances, then maybe they would've genuinely had something. Tears started to gather, and he rapidly blinked them back.

"Does that hurt?" Mather asked him when a rogue tear streaked down his temple.

"Yeah, more than I thought it would," Raiden whispered.

A melancholy feeling claimed him. He was used to being on his own. He was flexible and good with change. Why was this bothering him? Ash and Stone were supposed to be together. That had to happen. His soul demanded that they join up. And Raiden, he was supposed to be alone. The feeling must be the drugs.

Stone returned, and it was clear he had showered. His hair was still wet. He was in a spotless shirt, and Raiden envied how clean the other man was. He felt filthy in such a sterile place.

Ash jumped from her seat when Stone entered, followed by the blond. She paced by the door and glared at Baron's damp hair. Stone took the chair Ash vacated and watched the doctor work. When Stone tugged Raiden's ponytail out, the smell of coconuts wafted. Raiden inhaled deeply. The harvester ran his fingers through his hair like Ash had done.

Mather worked on his leg, but Raiden couldn't seem to care. Whatever the drugs were, they seemed to make the world blur, and all he could focus on was Stone's fingers. He inhaled again. The smell of coconuts took him to a happy place. A place where Stone and Ash were his, and everything worked out.

The other doctor stood at the foot of the table and did his blank stare as drops of moisture slipped onto his broad shoulders. Stone stared at a bouncing Ash. The silence got on Raiden's nerves. There was a tension between Ash and Stone that Raiden began to feel in his bones. The pain grew. They were gearing up for a fight. The fight would start in thirteen minutes.

"That joint pain must keep you awake at night," Baron broke the silence. "Looks like it's getting better. You look like you're growing new cartilage. Can people do that, Mather?"

"No, Baron. You can't regrow cartilage or bone."

"Oh."

Raiden wasn't listening. His joint pain had gotten better since he met Ash and Stone, except now it was all over the place. He was used to the ache before, but now the throbbing came and went with their fights, and their happiness, and their touch.

"All set," Mather tapped Raiden's foot. "I'll give you some tablets for your drinking water. Dump out whatever you have."

"We can leave?" Ash's brow furrowed. "That's it?"

"Just let me get Raiden some medication I want him to take. Wait here." Mather left with Baron trailing him. Silence descended.

"I can't wait to get out of here." Ash started back and forth next to the door again. "This was a bad idea."

"Why?" Stone glanced up at her.

"Because it was," she snapped.

"Foo-fur got the help he needed. What's the problem?" Stone stood.

"Are you gonna tell me who those guys are?" Ash stopped moving. "Is Baron your ex? They both seem into you." Her hand went to her gun. "Did you fuck them?"

Raiden stretched his shoulders as they tightened.

"I don't know what you mean. They're just doctors I met once. They check for things, injuries, and..." Stone shrugged. "They aren't into me."

"Why are you trying to bullshit me? Of course, you know these guys. Are they more of the men you've given blowjobs to? Did you get off in your shower?"

"What are you talking about? Ruffy threw up on me. I just showered because..." Stone paused. "More men I've...?" He threw his arms out. "How many people do you think...? I wasn't sucking Baron." He looked to Raiden. "Shit. Did you say...?"

"Did I say what?" Raiden rubbed the ache in his arm.

"What the hell is his problem?" Stone asked him.

"You just got a shower. That's all?" Ash paced by the door. "I bet that's what you got. Did Baron help you?"

"You want to shower?" Stone asked. "Is that your issue?"

Raiden's shoulder panged and stiffened. She was furious.

"Yeah, ice-for-brains." Ash seethed. "That's what I want. I want a hot *shower* just like all the ones you've gotten over the years. The ones I've had to watch, and now I see it again. It's never going to change, is it? Telling you everything won't change all the *showers* you're going to have. I've done this before. You'd think I'd learn. I want a fish and all I have is a badger."

"Am I high?" Raiden asked. He didn't understand her, and he could usually sort out Ash. Why did she keep saying "shower" in such a snide way? Why did she want a fish?

"I don't know. Am I high?" Stone asked him. He glanced at Ash. "I can get you a shower. I don't know about fish."

"Fuck a shower and the fish. I want to get out of here." She made another pass when Mather entered the room again.

"Stone, can I talk to you before you leave?" Stone made no move when the doctor addressed him. "Here are the water tablets." Mather handed a paper sack to Ash. His eyes popped back to Stone. "Can we talk in the hall?" he asked, as his eyes tracked Ash's hardened glare.

Stone followed the doctor out the door.

"You're too pale. You need to get under sun lamps." Doctor Mather's voice drifted from the hallway, and then there was silence.

Ash prowled like a hungry bear.

"He buggered him." Ash fumed as she passed Raiden's bed. "The blond. His hair was wet. And did you see the way Doctor Mather looked at Stone with all the 'I love you and miss you' vibe? Stone never stops. He wouldn't be with me if I told him the truth. He'd treat me like Felix did. First, we'd have sex, and it would be humpty-humpty, then he'd ditch me. Stone would never hit me, but he'd hurt me all the same. Hell, he could hurt me more when he deserted me. He'd run away when this all got too difficult. I wouldn't be able to trust him or lean on him." Ash was a boiling cauldron of emotion. "He sleeps with everyone. Men, women, whatever he can find that swings leg. I'd be ready to go out, and then Stone would drag some dumb, poor sap into his room. I'd have to sit there and listen to the pleasure Stone was giving."

"What does this have to do with wanting a shower?" Raiden wasn't in the mood to solve a puzzle. "Or fish?" He needed a nap.

"I don't care about a shower. All I'm saying is, why am I so stupid that I want a fish?"

"Did you ever consider that he sleeps around because all he thinks about is wanting you all the time? He might be trying to tame his dick because he's messed up about the one man he can't touch. You know damn well Stone would never treat you like Felix did. He'd never intentionally hurt you. He loves you. He'd never leave you."

"Did I say I wanted logic?" She threw herself down in the chair next to Raiden's bed. "You both think I'm a nutter, don't you?" Tears gathered in her eyes. "I like showers, but I'd get caught," she sniffled. Were they back on that again? Raiden could barely keep up.

"If you told him the truth, you wouldn't worry so much about being caught naked."

"No more logic." Ash slumped in her chair. "Just let me be miserable."

"You've been miserable for years, Ash." Raiden tipped his head and wiped the tears collecting on her lashes. "Why not try it my way and see what happens?"

For a split second, Raiden thought about telling her about the sex he'd had with Stone and how Stone had spent the whole time talking about her. At the last moment, he decided this might not be a good time for that. He scooped up her hand and drew her toward him. He kissed her lips softly, and a smile tugged at her lips.

"Stone loves you, and he wants you. I don't think he has as much sex as you think. He's hung up on you. Mather is nothing to him, I promise you."

"Stone makes me crazy. I saw the way the blond looked at him."

"If this is bothering you, why don't you do something with Stone? Maybe it would help. It might tame the tension between you and him."

"What are we talking about here?"

"I'll give you a second." Raiden sat up and reached for his pants. He pulled them on and then scooted to the end of the table.

"You want me to have sex with Stone? How do I do that?" Ash stood and stepped between his legs.

"Would you like me to draw you a picture?" Raiden grinned.

"Blast it, Raiden. You know what I'm asking." She snuggled into his shoulder. "He'll know I'm a woman, and it will just end up as a fight. I'm not ready for that yet. Maybe tomorrow."

"I was thinking a kiss, Ash."

Ash tipped her head and brought her mouth to his. She brushed his lips.

"Not kissing me. I meant Stone. Maybe instead of punching him, you could hold his hand or kiss him."

"Is the man I'm bound to telling me to fool around with another man?"

Raiden laughed. "I think I'm drugged. I have no idea what I'm saying." Raiden brought her tighter into his embrace and licked her lips playfully. "I don't even know what fish has to do with anything." He'd missed this. His whole body felt amazing when she was in his arms.

"I told you I thought I could change Felix. But if you have a badger, you can't expect it to become a fish." She sighed, and her shoulder dropped.

"Ash." Raiden hooked his uninjured leg around her knee before she moved away. He held her to him. "Stone and I aren't badgers or fish. We're just men. And Stone is a good man who loves you. Just think about touching Stone before we split up. If it feels right between you, then you'll know how you feel about all this. Think about it." Raiden pressed his forehead to hers. A tiny part of him secretly hoped that Stone and she would flop. Perhaps she would kiss him, and there would be no chemistry. Raiden closed his eyes and pictured her telling him that she would like to keep him.

"You're right. You're not a fish. You're my moth, bridge, nanny." Ash giggled.

"Don't forget slush-head."

Ash laughed.

"We can leave." Stone's voice made Raiden's eyes pop open. Stone stood in the doorway looking fierce and ruggedly handsome. Raiden stared at his biceps as he threw his coat over his shoulder. It was a wish in vain that Ash wouldn't want Stone. Raiden would be saying goodbye the second Ash and Stone got together.

"Thanks for talking to me, tough guy." Ash kissed Raiden's forehead and then looked up at Stone. "If you wanna win?"

"You gotta bet." Stone exhaled, and then he held up a palm-sized orange bottle. "I got some pills Mather wants Beethoven to take. And I got us a place to hang out for tonight. Our train left, so we can sleep somewhere other than with the platform rats."

Raiden nodded. That's what he needed. A place to sleep, and then he'd work on the Stone-Ash puzzle tomorrow.

Chapter 19

The hospital was a maze. The water base was just as confusing. Even if he hadn't been given potent pain medication, he would still have no idea where they headed.

Stone let him hobble until they left the main exam rooms. As soon as they hit the hallways, the burly harvester scooped him up, and Ash took his pack. No amount of his complaining made any difference. Oddly, the ignoring made him feel safe and part of their group. Perhaps he was just getting used to them.

They didn't go out the way they came in. Instead, jumbo steel doors opened to cement arches. Stone led the way like he knew this base. Ash grew more agitated as Stone lead them through the maze. Her anger was like invisible spikes. Raiden could feel her growing fury in his bones. If Raiden had met her on the train like this, he would be expecting insults hurled his way. She didn't insult Stone. In fact, she became more and more silent as they walked. He could virtually see her retreating inside of herself. Pain was her cloak, and she wrapped herself in the folds. She didn't tease, she didn't hit, and she didn't insult. Raiden hated it.

When they reached the molded white plastic door set into the brick, Stone let Raiden stand so he could fish out a key from his pocket. Ash waited until Stone helped Raiden across the threshold before she followed them. Raiden leaned on the table by the entrance as Ash squeezed past the door jamb like a fat man. As soon as she entered, she set Raiden's pack by the table. She didn't take off her own.

Inside the room was a tiny kitchen area with a table. Raiden leaned on the wood while he looked at the pictures hung on the walls.

"Sit." Stone pulled out a stool from under the table. Raiden complied, but his eyes sprang to Ash. Her hands went to the straps of her pack, and she held on to them for dear life. Her eyes leapt around the kitchen then to the bathroom. He noted Ash didn't enter more than a few steps. The door closed behind her and she shifted uneasily.

"That wall is a bed." Stone walked to the furthest wall and pulled on a rope. The flat wooden slats dropped down to reveal a mattress with a blanket tucked in. "Pillows," Stone continued. He grabbed white balls of fluff from out of a cabinet next to the bed and then threw them on the center of the blanket. As he kept talking, Raiden thought he seemed as nervous as Ash. He strode to the opposite side of the room. "Bathroom. There are a washer and dryer in there. It's small but it works." Stone walked back to the kitchen area and opened the fridge. His head disappeared behind the white door. "I can make dinner. My mom taught me to cook." He paused, and then his head popped up to look at Ash. "Are you hungry?"

No one responded. Raiden studied the room. He scanned the photos on the wall of Doctor Mather and spotted the doctor's scrubs hanging on hooks next to the bathroom. He knew where he was. He supposed Ash did too. She wasn't happy about it.

"I need to eat to take that medication," Raiden said to cut the tension. It was a feeble effort. He wasn't in the mood for their two-year-old issues. Raiden just wanted a hot shower, food, and more medication. He didn't want to feel the growing pain in his limbs because Ash didn't want to be in Doctor Mather's private quarters.

"I'm not hungry." Ash crossed her arms over her chest. "You've been here a lot?"

"Once or twice." Stone closed the fridge and copied her stance.

"Doubt it," she scoffed. "You've slept here?" Her lips became a grim smile. "Of course, you have. You know where his pillows are. I bet you didn't do much sleeping."

Raiden's shoulders began to throb. *Skit.*

"I thought you wanted a shower?" Stone glared at her. "Here's a shower and a place to crash. I don't get you, Winsor. What the hell is your problem? Is this about the fish you were bitching about?"

"You're my problem."

That was the most accurate statement Raiden had heard since he had met them.

"I'm going to stop you both right now before this starts. I don't have the energy for your fight." Raiden held up his hands between them. His shoulders and knees screamed. He wasn't going to watch them bicker until one stormed out of the room.

"Stay out of this, Scooby-Doo. This isn't your snowstorm." Stone leaned over the table.

"Are you sure about that, Stone?" Raiden raised an eyebrow. It was a low blow, but he would bring up what happened if it got him a little rest. "I could be talking to Ash about all sorts of snowstorms."

Stone slowly shook his head. He got the message.

"Stay out of this, Raiden," Ash snapped. "This is for me and Stone to work out on our own."

"On your own?" Raiden laughed. "You're shit at working out anything on your own. Sometimes, I think you haven't been trekking together for two years, and you just met." Raiden stared hard at Stone as his laughter died. "I know how much you both love to ignore me, but we aren't doing that tonight."

"Ignore you?" they said in unison.

Raiden held up his hand again and took a deep breath.

"Ash, Stone didn't have sex with Doctor Mather. If you're jealous, you don't need to be. He doesn't sleep with as many people as you think. And I'm not putting up with a tantrum. If you want Stone to stop fucking, then just ask him to do that. You could also help him out with that. You know how to make a deal. Make one that works for you and stop pouting." Raiden turned to Stone as he got up from the stool. "I'm going to shower. Stone, tell Ash who Doctor Mather is so he takes off his pack. Stop trying to pretend like you don't care about Ash. No one is buying your 'I don't love him.' You're not as complicated as you think you are. You're just a man with his heart on his sleeve trying to play games to get Ash to notice him. I'm not going to spend the night listening to him freak out, and your moaning that you can't have him."

Both Ash and Stone stared at each other across the table after his outburst. Raiden grabbed the pain meds and popped two of them before he opened his bag. He stretched his shoulder. He'd take silence and sexual tension. At this point, it was better than fighting.

"Who's Mather?" Ash slipped her pack off her shoulder and set it down.

"Mather is my brother. Mather Stone." Stone reached into his pack and pulled out a pink bottle. "I have two brothers. My eldest is a council member, and Mather's a surgeon here."

Ash studied Stone and then looked to Raiden. "How did you know that?"

"Mather and Stone have similar eyes, and I think that's a picture of Stone as a little kid on the wall." Raiden pointed to a frame near the bed. "And Mather plays the guitar." He pointed to the instrument leaning against the counter. "It's not a complicated puzzle."

Ash walked over and her eyes jumped from photo to photo. "Oh."

"And Doctor Mather seemed overly concerned about Stone's sexual safety." Raiden pulled out a pair of loose sweat pants and a large fluffy sweatshirt. "I felt like it was more than just a routine doctor question when he asked us to give him a blood sample so he could check for sexually transmitted infections."

"He did what?" Stone's Adam's apple bobbed when he swallowed. "I told him we didn't…" He pointed back and forth. "And I said that the three of us…" He waved in a circle. The pink bottle almost shot out of his hand.

"He didn't believe me, either." Ash shrugged. Raiden thought it was a good thing at least one of them understood Stone's hot air and arm-waving.

"Ash, you would've seen the resemblance, too, if you hadn't gotten so mad. I swear you two do need a bridge." Raiden pushed away Morgan-Roth's words and opened his pack and pulled out his toothbrush. "Marion Stone, meet Ashley Winsor."

"Ash is short for Ashley? I thought it was Ashton." Stone gave a startled laugh and then handed Raiden the pink bottle. "You have a girl's name like me?"

Raiden read the label. Mango Passion Soap. He smiled.

"I don't have a girl's name. I have my name." Ash glared at Raiden. "You're a blooming hophead."

"You're welcome." Raiden grabbed the last of his clean clothes and started for the bathroom. He didn't even care what a blooming hophead was. "I'm hungry," he tossed out when he reached the room.

"I'll cook. Mather told me he had some fish." Stone grinned like an idiot while he opened the fridge. "You thought I had sex with Mather, and you were jealous?" He smiled at Ash. "Do I make you jealous a lot?"

"And Ash thought you showered with that blond." Raiden grinned. "Because his hair was wet."

"Blast it, will you take a shower already?" Ash griped. "I'm gonna tape your mouth shut."

"Baron?" Stone looked thoughtful. "I didn't touch him. He's not into men, as far as I know. And I wouldn't do that anyway. His hair was wet because I couldn't get the shower nozzle to work. I asked him to help me. I guess, the doctors had some plumbing problems in the lounge, and someone forgot to turn the water back on. It was an accident and the nozzle sprayed Baron in the face." Stone paused. "It was funny."

Ash looked like she didn't think any of it was funny, but she pulled out a stool and sat. She crossed her arms over her chest.

"I don't get jealous a lot. I just hate all the slobbering nutjobs you bring back to your room all the time."

"I give some blowjobs, not all the time." Stone glanced at him and then back at her. "I don't do…" He fidgeted with his hair. "I didn't know you wanted…" He sighed. "I haven't been…" Stone scrubbed his hand over his face. "Just tell me what you want. You want me to be with…?" Stone pointed back and forth between them. "Just say so."

"I'm saying so." Ash lifted her chin. "Just us."

"Would you look at that? You're already getting to know each other." Raiden grinned as the pain in his body melted away. "I'm glad I could introduce you." He opened the door to the bathroom.

Ash gave him the finger. He laughed.

"I'll give you both a second to get to know each other." He sailed into the bathroom.

"I don't need your shitty seconds," Ash called as he closed the door.

Raiden had just gotten fully naked and turned on the stream of water when the door to the bathroom opened.

Ash slipped in, and his cock automatically started to fill out. He groaned.

"What're you doing in here?" He turned away from her and got into the hot stream of water. He peeked past the curtain. She stood by the sink.

"I wanted to make a deal with you. Something you want in exchange for something I want."

"While I'm in the shower?" Raiden opened his new bottle of soap.

"While we're alone." She glanced at the curtain. "I can see your outline. You're hard? You want to have sex? Now?"

"When you're around, I always want to have sex. Damn Weaver." Raiden made sure his bandage didn't get wet. "Now, what's the deal so I can finish my shower alone?"

"Deal?" Ash stared at the curtain. Was the cloth see-through? Her eyes turned a deeper silver. When they popped to his face, his eyebrows rose. "Right, I wanted to…" She moved her hand back and forth.

"You're talking like Stone. I don't speak arm-waving. What do you want?"

"I thought about what you said." Ash turned away from him and sat on the counter. "About how I'd have to touch Stone if I'm going to ask him to stop sucking off every harvester he meets."

"You want my permission?"

"Ash Winsor doesn't need your permission to do anything."

"Fine. Whatever. Tell him the truth. Have some sex." Raiden closed the curtain. He began to wash his hair. "Maybe, if the two of you fuck, it might calm down the drama." Ash and Stone could make him as insane as his father. He created a lather and stood under the hot spray.

"I'm not ready to tell him yet."

"Right, you'll do it tomorrow," Raiden called over the water. Ash shoved the curtain aside, and Raiden raised one eyebrow. "That's a 'no' to showering by myself?"

"Will you help me or not?'

"Help you do what?" Raiden ran his hands over his nipples and then down his stomach toward his cock. Ash's eyes followed his hands.

"I thought I could suck him off. I could see how it went. If it's a calamity, then I could tell him we're staying friends. I wouldn't have to ever tell him I'm a woman."

Raiden wanted to point out that hiding her gender indefinitely wasn't a realistic plan, but he didn't. He stepped out of the shower and grabbed a towel.

"If you think I'm going to stop you, I'm not. Go ahead. You're right, big, bad Ash Winsor. You don't need my permission. Suck whoever you want." Raiden couldn't very well say 'no' anyway since he'd had full-blown sex with Stone. On some level, he wanted her to fool around with the other man to ease his guilt. Even if it was illogical, he thought he would feel a hell of a lot better if, when Raiden told her he had Stone inside of him, she had done the same thing. Maybe the conversation wouldn't be so bad. He was grappling at a thin ledge.

"I don't know how to give one. I've never done it." She glanced at the shower like it was the most beautiful thing she had ever seen. Her silver eyes shot to him.

"Do you want a shower?" Raiden asked. "I thought when you said shower all snide at the hospital you were talking about Stone having sex. I thought it was a metaphor."

"I was mad at Stone before," Ash agreed, "but sometimes I just wish I didn't have to hide all the time. After my parents died, my uncle made the plan to hide me as a man, so I'd be safer traveling the trains. Back then, I thought it was a great idea, and we needed the HOCs. Now it's been years, and some days, I get tired of always worrying about getting caught." She turned her back. "It's my problem, Raiden. Forget about it."

Raiden brushed his teeth. He wasn't going to forget about it. A shower was such a small thing to make her happy.

"Just shower. I'll hang out with Stone so you don't get caught."

"I don't have any clean clothes." She gave a quick glance to the curtain.

"The two moths can hang out." Raiden handed her his sweatpants and shirt. "We can giggle like twelve-year-old girls." He grinned at her.

"Wait." She held the clothes as he started for the exit. "What about my deal?"

"What deal?"

"Will you teach me how to give a good blowjob? I know you did it with Doug. I've never done it, and Stone will know if I'm not skilled. People talk about how amazing Ash Winsor is in the bedroom. Weaver and I worked on that lie for three months."

"Would I be wasting my time if I said tell the truth?"

"Yes." She looked at him like he'd lost his mind. A knock sounded. Raiden wasn't surprised. They were always interrupted. He tightened his towel and then opened the door.

"I panfried fish and veggies." Stone glance from him to Ash. "Just don't eat Mather's applesauce."

"Your mom really taught you how to cook?" Ash asked.

"See how fun it is to get to know someone and tell them the truth about who you are?" Raiden grinned.

"Stuff it, Fido." Stone sighed. "Just come and eat and leave me and Ash alone. That is if you can do that."

"Doubt it." Raiden glanced back and forth between Ash and Stone.

Stone closed the door.

"Can we make a deal? What do you want Raiden? I could get anything for you. You've like zero gear and no HOCs. Just teach me, and I can get you anything you want."

Anything? What he wanted was Ash Winsor. He wanted to never get separated, but everything they talked about was about making a stronger relationship with Stone. He couldn't ask for that.

"Go ahead and shower." Raiden reached for the door handle. "I'll keep Stone busy. I'm hungry, and he can cook, apparently." He glanced back at her. "I'll help you. Just give me a second."

"Take all the seconds you need." She smiled. "Thanks, tough guy."

Chapter 20

"Did you tell Ash that we had sex?" Stone set a plate of vegetables down on the table in front of Raiden. Steam rolled off the fillet.

"No."

"I just can't face that right now. Maybe tomorrow."

"Yeah, tomorrow." Raiden took a bite. "None of us are so good with the truth-telling. We can all do it tomorrow."

"What does that mean?" Stone sat across from him.

"You and Ash just lie to each other, and then you wonder why you can't get closer."

"We get along fine. We're close." Stone played with his fork.

"Yeah, so close." Raiden's look must have displayed his skepticism.

"We bicker a little. But he's also my best friend." Stone set a pot of rice next to his plate and then started to shovel food into his mouth.

"Most of the time, a simple 'best friend' doesn't make you so flustered you wave your arms like a spastic."

"He makes me forget what I'm saying mid-sentence."

"You make him crazy. He makes you forget words. If you'd just both admit you love each other, that might be the start of heading in the right direction." Raiden paused. "You admitted it to me."

"I don't know what to say to him." Stone picked up his dishes and set them in the sink. "I tried to talk to him once, and he called me a…"

"He called you a twelve-year-old girl? I get it."

Stone licked his lips as he scanned Raiden. "Why are you wearing just a towel?"

"Ash took my clean clothes." Raiden tugged his towel tighter. Stone's eye traveled over his chest. The blatant invitation in Stone's eyes had his skin warming. He adjusted in his seat. If he got hard, the towel wasn't going to hide it.

"I need to find you a shirt. In fact, I need to get you a pack-full of clothes."

"Thanks for the soap." Raiden smiled.

"I liked the smell. I could still smell it on me after you left, when…" Stone's eye traveled over Raiden's torso again. This time he knew exactly what the other man was saying.

"I could smell coconuts on my skin, too."

The door to the bathroom opened. Ash stepped out in his sweatpants and giant top. She looked beautiful. No matter what she had on, Raiden liked it. His dick nudged him, but he pushed the stiffening pole down. She wanted to be with Stone, not him. It was right they were together even if they went about it all wrong. Ash and Stone were still deeply involved, and he wasn't sure where that left him. All he knew for sure was that he wouldn't get in the way of love.

Ash sank down in the seat next to them and scarfed down the meal Stone had prepared. Stone made fun of how much she ate. She called him names. He teased her about fish. She threw a handful of rice at him. The two of them fell into the typical bickering and teasing that Raiden was used to.

As he listened to them mock each other, he wondered how he was ever going to get them close to doing anything romantic. They treated each other like brothers. Stone did none of the things that Raiden would consider as adoring or amorous. When Stone mentioned how fat Ash was, she threw her fork at him.

If Ashley wanted to suck Stone off, Raiden had no clue how to even get them started. He left the table when the two of them began to gather the empty plates. Sitting on the bed, Raiden watched Stone push Ash's shoulder. He considered the fact that he should be jealous of how close they were. He should think of Ash as his and not want her to touch Stone, but he couldn't seem to do that.

Whenever he thought about her, he thought of her in terms of a pair. She was always with Stone. They were a package deal. He never thought that way when he thought about Morgan-Roth. Only Stone. He wanted her to be happy, and if he wanted Ash to be happy, then he wanted that for Stone too. Once Raiden was gone, he wanted Ash to have not just a friend but a lover. That's what she needed and so did Stone, even if he wouldn't admit it.

Stone snapped his towel at her as she sprayed water at him. Raiden rolled his eyes. This was as far from sensual as they could get.

When they were finished cleaning, Ash went over to her bag and pulled out Raiden's puzzle cube. She climbed up on the bed and sat next to him.

"What's that?" Stone stood at the foot of the bed, and his eyes tracked her slim fingers as she spun the cube. "I saw you playing with it before."

"Morgan-Roth gave it to me. It's a toy. You gotta make all the sides one color. See I got one." She held up the yellow side.

"Let me try." Stone held up his hand, and Ash tossed him the puzzle. The harvester turned the cube around and around. All the sides changed colors. No longer was the yellow put together.

"Thanks, ice-for-brains. Now none of it is right." She scooted next to Raiden. He noticed that when Ash felt cuddly, she came to him. She'd moved to his arms at the hospital, and she had stroked his hair back on the train. Why could she cuddle with him and not with Stone?

Ash lifted his arm and set her head on his shoulder. He obediently wrapped his arm around her shoulder and squeezed her to him.

Stone flipped the cube in his hand, and then he glanced up. His eyes dimmed at the way Raiden held Ash.

"Here." Stone tossed the cube and Raiden caught the toy in midair. "You try it." Stone's eyes raked Raiden. The harvester was angry. Raiden's knees began to ache. Fan-fucking-tastic.

"No thanks." He handed the puzzle to Ash.

Ash resumed playing with the cube as Stone pulled on his coat. Ash didn't notice until Stone grabbed his boots.

"Where are you going?" Ash glanced up when Stone reached the door.

"The bed only has space for two." Stone paused for a second and waved his hand. "Not three."

"Stone, wait." Raiden glanced at Ash. Her lips were pressed into a hard line. She wasn't going to speak. *Helvete.* Raiden sighed. Quickly, he would have to think of the right thing to say. "Let's make a deal."

Stone faced him and crossed his arms over his chest. "What deal?"

"If I solve this puzzle toy," he gestured to the cube, "then for the rest of the night, you have to stay here, and you and Ash have to do whatever I say. Follow me."

"And if you don't solve it?" Stone studied Winsor.

"We do whatever you want. We follow you. If you want to leave fine, or if you just want to roll the dice, whatever."

"Ash?" Stone's eyes went from the toy to her beautiful eyes. "You want to play this game?"

"I don't care." Ash shrugged like it didn't matter. She was such a liar. Raiden could feel the tension in her shoulders.

Stone shook his head. "No deal."

"Wait," Raiden called. *Fanken*, what now?

"What?" Stone turned around and set his boots on the stool by the table.

"If you leave," Raiden paused, "Ash and I will talk." It was a dirty trick, but Raiden was past caring. They were all liars at this point. He wasn't telling Ash the truth about being sexually attracted to Stone and fucking him. She was lying about her gender. Stone was hiding his love for her. As far as he was concerned, it was time to play dirty. All bets were off.

"This is a stupid bet. You can't solve this. It would take you days." Ash handed him the cube. "I've been working on it, and I only got one side." She glanced at Stone. "If you want to leave, leave. I'm used to you being out all night."

Raiden wasn't giving up that easy.

"I'm not going to sit here all night and watch you hold Ash while you play with a puzzle," Stone stated flatly.

Ash's and his eyes met. That might've been the most honest thing anyone had said since Raiden had met them. That's what was really going on. Stone might be playful with Ash and push her, but that wasn't what he truly wanted to do. Stone wished to hold her, and Raiden annoyed the shit out of him because she picked him for that kind of embrace. Well, things would change tonight. Tomorrow they would head to H.S.P.C. to find Weaver, but before they went their separate ways, Raiden would see a few honest reactions from the two of them.

"All night?" Raiden held up the cube and studied it. "If I can solve this cube in an hour, I win."

"Fuck an hour."

"Thirty minutes?"

"Twenty"

"Deal."

Stone shrugged out of his coat and threw it over the stool and his boots. Standing at the foot of the bed, he crossed his arms over his chest. Raiden held his smile. He didn't need even twenty minutes.

"And if you can't solve the puzzle, you'll leave Ash..." Stone waved his hand back and forth. For once, Raiden understood what he was talking about.

"Fine. I'll sit at the table."

"This is stupid," Ash griped. "You can't solve this in twenty minutes. What's the point of this bet, Raiden?"

"Did you want my help or not?"

"I should've never asked a slush-head for help with a man with ice for brains," she grumbled.

"Say start." Raiden looked at Stone.

"Start."

Raiden flipped the cube through his fingers. He spun the plastic side one way, then the other. Ash leaned back on one of the pillows. Stone glanced at the clock on the stove in Mather's kitchen.

Stone kept an eye on him as he went to the kitchen for a glass of water. Just as Stone came back to the foot of the bed with the cup in his hand, Raiden had all the sides solid colors.

"Done." He tossed the cube to Stone.

"You cheated." Stone held up the puzzle. "You've done this before."

"The moth has hidden talents." Ash grinned.

"It's not cheating; it's my bridge skills." Raiden lifted one eyebrow at Stone. "Are you staying?"

"You win." Stone stared at his water. He looked like he was preparing for the most painful night of his life. "What're we gonna do, Kipper?"

Chapter 21

Stone cocked his hip against the table in the kitchen. He swirled the glass of water in his hand as he stared at the bottom of the cup.

"I'm waiting." Stone glanced at the two of them. "What're we gonna…?"

Raiden hadn't thought this far ahead. He'd figured out a way to get Stone to stay around, but how would he get Ash and Stone to get past teasing like siblings and on to being lovers? A deep piece of his soul insisted he help. Raiden was confident that the part of him that demanded he connect Stone and Ash was the same part of him that ruled the pain in his joints.

He would start with showing his dice. Maybe he could skip some of the long-drawn-out jabber if he set his intentions out there.

"Tonight, I want to watch Ash give you a blowjob." There it was. Raiden would see how that went over. He was out of ideas.

Stone spat the water out of his mouth. He coughed and bent over. "Are you still drugged up?"

Ash sat up on the bed and stared at him with horror etched on her face. "What the fuck, Raiden?" Ash snapped. "You chowder-head."

"You both made the deal. I said that for the rest of the night you have to stay here, and you and Ash have to do whatever I say."

"I didn't—" Ash sputtered. "I only said—" She stopped abruptly.

"No dice." Stone stared at his glass. "I never said I'd do that."

"Fine. Back out of the deal." Raiden threw the challenge out. "I'd be able to do it."

"I didn't say I couldn't do it. I can do whatever you can do, Pooches." Stone glared at him. "That wasn't the deal."

"I said do whatever I want. You follow me." Raiden reminded him.

"That doesn't mean I'm going to force…" Stone flapped his free hand.

"I never said force. Ash is into it." Raiden's eyes flipped to Winsor.

Ash dropped her eyes to her hands while she held the cube toy. She didn't look at either of them. Raiden wished he knew what went on in her head. She had asked for his help. He'd cut through all the shit. Isn't this what she wanted? Didn't she want to fool around with Stone? He would teach her using hands-on training.

When she still didn't speak, doubts plagued him. He tried to recall the conversation in the shower. He thought he understood. Did he push too much?

"Ash doesn't want to do that. I won't make him do anything he doesn't want to do." Stone slammed the glass down on the table. "Fuck you and your deal." He picked up his coat.

"How do you know what he wants?" Raiden asked Stone.

"I've trekked with him for years." Stone shrugged on his jacket.

"Years, yet you both don't know each other." Raiden's eyes narrowed. He silently dared either of them to deny it.

"I just mean that if I was what he wanted, he would've told me by now. I don't know what you're trying to do, Alpo, but I'm out." Stone picked up his boots.

"Never pegged you for a marshmallow." Ash lifted her head. Her chin rose. Raiden wanted to praise her. "Go ahead and leave if you want. I'm no softy. If Raiden wants to throw down a challenge, I'll pick it up. If you wanna win, you gotta bet."

Stone and Ash stared at each other for what felt like years.

"I'm no marshmallow." Stone set his boots on the stool again. "I don't give up and melt."

Raiden held in his grin as he plucked the puzzle cube from Ash and tossed it to the floor. Stone was silent for a few minutes; then he shrugged out of his coat and tossed it over his boots.

"You're in?" Ash's question was just a whisper.

"I'm not backing down from a deal; it's just that Ash doing that to me doesn't seem right. He's King Winsor." Stone visibly swallowed. "I should suck Ash off. I should be on my knees for him."

Raiden considered what he said. Ash wasn't a god. She was just a woman, a fantastic woman, but a woman all the same. She wanted love, not worship and not friendship.

"Tonight, Ash doesn't get to be Ash Winsor, king of the trains." Raiden glanced at her. "He can be just Ashley, and you can be just Marion, and I'll be—"

"A slush-head." Ash shoved his shoulder.

"Fine." He let out his grin. "Are you both in?"

"Whatever Raiden wants me to do, I can follow." Ash stiffened as her chin tipped up another notch.

"No one is calling me Marion." Stone threw out his arm at Ash. "What if I just…?"

Raiden rubbed his temple. He didn't want to spend the night deciphering arm gestures. If he let this go, Raiden had the idea that Ash and Stone would get out paper and pen and write up a formal agreement. That is if he could understand the gap-talking and flapping. They would be doing whatever they could to procrastinate. Ash might even say she would fool around with Stone *tomorrow*. Raiden could feel their trepidation in the form of ankle throbbing. It would be morning before they got close enough to touch. He supposed he would have to make a move of some kind. It was a good thing he was flexible and could flow with change.

"What if you just stop fluttering like a bird and come over here, Stone." Raiden loosened his towel. "You can touch me. My dick is available. I'm not a marshmallow." He pulled the terry cloth open and settled back. "One of you can be on my right and one on the left. Back to me being a bridge."

Stone and Ash both stared at his rock-hard dick pointing at the ceiling. It felt awkward to have their eyes eating up his exposed skin, but he reminded himself they had both seen him naked before.

"I thought—" Ash paused. "Am I going to just sit here and watch Stone?"

"You can help Marion." Raiden started to run his hand up and down his shaft. "Just to start with." He closed his eyes for a second. The idea that they could both touch him made his entire body tremble with excitement. This might be about Ash and Stone, but he wasn't the kind of man to cheapen a gift.

"Don't call me…" Stone swallowed again as his eyes followed Raiden's hands. Raiden lifted one eyebrow when Stone stopped speaking.

"Don't what?" Raiden smiled. There was something amusing about seeing Stone lose his thoughts mid-sentence because of Raiden. He slid his fingers along his balls.

Stone licked his lips. "I forgot what I was gonna say."

Ash turned to face Raiden. He intertwined her fingers with his and placed his member in her palm. Her hand was warm, and Raiden shivered with growing desire. Ash licked her lips as Raiden started a slow up-and-down skimming of their hands together.

"I like that, Ash. Do it again."

Stone was still rooted to the spot.

"Are you staying?" Ash turned her head.

"I'm staying." Stone crawled up on the bed. Raiden moved his legs apart so Stone could settle between them. "Is this okay, Ash? You two are tied together. Is this…?"

"Forget that for tonight. Let's forget all the rubbish for now." Ash stared into Stone's eyes. "Just make good on the deal."

"I'll make good on it." Stone ran his hand up and down Raiden's thighs. Raiden got goose bumps. "Do you want to watch me with Spike?"

"Yes." Ash tugged on the piercing in Raiden's ear. Raiden held in his chuckle. She wasn't backing down. He loved how brave Ash was. He loved her, maybe as much as Stone did. In this second, he simply wanted to help Ash and Stone and take a little of his own bliss while he could.

Raiden's feeling of winning was short lived. He couldn't concentrate on his success with the two of them running their hands over his rapidly heating skin. Raiden inhaled the smell of coconuts when Stone curled forward and took the head of Raiden's cock in his mouth. *Helvete*, that felt amazing. Ash pinched his nipples until they stood at attention.

As Raiden's hips rose off the bed, Stone suckled his head and then swiped with his tongue. Stone's tongue deserved an award. Raiden whimpered as he let go of Ash's hand. She still held the base of his dick. He opened his eyes.

Ash and Stone had woven their fingers together. They fondled his shaft, making his head spin and his skin tingle. When Stone sat back, Ash leaned forward.

To Raiden's astonishment, Ash kissed Stone.

They ignored him as they kissed hungrily. Raiden enjoyed just watching them. Their heat was like sitting right next to an old barn set ablaze.

Ash opened her eyes and pulled back. She gave a quick shy smile to Raiden before she turned to Stone.

"I want to suck you, Stone. Just like Raiden said," she breathed. "I've wanted to do that for a long time." Her eyes stayed on Stone, and then she sent Raiden a fleeting glance.

"Good, Ash," Raiden encouraged. "Tell him what you want."

"I never thought…" Stone reached for her, and she linked her fingers with his. "You're Ash Winsor, and I should be the one who…"

"I know I'm Ash Winsor." She studied Stone's face. "But tonight, it's Ashley, okay?"

Raiden felt a fresh fight start in his knees. He sat up as a sharp pain in his shoulder practically killed his hard-on.

"Come here." Raiden grabbed Stone around the waist. Stone let Raiden manhandle him. "I want to watch Torch. I told you that. Follow me."

"I would've never pegged you as cocky in the bedroom." Stone settled on his back in the middle of the bed.

"I have hidden talents." Raiden unzipped Stone's pants as Ash pulled off the other man's shirt. They had him stripped naked in the center of the bed before Stone could even speak.

"I should...?"

"Stop talking." Ash bent her head and kissed Stone's neck. Stone groaned and tipped his head to the side to give her better access to his skin.

Raiden angled over Stone's dick and ran his fingers along the enflamed crown. A drop of pre-cum had worked its way toward the base of his shaft. Raiden followed the gleaming wetness with his thumb and then caught the droplet. He licked the bead. The taste of Stone was better than he'd ever imagined.

Bending forward, Raiden fed all of Stone's thick length into his mouth. The harvester was bigger than any man he had taken, but he relaxed and sent the throbbing shaft all the way to the back of his throat. He could feel the hardness of the head as the other man thickened and pulsed.

When he glanced up, Ash and Stone had begun to kiss each other like this might be their last chance. Ash held Stone's hands to his sides, and their fingers were still intertwined. Her oversized sweater brushed at Stone's naked chest. Stone's hips rocked under Raiden's suckling mouth. As Raiden started to draw on the skin, one of Stone's hands yanked out Raiden's ponytail. Stone placed his palm on the back of Raiden's head and tunneled through his hair. Raiden grinned. Stone and Ash both wanted his hair down.

Watching Stone's tongue licking wildly at Ash's mouth caused the hammering in Raiden's dick to intensify.

No longer did his joints hurt, all he could feel was sexual tension and growing need. The desire from Stone and Ash reached a breaking point, and Raiden joined them at that pinnacle. He wanted to command one of them to make him come, but he couldn't speak around the shaft in his mouth. His eyes stayed on the hungry way Ash and Stone kissed each other.

Raiden began to buck his hips. He rubbed his cock against the bed. This was the most erotic vision he'd ever seen. All he could think was he wanted more.

Ash buried her head into Stone's shoulder. The other man squirmed trying to go deeper into his mouth. Yes. This is what he wanted to see.

Stone's shaft hardened. His climax was just under the surface. Raiden's own rose. He gripped the base of Stone's cock and squeezed.

"Shit." Stone sat up dislodging Ash. She sat back on the bed as her eyes widened in puzzlement.

"Do you want to stop?" Ash asked.

"No," Stone growled. "I want Spike to stop messing with me. I could've come."

"If you want to come, talk to Ashley. I'm not helping you." Raiden leaned back. "Ask Ash. In fact, beg."

"You're a..." Stone panted. His eyes gleamed with lust. The other man had been damn close to exploding, but Raiden wasn't going to let him. Ash would have to help him finish. "Ash?" Stone's eyes turned to her. "I need…" Stone trailed off, and then his eyes dropped to the blanket.

Ash pointed to the other side of Stone. It was a regal command for Raiden to get out of her way. Raiden grinned as he moved to Stone's side. He knelt next to Stone's knee while Ash took up the space between Stone's legs. She was on her knees, but Raiden set his hand on her back until she settled flat on her belly between his legs.

"Lick him here," Raiden whispered in her ear as he pulled Stone's legs further apart. "He'll like that." Raiden's fingers swirled around Stone's sack and down toward his hole. "I want to see him squirm."

"You're a dick-head in the bedroom, Spike," Stone moaned as Raiden played with the other man's balls.

Ash ducked her head between Stone's legs and her pink tongue probed at Stone's balls. He moaned and lifted his hips. Her head tipped to the side as if she considered his taste.

"My turn." Raiden bent his head and ran his tongue leisurely on Stone's chest. "I could get Stone screaming." He sucked one of Stone's nipples into his mouth. "I could get you both to beg me." His teeth nipped, and Stone bowed his back.

"You're a punk." Ash shoved Raiden's shoulder.

"Ash doesn't have to—" A grunt finished Stone's sentence when Ash ran her hand over his waiting shaft.

"I know I don't have to do this. I want to do this and I can lick you as well as Raiden can," Ash murmured before she sucked Stone's sack into her mouth. Stone gasped as she licked until his balls were coated in saliva.

Raiden's fingers twitched to touch her. His heart began to ache. He couldn't keep sitting next to Stone. Raiden shivered as he wondered what Ash would feel like under her clothes. Was she wet for them? Was her skin as smooth as he remembered?

Moving to the end of the bed, Raiden lightly pushed Ash's legs apart and climbed onto the mattress between her calves. He used his right hand on Stone's thigh to part his legs just a little more.

Stone's eyes were closed, and the other man kept up his constant moaning as Ash's tongue bathed his balls. Raiden angled over Ash's head and took a hold of Stone's lonely shaft. He began to pump the other man in his fist. Ash's eyes followed Raiden's movements, but she didn't stop licking. Drips of pre-cum clung to Raiden's fingers. He swirled the mess.

"Please." Stone lifted his hips and Raiden let go.

"I'm not going to make you come. Ash is."

Stone sat up and glared at him. "Shit."

"Tell Ash that you want him." Raiden met the other man's angry gaze unflinchingly. "Tell him. Be honest. Try out honesty." He began to suck on his fingers removing Stone's wetness.

Stone's eyes dropped to Ash between his spread legs. "I want you, Ash Winsor." He looked vulnerable. "You can fuck me if you want." His voice was whisper-soft. "I'm yours."

Ash glanced behind her at Raiden. He stayed knelt between her knees. Her eyes studied him for a second, and then she settled back on Stone.

"If you wanna win..."

"Fuck that. I'm winning right now," Stone growled. "Please, Ashley."

"I feel like I'm winning too." Ash wrapped her lips around the head of Stone's cock. Raiden figured Stone must be so hard up, she might not even have to suck all that much. Stone might explode just because he was finally getting what he wanted. Ash Winsor.

Stone flopped back on the pillows and arched his back. His curved back and thrusting hips sent another inch of his shaft into her mouth.

"Nicely done, Winsor." Raiden took Ash's hand, and together they held Stone's dick. Saliva made the harvester's cock glisten. He slid Ash's hand through the wetness. Up and down, they slipped over the skin. She took over the rhythm Raiden set. The sound of her sucking became his new favorite song.

Ashley's large sweater had risen slightly exposing a narrow band of beautiful skin above her loose sweatpants. The flesh drew his eyes away from the erotic view of Stone's cock gliding into her mouth. He ran his hands over her soft skin and under the waistband. Ash lifted her hips off the bed and spread her legs a little wider. Raiden smiled at the silent invitation.

Running his hands around her waist, he then leaned his chest to her back. Rubbing against the material of her top, he kissed her neck as he inhaled that scent of sunshine and Ashley. His tongue searched for her earlobe. Easily, he nestled his palm under the fabric of her pants and underwear and then pressed to her mound. His fingers combed through the damp curls until he located her clit. He'd memorized the sensitive nub's location. He petted the wet flesh. Her hips started to rise and fall against his hand.

"I like watching you and Stone," Raiden whispered in her ear. "I'm hard." Stone was still a puddle on the bed. His eyes closed in ecstasy as she worked her mouth over his head.

Raiden took Stone's distraction to his benefit. He worked a finger into the warmth of Ash's body and began to slip her pants down. He shouldn't be risking her secret, but those damn heartstrings whispered this was a good idea. It was like there was an imp on his shoulder hissing that Ash was his too.

Her hips wiggled. The fabric reached her knees and Raiden paused to admire her rounded ass. He wanted to strip her naked and sink his teeth into every part of her. He wanted to watch Stone suck her nipples until she screamed. If he could've stripped her naked right now, his mouth would be on her wet folds in a heartbeat. If he could, he would swirl his tongue around until she begged him to never stop.

His cock throbbed, but she would never forgive him if he was the one to expose her secret. Raiden had to be careful. He added a second finger into her hot channel and rubbed back and forth until she panted around Stone's cock. *Fanken*, but he wanted to be inside of her deep and climaxing.

"Don't stop, Torch. Make Stone come for you. Make him scream and beg." Raiden's hand left her slit and slipped up her shirt. Through her bandaged chest, he squeezed and kneaded her breast. She shuddered under him and her ass rose up to press against his cock. His pre-cum marked her satiny skin. He would remind her he was there, naked and hard.

Raiden slipped his cock between her ass cheeks as she came up partly on her knees. His dick found her waiting warmth, and he sank the first inch into her wetness. Raiden pressed her back down flat to the bed as he rotated his hips into her heat.

Ash groaned, then gasped. Stone's eyes popped open. Their eyes met over Ash's head. Ash let Stone's cock slip from her mouth.

"Ash?" Stone spoke to her but stared at Raiden. Stone's hand stroked her cheek. "Is he hurting you? Should we stop?"

"No stopping. Raiden feels good. More." Ash buried her face into the side of Stone's thigh. Stone tunneled one of his hands into her hair. "Raiden, move."

"Not until Stone's back in your mouth." He continued to stare into Stone's intense brown eyes.

"Raiden *is* a punk." Ash lifted her head, and finally Stone dropped his eyes. His palm petted the back of her head.

"Move for Ashley, Spike." Stone looked at her as he stroked her cheek. "Make it good for him. I want to see him come."

As if in slow motion, Ash wrapped her lips around the head of Stone's cock again. Stone's hands went to her hair. Raiden bent forward as her channel hungrily tightened around his dick. He sucked her fingers into his mouth until they were as wet and slick as Stone's cock.

Raiden thrust his erection forward and Ash whimpered around Stone filling her mouth. Stone threw his head back. When his back arched again, Raiden guided Ash's slim fingers to the other man's hole.

"Touch Marion here," Raiden whispered as he started to rock forward. He started to plunge in and out of her body. Closing his eyes, Raiden buried his face into her neck as the feel of her seeped into his soul. He inhaled her scent, and that feeling of sunshine and warmth encased him.

"Yes, Ash," Stone called out. "More."

Raiden opened his eyes and was mesmerized as he watched Ashley. Ash used her wet finger to breach Stone's hole. She licked at his head and added a second finger. Stone rocked on her hand.

"Curl them up this way." Raiden moved her hand to the position he knew would make Stone shout. It worked. Stone started to beg and gyrate on her fingers. "You can make him scream for you."

Raiden continued to drive into her body pressing Ashley into the sheets. She began to pant with every hard stroke, and Raiden knew she would come soon. He prayed she didn't scream, yet if she did, he didn't care how he would explain that to Stone. He just wanted to feel her walls clench around him.

Ash lifted her hips, and he surged forward. His head spun and sweat dampened his skin. *Fanken*, if he did that again, he would climax.

"I'm going to come," he groaned. "My hot torch, I want you." He licked the skin of her neck and nipped lightly at her shoulder. He couldn't stop the way her body possessed him when he was inside of her. He thrust helplessly. Raiden wanted to make this last, but that wasn't going to happen.

Stone shouted just as Ash lifted her head and cried out. She milked Raiden's cock until Raiden stopped breathing. Stone climaxed. A rope of semen shot up. On instinct, Raiden drove deep into Ash as her body held him captive.

The sight of Stone's cock, with shining ropes of white spurting from the tip, called to him. Raiden bent over Ash's shoulder and engulfed the other man while his hips continued to drive forward. He sucked ruthlessly, gaining another shout from Stone.

Ash shuddered and clenched around him until Raiden thought her body might keep him in bliss forever. He panted and groaned as Stone's dick slipped from his lips.

Licking off every drop of Stone, Raiden thrust once more into Ashley. Another shudder cascaded down his spine as he pulsed deep inside of her. With a final tremor of pure gratification, he slipped from her warmth. His whole body tingled. Nothing hurt. He felt like he was flying.

Ash pulled up her pants but stayed between Stone's legs. Stone collapsed back on the bed with his hands still wound in Ash's hair. Ash used Stone's thigh as a pillow. Raiden rolled to the side and set his head on Stone's belly. He couldn't seem to catch his breath. Stone seemed to be having the same problem.

"I'll move. Give me a second." Raiden yawned.

"You can stay just like that, Spike. I like you with us."

Chapter 22

Someone poked his shoulder. Raiden groaned as he opened his eyes. Ash stared down at him. She was back to man mode, fully dressed.

"We have a train to catch."

Raiden sat up and glanced around. Last night crowded into his brain. Some part of him hoped Ash would still be curled around him, and Stone would be snuggled with him. Instead, he was alone in the center of the bed.

Stone came out of the bathroom fully dressed. He folded a buddle of clothes in his hands. He didn't look at Raiden at all. It wasn't the normal ignoring him to stare lovey-dovey at Ash. It was too deliberate. Stone knew he was there still naked in the bed, and he purposely averted his head and walked away. Stone began filling Raiden's pack with clean clothes.

"You want to eat?" Ash asked. "You should eat if you want your meds." Raiden glanced to Stone and then back to Ash. "Your clothes are on the table."

"I thought you slept in till noon." Raiden stood and stared stupidly at the neatly folded jeans and shirts on the table. What the hell was wrong? Everything felt off.

"Not when he has a train to catch," Stone said, more to Raiden's pack.

As Raiden dressed, Stone offered him more pain pills. Raiden declined. His head had been fuzzy last night, and already, he felt like there was something very wrong with Ash and Stone. He wanted to be completely sober while he travelled with them today.

"How long before we reach Headquarters?" A dark thought hit Raiden. It could all be over today. They could be split today. What was worse, he couldn't even tell if Ash and Stone were looking forward to that or not. They seemed just as distant as before. No, even more so.

"The train will reach Dallas later this afternoon." Ash pulled her pack onto her back.

Raiden thought about dragging his feet and missing the train. They would be split by tonight? That was too soon. He needed more time.

As Raiden yanked on clean clothes, he glanced to Stone's somber expression and to Ash's quick movements. They both walked around the apartment like the other one wasn't in the room. Raiden's knees started a dull ache. It wasn't a fight, but the distance was clearly there. They were unhappy.

Raiden sighed as he finished packing. It would be good to split up tonight. Once Stone and Ash were solidly together without him in the middle, then they would be settled in their relationship. The two of them carried so much pain with them that Raiden could see it. Hell, he could feel it.

"Follow me." Stone helped Raiden pull on his pack, and then they left the apartment.

As they made their way back to the platform, Raiden noted that they didn't hit each other. They didn't bat or tease. They didn't insult or joke. Stone and Ash were eerily polite. The frosty courtesy was shrouded in sadness.

When they reached the train, and he had them in a private room, Raiden would find out what was wrong. If they regretted that the first time they were sexual with each other he was with them, he would simply explain that soon it would be just Ash and Stone. He'd be out of the picture. They plainly needed to talk this morning. He would help the conversation and puzzle them out. Morgan-Roth was right. He'd be their bridge.

When Raiden's eyes alighted on the train waiting at the end of the tunnel, his heart sank.

So much for a private room.

"We're taking *Catboat*?" Raiden already knew the answer.

Stone and Ash climbed the couple of metal stairs onto the train, and then Stone turned around to help him. This was the first time Stone had touched him all morning. Raiden had thought that the man would be all over him while he struggled to put on his pants, but so far, Stone had acted like Raiden wasn't even with them. For the way the two of them appeared, they could all be traveling alone.

Stone let go of his arm as soon as he was on the train. The three of them walked to the second cargo car before Ash pointed to an area where two crates were nestled.

Stone took his coat off and threw it down. He sat with a plop.

"I'm gonna make some money," Ash murmured. "Fresh snow around here."

Ash didn't wait for them to answer. She strode out of the train car, head held high. Raiden wobbled on his bad leg as he watched her disappear out the farthest door.

Once Ash was gone, Stone stood and helped him slip off his pack. He scooted over, and Raiden sat next to him on his coat.

The engines made a whine as they started up. For a second, Raiden wondered if Ash had just ditched them. He tossed that thought aside. She wanted to be split from him. They had decided that from the start when he found out she was in love with Stone. She wouldn't leave when they were so close to doing what she wanted. Would she?

"I'd leave too, but I lost all my money the night I…" Stone sighed.

Why were they so eager to get away from him? Rejection wasn't a new feeling, but he had to admit this time the dismissal stung. Last night, he must have misunderstood what happened. They must have hated having sex the way they did. They were trying to not touch, talk, or be with him. He'd made the wrong call on what would be good for Stone and Ash. He should've never gotten involved. Some bridge he turned out to be.

Raiden scooted his pack over and fished in the side pocket. He should've not pushed with the puzzle. He should've let them figure out their fucked-up relationship on their own.

"Here." Raiden tugged out all of Stone's money and his dice. "Leave." He set the stack of HOCs between them. His heart started to beat faster when Stone didn't make any move to pick up the cash and walk away.

"I don't want your money."

"It's not my money." Raiden's brow wrinkled. "It's yours. I took it so you wouldn't lose it while you were on your bender. Here." Raiden pushed the HOCs closer.

"After what I did to you?" Stone pushed the cash back. "You can keep it."

That hurt roughly as much as the rejection. Raiden crossed his arms over his chest. "When you offer someone money in exchange for sex, you turn the receiver into a prostitute. I don't need another Doug. I'm not a whore."

"I'm not Doug." Stone scooped up the stack of bills. "In fact, now I'm gonna count it and make sure it's all there." He flipped the money in his hand.

"You have your money. If you want to ditch me, go. Follow Ash." Raiden couldn't keep the pain out of his voice. He expected Stone to call him a twelve-year-old girl.

"I don't want to ditch you." Stone lifted his head from counting his bills. "That's fucked up, isn't it?"

"What's fucked up?"

"That I don't want to ditch you. That I don't want..." Stone leaned his head back against the wall. "I don't know what to say or do. Can we just pretend like last night didn't happen? You were naked and I..." Stone stared at the ceiling. "Ash was there..."

"No deal." Raiden grinned. Confusion he could handle. "Are you going to tell me what's wrong?"

"I don't know what's wrong. It feels... Now I think I want..." Stone waved his hand.

"Did Ash talk to you?" Raiden tried to figure out how to ask if Ash had told him the truth.

"Talk to me?" Stone stared at the door where Ash had disappeared. "About what?"

"Did you fight before I got up?"

"No." Stone sounded miserable. "I wish we had."

"What happened?"

"I fucked this up, didn't I? I thought I was past making a mess of my life. I don't steal anymore, and I don't drink often, but you know, you can make a huge mess out of your life completely sober."

"What's wrong? What mess?"

"I'm confused, and I think Ash feels guilty. He's supposed to be with you, and I was in his mouth. It's all I can think about. I just keep picturing you thrusting into him from behind. I can close my eyes and feel him."

Raiden felt his pain. Last night, he didn't think sex would make their relationship more complicated. Apparently, Raiden had made the fragile bond much worse.

"We shouldn't have done any of it," Raiden whispered more to himself. "This is my mess not yours. Don't worry. Ash and I will be apart soon. I'm going to leave."

"Yeah, you're going to leave." Stone rubbed his eyes. "You want to separate from Ash. Leave us."

"Yes." Raiden hoped that would make Stone feel better.

"I'm going to start a game of Boxcar Dice. I've gotta go." Stone scrambled to his feet as he scooped up his dice. "Stay off your leg."

He vanished into the opposite train car.

Raiden stared after him. Stone hadn't used even one dog insult.

Chapter 23

The mass of people on the long cement platforms in Dallas overflowed in every direction. Raiden had never seen that many humans in one place. The train station in Dallas was a major hub. Trains that headed deep into the Northern Earth Dens dropped people off and picked people up. Harvesters piled onto *Cutter*. Raiden had heard that *Cutter* traveled to Harvester's Paradise. From the sea of men fighting to climb on board, he thought Mexicali must be a utopia.

Ash and Stone still didn't speak as they weaved through the hordes that pushed to get on the train they'd just exited. They equally had to navigate the men and women flowing onto the platform.

Their silence was unsettling, but what was even sadder than the quiet was they had stopped touching. He'd changed them, and he didn't know how to put it back. Raiden kept hoping for a playful punch or a shove. He even held out hope for an insult or two.

The cement enclosure that housed the trains and the platform opened on both ends by huge archways. Raiden stared at the openings as they crossed out into the sunshine.

Stopping abruptly, Raiden stared at the gray sky. There were places where white clouds floated and parted. Raiden had never been outside without his face mask and goggles. He'd felt the heat of the sun on his clothes, but never on his bare skin. His eyes started to sting. Sunlight filtered down between collapsing buildings. He squinted and took a deep breath.

"It kind of fucks you up the first time." Ash stopped, and her eyes bore into his.

"First times can be hard." Raiden glanced at Stone.

"Follow me." Ash turned around and began to stride down a paved street with broken lamps and downed telephone wires. The three of them snaked through the crowds, and Raiden spotted a mix of young and old and poor and rich. Men with the blue-gear bracelets spoke to women and children. Raiden had never seen so many H.S.P.C. agents.

"Maybe you two should put your guns away." He spoke in a low tone to Stone as they passed a store selling skinned squirrels.

"I'll make you a deal." Stone grinned. "You tell Ash to do that, and I'll watch."

"No deal." Raiden smiled back as they kept moving. His leg had started to feel better, but now, the walking had begun to reawaken the pain. He began to limp as they headed past decrepit houses and burn barrels.

Fewer and fewer people dotted the landscape the further they hiked away from the train station. Stone took Raiden's pack off his shoulders.

"Do you know where you're going?" Raiden asked Ash when she took a gravel path.

"Of course, I do, slush-head." She pointed to a huge skyscraper that loomed above the skyline. "That's HQ. Morgan-Roth said Weaver went there. We meet him and tell him to split us. I have plenty of money to negotiate. That's what you still want to do, right?"

"That's right," Raiden said distractedly. He halted and stared at the sleek cement-and-glass tower that touched the clouds. So that would be where this would end? They would go their separate ways? He gave a sad smile. What was he so upset about? That was the plan from the beginning. He'd had some good sex, so what? And he got to know them for a few days, big deal. This was right. They would be together, and he would go back to trekking and sending money to his dad. He liked to travel around. He'd be fine.

"After we get separated, I might stay here for a day or two and rest up." Raiden said the words more to comfort himself. He had to make this feel right. "Maybe I'll head to Harvester's Paradise."

"I heard the betting there is glacial," Stone tossed out.

"I don't know where I'll head next." Ash wouldn't look at Stone. She didn't say "we." She said "I." His heart sank. Somehow, he had made a gap between them. Morgan-Roth was wrong. He was a crummy bridge.

The limping got more pronounced until Raiden was forced to fall behind. Ash and Stone noticed when he slowed and leaned against a charred stack of half-melted microwaves.

"We have to slow down." Stone wrapped his arm around Raiden's waist. Raiden leaned into the other man. He smelled like coconuts. The scent went straight to his cock. With the way he was pressed to Stone, he figured Stone noticed. He didn't say anything, but their eyes met.

"If we don't get moving, we'll have to stay together another night." Ash looked thoughtful. He couldn't tell if she liked the idea or not.

"We'd need some place to stop where we won't get robbed blind." Stone glanced around. "It's quiet now, but at night, we'd have a fight on our hands."

"Not like we haven't fought together before." Ash smiled at Stone. The little lift of her lips cheered Raiden. If they could have an extra night, it would give him time to think of a way to fix everything.

"Yeah, you and I've fought, but this time, we'd have to protect Pedigree."

"No one needs to protect me. I can fight. I just need to rest." He grinned.

A rickety blue pickup rumbled behind them. The bald tires splashed in a puddle of mud and then slowed.

"Ey! Winsor," a man called while hanging his head out the window.

Raiden turned. He recognized the man from Bosstown.

"What the hell are you doing here, Essie?" Ash took a few steps closer to the window of the truck when he came to a halt next to her. She talked over a young twenty-year-old with bright-orange hair who lounged in the front seat. "I thought you left a while ago."

"I missed my train for a young, hot thing." Essie shrugged. "Where're you headed?"

"Headquarters."

"Aren't we all?" The man with orange hair lifted his head and eyed Winsor.

"I'll give you a ride. Hop in the back." Essie used his thumb to point.

"Do you know what day it is? Hunter is at HQ." The man in the seat next to Essie spoke in low tones. "I'm going to go. You can give them a ride."

Ash took a hasty step back as the man with orange hair got out of the truck. Raiden glanced over to Essie, and when he looked back, the orange-haired stranger was gone.

"Where did he go?" Raiden stared down the empty street.

"He's fast, like gifted fast." Essie turned in his seat. "Hop in the back," he repeated.

"Thanks, Essie." Ash waved to Stone. Stone wrapped his hand around her waist and helped her into the back of the truck. For a fleeting second, Stone let his hands linger before she shoved him. His eyes dropped down and his shoulders sagged. Then he turned to face Raiden.

"Hop in, Bandit." Stone lifted him into the truck and then threw their packs into the bed. Stone climbed in, and Ash settled next to the cab. As soon as they were seated, Essie pulled the pickup away from the curb, and they rumbled toward the headquarters building.

The truck made quick time to the skyscraper. Raiden kept hoping for a flat tire. At the front of the building, there was a mob of people shouting. The crowd blocked a massive steel gate, and Raiden stared up at the huge cement wall that surrounded H.S.P.C. headquarters. Every few feet, sentries stood guard. Some of them talked to the men and women assembled next to the gate. Raiden thought he'd never seen that many guns before.

Essie didn't stop at the front and continued around the building.

"Where're we going?" Raiden called to Ash. "Don't we want to get in?" Not really, he added in his head.

Ash glanced around.

"Essie." She got up on her knees and leaned around the cab toward the driver window. Raiden couldn't tell if Essie talked to her or not. He couldn't hear anything over the rumble of the truck.

They splashed through more puddles, and Stone's face was unreadable.

Just as Ash turned around and sat, the truck took the next corner around the building. His eyes widened. That wasn't what he thought the back of H.S.P.C. Headquarters would look like. Stone grabbed his hand as his other hand went to the gun on his hip.

Raiden changed his mind. Now he decided that was the most guns he'd ever seen in his life.

Chapter 24

All along the high wall surrounding the H.S.P.C. HQ building armed men stood with weapons of every size, shape, and caliber. There had been a few by the main gate, but this looked like the start of a gun battle that would take months. Raiden couldn't even count them all. Every rifle had a parade of parked sleek black cars in their sights. Armed men surrounded each vehicle as well. Raiden's eyes bounced from barrel to barrel. He didn't think there was one person who didn't have a weapon aimed at him. Except maybe them. That was until Essie turned off the truck.

Even before the engine went silent, all eyes turned to them. Raiden gulped.

"Essie, you're late." A man with thick horn-rimmed glasses pushed away from a metal door. "I expected you much earlier." The stranger strode toward their pickup like he wasn't walking through a battlefield.

"Time is relative, Doctor Gears." Essie pulled a blue pipe from his coat and lit it. "It doesn't matter." A curl of smoke hung between the two men.

"Who's this?" The man with glasses eyed them.

"They needed a ride to HQ." Essie drew on his pipe. "This is Ash Winsor," smoke puffed out of Essie's nose. "And that's Stone and Mutt."

"Ash Winsor?" Gears turned to the truck and faced Ash. A smile hung on his mouth. "I've heard of you."

"Who hasn't?" Ash hopped out of the truck with a smooth swing and then pulled on her pack. "Gears? Nice name."

"You're a doctor?" Stone swung out of the truck bed after Winsor and then turned to Raiden. "Are you waiting to close up bullet holes?" He held out his hand to Raiden, as his eyes flipped to a machine gun mounted on the wall.

"That's what I was just thinking." Raiden let Stone help him to the ground. He leaned on his good leg and reached for his bag, but Stone wouldn't let him take his pack. They got into a tug-o'-war, and finally, Stone let go. "It's not Mutt. My name is Raiden." Raiden pulled on his sack himself. Showing weakness in front of this many guns seemed like a bad idea.

"I need entry into Headquarters, Doc." Ash took a spot directly in front of the man Essie had referred to as Gears. The dude pushed up his glasses and tipped his head like he read her. He opened his mouth, but a man behind him spoke before he did.

"There's a gate for requesting entrance." A man with hair the color of red flames came from the metal door on the wall. His thick-muscled frame matched Stone's, but he didn't match Stone's extra five inches. Even if he was the same height as Ash and Raiden, he was still intimidating. He was armed to the teeth. Raiden placed a hand on Ash's shoulder, but she shrugged him off. "Go to the main gate."

"There is a gate, but here is a door." She waved to the door and glared. "I'm here to meet someone."

The man with red hair crossed his arms over his chest and lifted one red eyebrow.

"Why am I always here for this bullshit?" The redhead glanced at Gears. "I'm starting to think this is 'coz of you."

"I didn't invite them, Mac. They aren't here to meet me." Gears turned back to them. "This is Mac. He's in charge. You're going to have to clear it with him."

"I plan to see Weaver Yazzie." Ash could have been made of granite. "We have business." She wasn't moving, and that was clearly not a request. Her statement lifted another eyebrow from the redhead.

"Sometimes he goes by the name of Arrow." Raiden added. Gears studied Raiden then Stone.

"Archer!" From the door, the most beautiful woman Raiden had ever seen floated toward the parade of armed vehicles. She threw her arms out and spun as her long skirt fanned out. Abruptly, she stopped by the car in front of them. After she ducked her head into the car window, she then popped it back out and looked at them. Her mouth split into a generous smile.

"Hi, Mac!" She pranced over to them, and then hugged Doctor Gears. Raiden thought it was surreal that no one seemed concerned about the sheer volume of firepower. "Did Mac bring friends for a visit?"

"Mac doesn't have friends." Gears chuckled. "We should talk about that."

"I'm stuck in the middle of a conversation while there are enough guns to start a war," Mac snapped. "Yet you want to ask me about my friends?"

Raiden agreed with Mac. This seemed like bad timing.

"Don't worry." The beautiful woman tossed her long white-haired braid over her shoulder. "Rumi says—"

"No. No Rumi. No quotes. Stop it, Luna." Mac threw his hand up. He shot a stony look to Ash. "You're not entering my HQ. Weaver Yazzie was given Snow Flu for study by the H.S.P.C. for crimes committed with The Originals." His eyes darted to the line of cars. "Move along, strangers. I don't need trouble."

Ash's back snapped straight, but Raiden wasn't sure if it was the reaction to the news or being told to move along. Raiden's eyes flipped to the blonde. That was Weaver's braid in her hair. He knew it. Should he say that he thought they were lying? If he stayed quiet, maybe he could just stay with Ash and Stone.

Stone would never forgive him if he stayed with Ash. *Helvete*, he loved Stone and cared about the other man. As much as Raiden was sure that over time Ash and he could become very happy with Stone, Raiden had his doubts that Stone would ever want to share Ash Winsor. The man had wanted her for too long. Raiden would never be anything other than the home-wrecker who stole Ash.

"Move along?" The blonde pouted. "We're not all strangers in life. We are connected, Mac."

"Save it," Mac grumbled.

Stone shook his head slowly. Raiden's heart dropped. No. If there was a way for him and Ash to separate, then they should. If they were lying, Raiden should find out.

"We can figure out another way to untie our heartstrings." Raiden leaned on the truck to take some weight off his bad leg. Pain started to throb in his knees and shoulders. Was it a storm? He glanced at the gray sky. He couldn't tell. He never could figure out what the pain was attached to. "Let's just go and let them get back to whatever this is." Raiden pointed to the guns and the line of parked cars.

Stone nodded his agreement as his eyes scanned a guard with ammo as a necklace.

"Wait." Gears pushed up his glasses as he eyed Raiden. "You're the man Weaver tied to Ash Winsor. Your heartstrings are attached." He kept studying him. Raiden squirmed under his intense stare.

"How do you know that?" Ash stepped between them in a protective gesture Raiden found endearing.

"I'm Nova's father." The doctor paused. "She told me about her train ride. I've lots of questions about your connection. I just started studying Conpar and gifts. It's truly fascinating."

"What's Conpar?" Raiden asked.

"Who cares what it is." Ash crossed her arms over her chest. "Can we see Nova?"

"Don't give me the 'it's fascinating' crap, Gears. I know what you're thinking. No." Mac bristled as the parade of black cars started to pull away. "Come back later."

"Oh, no." The blonde scooted around Ash and pointed to his leg. "You're bleeding. Look, Mac. Our new friend needs help."

"New friend?" Mac groaned.

Raiden shifted and looked down. The beauty was right. His jeans had small blots of blood seeping through the fabric. Stone was at his side as soon as the words were out of the woman's mouth. Ash turned around and wrapped an arm around him.

"Give me your pack, and lean on me," Stone said.

"I'm okay." Raiden shook his head.

"Doubt it." Stone reached for his arm.

"You should sit down." Ash gestured to the truck.

"I'm Luna." The woman smiled again. "I could just look at your injury. Check for infection. Right, Mac? Look, Hunter just left. We could help our new friend now." She didn't even look at the burly man still grumbling behind her. "That would be okay?"

"He's fine," Ash snarled. "Back off, Barbie."

Raiden grinned. He was fairly sure Ash was being jealous. Luna didn't seem to notice.

"No, no." Luna smiled. "Luna, not Barbie."

"Cleanliness is next to godliness." Gears pushed his glasses up his nose. "Can she just hold your hand? She is exceptionally good at this. We've been practicing."

Holding people's hands took practice? Raiden shrugged. He supposed it wouldn't hurt.

"Thank you, my match." Luna beamed at Gears. "I am improving."

Ash stepped aside just as Mac heaved a sigh.

"One day, this jaw-jacking is going to get you all shot," Mac grumbled under his breath. "Since they left, go ahead, but then we're going inside."

Luna held out her hand. Ash kept glaring, and Stone joined in. Out of curiosity, he placed his hand on Luna's. He shrugged at both Ash and Stone.

Just as their palms touched, Raiden had another surge of pain in his joints. There was something wrong, but he didn't know what. He looked at the sky. A storm? Gunfire? A polar bear? He glanced at Ash and Stone. They seemed fine. Whatever the problem was, it would happen in three minutes twenty-four seconds.

Luna's eyes widened, and then she squeezed his hand tighter.

"You could come in, and I could mend the wound on your leg." She smiled at Gears and still didn't let go. "And you can talk to them about Weaver."

Raiden's eyes narrowed. "I thought you said Weaver was given Snow Flu."

"He was." Gears assured him. "But I was curious about the binding ceremony you went through."

"It wasn't a ceremony. Weaver didn't even ask," Ash griped.

"No." Mac shifted uneasily. "Get checked in at the main gate." His head flipped to Ash and Stone. Raiden had the idea that Mac knew they were armed.

"I agree," Stone said. "I'll fix up your leg, puppy-chow. Let's go."

Raiden nodded. There was a tension in the air that didn't have to do with the armed men on the wall around HQ. The issue must be a storm. They did need to leave and now.

"Wait." Luna's hand tightened when he tried to pull his fingers away. "Gears would like to talk to you a minute. Please? I could look at your leg and the bruise on your ribs. I'll make it better."

"Bruise?" Ash asked.

"Must be from when Doug punched me."

"And," Luna continued, "I can even ease the discomfort in your…" Her slim eyebrows drew together. "I don't know the word. I'm not a doctor like Gears. I'm just a healer." She glanced at the man with glasses. "What's the medical word for your asshole?"

Gears pushed up his glasses. "Rectum?"

All eyes turned to Raiden.

"I'm fine." Raiden knew he shouldn't, but his eyes jumped to Stone.

"Your ass?" Ash glared. "Your ass is hurt? What happened?"

"Luna, we talked about how people don't like to discuss personal medical problems in a group setting." Gears smiled at her. "We can work on that."

"Just leave their asses alone," Mac growled.

"I know we talked about it, but I just thought if they wanted to have more rough sex I could make it comfortable, and then you could talk about—" Luna was cut off by Ash.

"Rough sex?" She scanned Stone and then him. Her armor was back on in full force. The pain in Raiden's limbs reached a breaking point. *Skit*, this was an overturned train. He yanked his hand from Luna. No more of that.

"My ass is fine." His eyes scanned Ash's expression. "Honest." Thunder rolled through his limbs.

"Ash, listen," Stone sputtered quickly. His words tripped over themselves. "I was gonna tell you that I forced…" He waved his hand. "I was drunk when Puddles came in and…" He rubbed his forehead. "I didn't mean to…"

"You forced him?" Ash flipped her coat back. "You raped Raiden? You hurt *my* Raiden?"

"*My* Raiden?" Stone looked like someone had just belted him in the stomach.

"No, Ash, no." Panic struck Raiden like a frying pan over the head. "Let's talk."

"Fuck talking." Ash drew her sidearm with a quick spin. When she did, all the weapons turned to aim directly at her. Three men from the wall shouted for her to put it down.

"Drop the gun," Mac commanded. The huge man took a step directly in front of Gears and Luna. He shoved them behind his back. Raiden didn't know what to do. Should he protect Ash or Stone?

"Listen to me Ash." Raiden grabbed her arm.

"He forgave me." Stone threw up his hands. "Please, Ash. I didn't know I hurt him at the time." His voice was whispered anguish. "I would never hurt him, I…"

"He did *not* force me." Raiden stepped in front of Ash's barrel. He pushed the gun down until it pointed at his knee. "It wasn't like that."

Ash's eyes filled with tears. "Did Raiden say yes?" Her eyes searched Stone's. "They have to say it, Stone." Raiden couldn't even get her to look at him. This was a bad time to be ignored. Luna grabbed Raiden's hand again and gave him a wan smile.

"No," Stone whispered. "He begged me to stop."

Ash's hand trembled, then after a few seconds, she dropped her arm.

Before anyone could do anything else, Mac moved. The redhead snatched Ash's pistol from her hand, disarming her. Ash threw a quick punch when the weapon was plucked from her palm. Mac caught her fist and flung her backward. She stumbled and then landed in a mud puddle.

Stone lunged. Raiden was positive he was trying to reach Ash before she fell. Mac reacted like the move was an attack on him. He grabbed Stone around the waist and tossed him to the ground. Mac pinned Stone before Raiden could get Luna to let go of his hand.

"That's it. I've had it." Mac glanced around. "You're all arrested."

"Arrested?" Luna tipped her head to the side. "It's not like they pointed a gun at us."

"They're armed, and they bug me." Mac gave an arm signal to the other guards. "I'm bringing you in." Stone was flipped over and tossed onto his stomach. More mud splashed. The redhead forced Stone's arms behind his back. "Disarmed," Mac growled.

Stone wiggled but didn't go for his guns. Raiden silently thanked him for that. Three guards appeared out of the doorway. They hauled Stone to his feet and held his biceps.

Raiden tried to let go of Luna to help Ash as she rose. Luna grabbed both his hands and refused to release him. Raiden wouldn't fight a woman. Ash wiped the tears on her face. Mud streaked along her cheek.

"You can take my gun from my cold, dead hands," Ash bit out at Mac.

"I accept those terms." The redhead laughed.

Ash raised her chin. Raiden pried Luna's hand off him. Just as the redhead grabbed the front of Ash's coat, Raiden grabbed the man's arm.

"Leave her alone, Mac." Gears pushed up his glasses. "This is like Karma."

Mac froze, but Raiden didn't take his hand off the other man's shoulder. What did karma have to do with Ash? Raiden took one deep breath, and then Mac dropped his arms. Raiden stepped away from Mac.

With a push, Mac shoved Ash away from him. She stumbled and then straightened. Raiden stared into her eyes as he offered her his hand. Maybe no one noticed the word "her" that the doctor had used. And by no one, he meant Stone. Ash took two steps closer to Raiden, but she didn't accept his outstretched hand. Her eyes darted to Stone held between the guards. Maybe Stone missed it?

"I didn't know you were a woman. Just go." The huge redhead crossed his arms over his chest. "Let him go," Mac commanded the guards who held Stone.

Raiden winced before he glanced behind him to Stone. There was no way he missed the female reference *that* time.

The storm was here. Raiden's legs and arms screamed. His joints stiffened so abruptly that Raiden didn't think he could walk. Leaning heavily against the truck, Raiden gulped down the excruciating pain.

"You're a woman?" Stone's voice was soft at first, but then the words rose to a shout. "You're a goddamn woman? You're a lying—"

Ash cut him off. "I'm a liar? You raped Raiden, and you planned to pretend it never happened."

"Just because you're fucked up about Felix doesn't mean…" Stone waved his arm around.

"I'm fucked up? Felix? You knew? How long?" She glared at Stone. "You never told me you knew?" she hissed. "Why didn't you tell me the truth?"

"Me? Tell the truth? That's rich. Fuck you, Ash Winsor. Don't you dare act high and mighty with me right now." Stone threw his arm around. "We even… in the bedroom… you should have told me. You're a lying sack of…"

"What does that make you? You always were a waste of my time. I can see why your family didn't want you." Ash turned her back on Stone and began to walk away.

Raiden could see how the words hurt Stone. The pain was written across his face. Stone took two huge steps and grabbed her arm before she passed the pickup.

Stone spun her around and shoved her against the tailgate. Tears of pain gathered in Raiden's eyes as his shoulders curled forward. His whole body hurt from head to toe, and the agony soared higher than ever before.

"I hate you, Ash Winsor." Stone threw his hands up when Ash shoved him. "I never loved you. You're the last person on this planet I'd follow anywhere."

"Fine with me. I never loved you either. I just put up with your pathetic shadowing me. What a waste of time. I should've never bet on you."

"Pathetic?" Stone stepped away from her like she'd slapped him. "Never bet on me?"

The pain skyrocketed. More tears stung Raiden's eyes. He slumped to the ground. The redhead rubbed his hands through his hair in agitation.

"I'm leaving." Ash glared. "I hope I never see you again."

"So am I." Stone adjusted his pack. This time he turned away from Ash.

"Oh, now you're leaving?" Mac's voice was drenched in sarcasm. "Right."

"Take my hands, Raiden." Luna knelt next to him. Raiden tried to breathe through the torment as his muscles stiffened. His joints felt like they were ripped apart.

"I'm fine," he panted.

"I can ease it." Luna held out her hand. "Take my hand and close your eyes."

"I can't." Raiden couldn't simply close his eyes and give up on Ash and Stone. His dad had given up and gone insane. Some part of him told him if Ash and Stone fell apart, he would as well. Raiden would have to explain to Luna that he had to puzzle out Ash and Stone. He was the only one who could.

"I can ease it," Luna repeated. Another seizure rippled through his system. Maybe if he could just take a second to dull the pain, he could think. He took Luna's hands and closed his eyes. Ash and Stone's yelling faded away.

Chapter 25

When Raiden opened his eyes, he expected to be next to a truck with Stone and Ash screaming their fool heads off.

He wasn't.

Scanning the room, Raiden didn't know where he was. He'd been placed on a small green cot. A metal counter sat across from him. A tiny clock sat on a table that could be considered a nightstand. There was a quiet tick-tock.

Raiden heard a noise, and a door on his right opened. Stone entered from what appeared to be a bathroom. His hair was damp, and he was in clean clothes. As the harvester paced the floor, Raiden thought there would be a hole in the carpet. Raiden closed his eyes as the dull ache in his body throbbed with each beat of his heart.

"Where are we?"

"We got arrested. They took our packs and our guns. We're locked in HQ."

"This isn't that bad, all considering." Raiden glanced at the clean room and paused. "I thought that redhead said we could leave. That Mac guy."

"That was before you passed out, marshmallow." Stone paced by the door like a caged tiger. Raiden figured his agitation wasn't due to the location. The room was far from a prison cell. Stone and Ash were still all kinds of screwed up.

Raiden studied the troubled harvester. "We got arrested because I passed out?"

Stone stopped walking for a minute. "No."

"What happened?"

Stone wouldn't look at him.

"What happened, Stone?" he repeated.

"Ash and I went from shouting to drawing our weapons to threatening each other. I called her a liar, and she called me a rapist. That Gears guy tried to get into the middle of it." Stone crossed his arms over his chest. "More guards came out. Mac was pissed. Luna held you and wouldn't let go. Ash yelled at her to stop touching you. Ash called Luna a name or two, ugly insults. You know how Ash gets when she loses her temper. She didn't want Luna hugging you."

"And then?"

Stone exhaled. "Then Mac demanded we give up our pistols, or he'd bring us in."

"And you didn't do as Mac asked?" Raiden knew the answer before the question was posed. "That guy was in charge."

"Ash gave him the finger." Stone dropped to the cot, and his head flopped to his hands. "You should've told me about her."

"And I'm sure wherever Ash is, she would say I should've told her about the sex we had."

Stone bristled. "That's different."

"Is it? You and Ash have said that to me before. It's not different, Stone. This is all the same," Raiden snapped.

"We're all a bunch of liars. We should all be asking for forgiveness."

"We are all liars, and it's never going to get better is it?" Stone rose to his feet. "I couldn't figure out my relationship with Ash in the two years I had with her. I'm never going to get Ash Winsor. You're leaving, and what the hell am I supposed to do? I should leave too. Fuck all this. I'm out."

There was a rap on the door, and Raiden sat up. *Helvete*, he didn't get a chance to talk to Stone. They needed to work out this problem. Raiden still believed it could be done.

Sighing, he glanced at the clock. Raiden had no idea how long they had been in this room. He stood and tried to stretch his muscles. They were stiff and objected to the movement.

Stone stared at him, and another rap sounded before they heard the jingle of keys. The door opened with a swish across the carpet.

Ash stood on the other side with Luna and Gears flanking her.

Raiden's eyes took in her frame. She wasn't wearing her coat or her many fluffy layers. She wore only a pale-blue V-neck shirt and black pants. The clothes clung to her curvy shape. There was no question about her gender now. Raiden knew she hadn't wrapped her breasts. She looked good enough to eat.

"We came to talk," Luna said as she entered the room first. Stone backed up and just gaped at Ash like he'd never seen her before.

Ash didn't look at him or acknowledge him. She crossed her arms over her chest and lifted her chin.

"I'm glad to see you're okay, Raiden." Ash walked toward him. When she got close, he pulled her into a hug.

His muscles relaxed some of the tension. She smiled but didn't hug him back. She shifted out of his arms.

"Now you're a full-on girl? Boobs and all?" Stone grumbled. "You're a real squall."

"Fuck you, ice-for-brains." Ash turned to face Stone. "I was tossed in the mud, and I don't have a pack. Deal with it."

"She's borrowing my clothes," Luna said brightly. "I brought her clean clothes just like I brought you." She smiled. "Ash has told us all about why you're here to see Weaver."

"Yes." Gears pushed his glasses up his nose. "Weaver was given Snow Flu and is no longer with us, but Arrow is here in HQ." He looked at each of them in turn. "If you want to meet with him, we can see him now."

The information must have been new to Ash. Her eyes widened. She looked to Stone, but he stared at the door.

"I don't give a shit what Ash wants to do. I don't follow *her*." Stone stood next to the exit. "I want my pack and my guns, and I'm leaving. I don't need to see anyone. I'm not tied to this snowstorm."

"As you wish." Gears adjusted his glasses. "Mac is outside the door waiting for you. I thought I'd give you the option after what I saw outside. I talked to him, and he said if you wish to leave he will escort you out."

Stone gave a brief backward glance to Ash. "I'm not betting on you anymore. I just lose." With a shuffle of his feet, he disappeared out the exit.

Ash raised her chin. Raiden didn't think she would cry with strangers watching, but he wasn't sure. She shrugged. He absolutely knew she was pretending like she didn't care.

"I thought that would happen once he knew." She grinned at Raiden, but the smile was a hard, cynical line to her soft lips. "This is for the best. I don't need a shadow. I don't need anyone. I'm better on my own. King Winsor, right?"

Raiden wanted to tell her this was all wrong, but he couldn't come up with a way to explain his attraction to Stone and her. He didn't know how to tell her she did need them. And maybe if she was right and she didn't need them, well, damn but he needed her. What was he going to do without her? If he had more time, then he could solve this, but it didn't look like time was on his side.

"Shall we go and meet Arrow?" Gears asked her. "He's a few floors above us. We can take the elevator. I like the stairs, but it's fine."

"Yes." Ash wouldn't look at him. They trailed Gears and Luna out into a wide hallway with a busy-patterned carpet. Armed H.S.P.C. agents passed them. They reached the elevator and stopped while Luna pressed the button.

"Ash," Raiden breathed. "About Stone…"

"No, don't, Raiden. We were never any good for you, anyway," Ash said as the door to the elevator opened. They stepped inside and started their climb to the upper floor. "I poisoned you with bad water. It was my canteen," Ash said after a few seconds. "Stone raped you while he was drunk." A chime interrupted her. The doors swished open. "We never gave you a fair shake. You're better off without us too. After this, I bet Doug looks good to you."

"Ash…"

"No, really, tough guy." She gave a sad laugh. "We dragged you all over and made you follow us. You had to listen to us bitch. We loved to have a row. Luna says the arguing messes with you. Who would ever want to live with that kind of pain? I get why you wanted to get here so much. After we left Mather's apartment, I was so hurt that you still wanted to do this. I thought, no, I'd hoped that the three of us could be... Never mind what I thought." Ash shook her head. "I just get it now. I wouldn't want to be stuck with someone like me."

"I didn't feel stuck with you, Ash." Raiden felt like he walked toward his execution. "What about Stone? Are you going after Stone? I thought he's what you wanted." Ash still wanted her best friend, didn't she? This was all wrong, and he couldn't figure out the puzzle. He should just shake her and tell her Stone loved her. He loved her too.

"Stone's gone." She shook her head. "I just want to be on my own. I never did figure out how to be with Stone, and that was years of trying. I can't do that with you, Raiden. I can't spend two years being someone else for you. I give up. I bet, and I lost."

Be someone else? Raiden didn't accept that. He wanted Ash the way she was. She didn't have to be someone else for him. He loved all of her... even her shadow. Before he could say all that, Luna spoke.

"Here we are." Luna opened a door into a huge office space with multiple desks in rows across the floor. On a far wall was a huge window with a thick blue curtain drawn closed. Medical equipment sat next to a door nestled in the corner of the room.

Gears pulled him toward the glass windowpane, and he dodged office chairs as he walked further into the room. The area was empty of people, and his eyes bounced around looking for Arrow. Raiden glanced to a clock above the elevator. The time blinked that it was after two in the morning.

"You can meet Arrow here."

Again, Raiden glanced around for his friend.

Luna pulled a cord. The drape over the window opened with a swish. Instead of seeing Dallas, Raiden stared at a room with a bed and a water pitcher. A few hospital items sat near the floor. A wooden screen moved, and Nova appeared. Her eyes weren't as red as Raiden remembered. They were brown.

"Raiden?" She gave him a smile. "I didn't expect to see you again."

"Raiden?" Arrow appeared past the screen next. "I heard you were here, and I didn't believe it." Weaver was in a wheelchair. He rolled past the screen and up to the window. He didn't look like what Raiden remembered. Weaver's skin was an ashen gray, and his hair was limp around his shoulders. He huddled under a blanket.

Nova sat on the edge of the bed, and Arrow stared at him. "You decided to come and see me?" Arrow tipped his head to the side.

"We came to pay you to unbind us." Ash stepped forward next to Raiden. "Your HOCs are in my pack."

"I'm sorry." Arrow's smile faltered. "I can't."

"What do you mean?" Ash hugged herself like she warded off the cold. "You said you could."

"I said he could," Nova piped up. She pulled a book out and curled up on the bed. She plumped a pillow. "I lied."

"You lied?" So, from the beginning, no one had told the truth about anything? Raiden glanced at Ash. What would they do now? His heart began to lighten. Maybe there was still a way to solve this. They could find Stone. The three of them could be happy together. Raiden glanced at the pain etched in Ash's face. She didn't want him and Stone. Now she wanted neither of them. If he was going to make her happy, the only way to do that was to disconnect.

"I don't think I can undo it. Your strings want to be this way. Your heart made up its mind." Arrow put his hand upon the glass. He squinted at them. "I could maybe rip out your heartstrings, or break them, but that would leave you lonely and sad. I've seen it."

"Lonely?" Ash gave a curt nod. "That's perfect. You can rip out mine. I don't want to feel any of this. I'll take lonely, over this pain."

"No," Gears spoke up from where he stood next to Luna. "I can't let a woman into a room contaminated with Snow Flu. Women are too important to take that risk even in protective clothing."

"Nova is in there." Ash pointed.

"I'm immune to Snow Flu." Nova shrugged. "Besides, this is where I need to be."

"That's bollocks. Being a woman is bloody shite," Ash snapped. "So, I have to stay like this?" She closed her eyes and hugged herself tighter. "I can't do this anymore. Now what?"

Raiden's bones ached. Ash's disappointment dug into his joints. He wondered if his heartstrings were ripped out, maybe he wouldn't feel the pain anymore. It hurt to know that Ash would always love and pine for Stone. He didn't care what she said about being better off or whatever nonsense she wanted to regurgitate. She would love that other man, and he would always be the one she was tied to.

As much as that hurt, he realized he had somewhere along the way fallen for Stone too. How would he live never having Stone around? He'd never be teased. He wouldn't be called silly dog nicknames. Stone wouldn't be there to sputter and arm wave. How could he hang around Ash knowing that Stone would never again call him Spike? Ash and he would always be messed up with Stone gone. Everything would be off, and he would never know how to fix it. The more he considered what Weaver said, the more the notion didn't seem like such a bad idea.

"You can rip out my heartstrings. If Ash wants us to be separated, I can do it." Raiden glanced to Gears. "I can go in, right?"

"Yes," Gears answered. "I could let you, but you're taking a risk."

Weaver placed his hand on the glass. His hair started to move like in a breeze. Weaver tipped his head from side to side.

"Are you sure?" Ash asked.

"I'm not sure about anything. I'm a lousy bridge, Ash. I let you down. King Winsor would be better off without me, not the other way around."

"I don't know what this will do to you." Arrow looked off between them and removed his hand from the glass.

"I couldn't figure out the puzzle of Ash and Stone. I couldn't even figure out where I fit in." Raiden gulped down the lump in his throat. "And I can't stay with you without Stone at your side." He glanced at Ash then to the floor. "I can't stay knowing Stone will never call me Spike. I'm sorry, Ash, but I think I fell in love with him. I think I love you both. I know it's fucked up, but I also know it hurts too much to be apart. Lonely is safer and less painful. I understand."

Arrow's eyes jumped to him. "I wasn't talking to you. I was talking to him." He pointed behind Raiden. "You're both tied to him as well."

Raiden spun around. Stone stood in the doorway of the elevator. The redhead pushed the button and the doors closed.

Stone slipped his pack off his shoulder and set it down by the door. Slowly, he walked toward them.

"All three of us are tied together?" Ash asked. "But Stone left that day. I don't get it."

"You were already tied to Stone." Arrow shrugged at Ash. "I'll admit I hooked you to Raiden, but Raiden and Stone did all those knots on their own." Arrow reached for a notebook and started to draw. "I don't even know how to braid like that."

Stone walked across the room. He stopped in front of the door leading into Arrow's sickroom.

"No one is going to get separated." He slapped his hands on his hips. "You'll have to fight me to get past the door."

"I told you, I could fight you and win." Raiden lifted one eyebrow.

Ash studied Stone. "But you said you hated me. You said you'd never follow me."

"I lied." Stone stared at his boots and paused. "I lied about a lot of things, I get that, but as mad as I am at you, I can't walk away. I want to run from my problems, but damn it, I can't. I'm going to keep betting on you, Ash Winsor." Stone glanced up and smiled. "Man or woman, it doesn't matter to me. I'd follow you to the ends of the earth, especially if you have Spike." Stone sighed. "I think he should introduce us again."

A smile hung on Ash's mouth.

"No." Raiden threw up his hands. "The bridge is out. The moth is dead. No."

"Do you want me to say I love you as much as I love Ash?" Stone asked him. "I'll say it." He came to stand in front of Raiden, and Stone reached out and squeezed Raiden's shoulders.

"You love me?" Ash grinned.

"Maybe." Stone turned to her and crossed his arms over his chest. "Do you love me?"

"Maybe." Ash copied his stance.

"Maybe isn't good enough. Maybe doesn't cut it. Try a little honesty." Raiden dropped his head into his palm. *Fanken*, they were always going to draw him in. He couldn't seem to help himself.

"I love you, Raiden. I love you as much as I love Ash."

Raiden jerked his head up at *his* name on Stone's lips. *Skit*. He liked that. A lot.

"Alright, you got me. I love Stone and you, Raiden. No maybe." Ash lifted her chin as if daring him to contradict her.

"When we left Mather's apartment and got on the train, all I could think about was your leaving us and how much that hurt. I can't do this without you, Spike."

Fan-fucking-tastic, he was never going to leave. He loved them.

"We can make a deal." Ash linked her fingers with Raiden's. "I'll start telling Stone the truth sometimes, and Stone can start being honest with me sometimes."

"Only sometimes?" Raiden asked her.

"Don't push it." She kissed his cheek.

"I can't push you two anywhere." Raiden groaned. He glanced back and forth between the two people he would never get away from. What was he even thinking? He didn't want to get away, and he knew it. They needed him.

"And what do you want me to do?" he asked. "What's the deal?"

"Be our bridge," they said in unison.

Chapter 26

Ash told Raiden she wanted to leave HQ this morning. They had been there for five days, and she said she wanted to catch the train. Gears offered them a room in exchange for researching their gifts. Raiden stared at the ceiling of the room and listened to Stone in the shower. He didn't want to leave just yet. There were still things that they hadn't worked out, and for some reason, he had the feeling that once they were back on the trains moving and trekking, those issues would fester. They needed to talk everything out before they yanked on their packs.

Raiden heard the shower water go silent. Ash had left the room an hour ago to talk to Gears and Luna. Gears wanted her to stay at HQ a little longer. The doctor had a full breakdown of Stone's gift of finding items by holding them and his side effect of being a kleptomaniac. Gears speculated that now that Stone had the two things he really wanted, Ash and Raiden, the need to neurotically have two items would probably abate.

Through talking to Gears, Raiden had discovered he never had the gift of knowing when snowstorms were coming in the first place. What he had was an attachment to Stone and Ash's safety and happiness. His side effect of pain came directly from his care for them. It was simply a bonus that when Ash and Stone were on the surface trekking, Raiden could sense a storm that might hurt them. Gears deduced that was why he wasn't always accurate. Raiden could only feel the storm as it related to Ash and Stone's wellbeing. The doctor said Raiden was unique. Never had he seen a gift that was limited to the people he was connected to, especially since Raiden had been connecting to Ash and Stone even before he met them or had become intimate.

Gears had learned all this about them, but the doc still had issues with Ash. He couldn't figure out her side effect. She was never lost, but he couldn't see anything that was a negative in her life.

While Ash was saying goodbye to the doctor and his match, Luna, Raiden was supposed to be dressing and packing. That's what Stone was doing, but Raiden stubbornly stayed in the center of the bed naked. He kept looking at the white ceiling. His shoulder ached. There was still some problem that had to be fixed, and he would solve the puzzle before he left. He wasn't leaving with anything hanging over their heads.

"Ash is gonna be mad if you're not dressed when she gets back." Stone came out of the bathroom in nothing but his black briefs. His rippled abs looked good enough to lick. The harvester headed straight for his bag and grabbed a pair of blue jeans.

"The deal is—" Raiden pointed to the bed. "In here, she follows me."

"Doubt it." Stone grinned at him as he pulled on his jeans. He buttoned them and came over to the bed. Stone leaned down and looked at him. "That cock of yours isn't gonna change her mind."

"Can it change yours?" Raiden reached up and grabbed Stone around the waist. He yanked him down to the mattress in one smooth motion.

"No." Stone laughed as he tried to catch himself. The two of them wrestled and Raiden let Stone pin him to the sheets. Stone sat on top of his thighs. Raiden's hard cock scraped between Stone's denim covered legs. He groaned.

"I win." Stone smiled.

"I think I win." Raiden reached up and wrapped his hand around Stone's neck. He pulled until Stone's mouth came close to his.

"You're cocky in the bedroom." Stone laughed before he kissed him. "Such a fucking punk."

"I'll show you cocky."

As Raiden kissed Stone, he thought about how in the last five days they hadn't done this. Stone had said he loved him, and he smiled and talked to him, but since his return, they hadn't truly touched. Stone had been attentive to Ash only. Raiden didn't mind. He liked the sex, and he enjoyed teaching Stone how to pleasure Ash, but he did miss this. Just kissing Stone was a thrill.

Stone's tongue speared into his mouth, and the harvester kissed Raiden in that same rough and hungry way that he remembered. Raiden couldn't wait until Stone had sex with him again. There were so many things they hadn't done yet. And everything would be even hotter with Ash there, naked and coming.

"Damn, Spike." Stone lifted his head, and his hand wrapped around Raiden's cock between his legs. "You do have talent." He started to pump his fist.

"I want you to fuck me again." Raiden kissed Stone's mouth and bucked into his hand. "I'll show you talent." He pulled his mouth away and unbuttoned Stone's jeans. "And I'll show you how hard you can come when I'm in your ass." Raiden's tongue slid over Stone's nipple. Stone's skin was still warm from his shower. He smelled like coconuts.

Stone's hand stopped moving, and he sat up suddenly. His lover placed his hand on the center of Raiden's chest and pushed.

"What?" Stone's brown eyes widened as his eyebrows rose into his hairline.

"What?" Raiden's forehead furrowed.

"You want to have sex with me?" Stone sputtered. "You mean…" He waved his arm. "In…?"

"*Fanken.*" Raiden sat up. "We don't have to. I was flirting with you. I guess, I did that badly." Raiden rubbed Stone's arms. "Just forget it."

"No." Stone cleared his throat. "I just thought Ash would do that one day."

"You know." Raiden grinned. "Ash doesn't have a dick? I mean, she's really good at pretending to be a man, but she can't pretend that." He chuckled. "Do we have to go over that lesson on her clit again?" He smiled as the memory made his cock fill out. "That was fun. I'd gladly show you how that works again."

"No, I get how it…" Stone paused. He didn't laugh, and his face held confusion. "I just thought…"

"You want her to get a strap-on?" Raiden still wasn't fluent in Stone-ease. "I think I know a harvester who has sex toys like that."

"Really…? I mean, no…" Stone lifted one eyebrow, and then he shook his head. "What I meant was that I've never let anyone fuck my ass."

"I know." Raiden drew him closer again. If that was a problem, he would gladly puzzle that out. "We don't ever have to do that. But if you want to, I'm here. That's all. I just want to be close to you."

"Close to me? You do sound like a twelve-year-old girl." Stone laughed. His head dropped down, and he kissed Raiden's neck. Raiden tipped his head to the side when Stone licked at the spike in his ear. "I'd be okay if you..." Stone kissed him again and licked at his mouth. Raiden moaned into the heat. He loved this.

"I should get a bucket of ice water and toss it at you." Ash's voice cut through Raiden's sexual haze, and he glanced over. "You're naked," Ash said flatly.

Ash stood by the exit. The door closed with a click.

Stone scrambled off Raiden like he just saw a polar bear. Raiden groaned when Stone's denim thighs brushed against his swollen dick. Stone quickly started to button up his jeans and wouldn't look at Ash or him. The upset harvester grabbed his pack.

Raiden's eyes met Ash's. That was weird. A light pang shot through his shoulder.

"What's the matter with you?" Ash asked Stone. "You can tell me. I won't get mad." Her eyes flipped to Raiden, and he smiled at her. It was good that they were getting more comfortable talking with each other.

"You might as well just say what's wrong. My shoulder is starting to throb." Raiden sat up.

In the last few days, Ash and Stone had come a long way in being open with each other. After they had both apologized and explained their feelings, they had talked about their lives and the reasons they made the choices they did. Both had been willing to reveal their hopes and dreams. For the first time ever, they shared things that made them vulnerable.

Even though Ash said she felt like a silly twelve-year-old at a sleepover, she still engaged with Raiden and Stone. It was useful that she started to see things—like when

Stone was distressed. She didn't push her best friend away, even when she was unsure. Raiden applauded her efforts.

"Spill it, Stone." Ash crossed her arms over her chest.

"What's the matter?" Raiden got to his knees on the bed.

"Nothing." Stone wouldn't meet his eyes.

"Doubt it." Raiden reached out and threw his hand over Stone's pack and tossed it to the floor.

"I'm sorry. I don't want to screw this up. I'm not going to fuck up again." Stone glanced to Ash, then to his pack. "I won't do that again."

"Do what exactly?" Raiden asked.

"I won't... with you... and Ash isn't..." Stone's eyes stayed on his bag. "Or never... even if I want to."

Raiden looked to Ash. He needed the interpreter.

"You think I'll be furious if you have sex with Raiden again?" Ash came over and set the pack aside.

"You were the first time," Stone pointed out.

They hadn't talked to Ash about how she felt about their mutual attraction. After Weaver had explained the heartstrings, Raiden thought their draw to each other was a nonissue. He wanted them both. He didn't think she was angry that they'd been fooling around, but maybe he was wrong.

"I wasn't mad that you had sex with Raiden." Ash glanced to him. "I knew you had from the start."

"What?" both Stone and he said in unison.

"I was looking for Stone, and I overheard a few harvesters say how Stone fucked Mutt in their room." She sat on the bed. "They were up in arms about it, so when I asked them what happened, they told me you took Raiden to their room and had sex with him. I knew it before we went after Raiden on the surface. It didn't bother me. At the time, I couldn't figure out why it didn't bug me, but now I know it was because of the strings."

"But… you were a squall." Stone sat next to her and Raiden did the same thing.

"I was upset because you said you forced him. I thought you hurt Raiden. I was fine if you wanted to have sex. I could tell you liked each other from the way you stared. You looked at Raiden the way you looked at me." Ash sighed. "Also, I knew you used his come to find him out on the ice. I didn't mention it because I wasn't ready to face the fact that I was okay with you two together. I kept trying to figure out why I wasn't freaked. I thought I was bonkers."

"I want to have sex with Stone. I might always want to do that." Raiden took Ash's hand in his. "I promise you, Ash, he didn't force me. If I didn't want to have him, I could've fought."

"Okay, tough guy." Ash nodded but Raiden didn't think it looked like she believed him. She glanced to Stone. "If you worked out what you did to him, that's all that matters. Just, from now on, I want you both to be heading in the same direction." She shrugged. "I assumed you would have sex again. I thought maybe at some point you might be doing things while you were inside of me." She gave another shrug.

Raiden instantly got hard again. "Let's try that now."

"No way." Ash let go of his hand and stood up. "We're catching the train, and you don't even have pants on yet."

"Doesn't Gears want you to stay?" Raiden asked. "He still doesn't know what your side effect is. We can stay, and I can figure out how to make Stone come over and over again."

Stone groaned, "Damn it, Spike." He adjusted the growing bulge in his pants. "You're damn cocky. I hope

Gears is right when he says this wanting sex all the time wears off."

"I hope he's wrong." Raiden grinned and leaned back on the bed.

"Gears figured out my gift to his satisfaction." Ash grabbed a pair of jeans off Raiden's pack. "No dice, Raiden. We can hop a train as soon as you're dressed."

"What's your gift and side effect?" Stone asked.

"I've never shaved. I don't grow hair on my arms or legs. The hair on my head has always been this short too. Basically, all the hair on my body never gets longer. What little I have anyway. I've great direction, but I don't have long hair. Unless, you boys change that. Gears said things could adjust, and I might have to cut it."

"That's it?" Raiden asked. "That doesn't sound bad. I thought side effects were all bad."

"Gears explained that it's like a lottery. You win some, you lose some. Sometimes the gifts don't even make sense. That gets under his skin. He said he met a man who had extra-long sensitive nose hairs. I asked if that was a side effect or a gift."

"Which is it?" Raiden took the pants from Ash and tossed them to the floor.

"He said he didn't know." Ash sighed. "The emergence of gifts is all new. He's writing a whole book on it."

"If the nose-hair guy is in the book, I don't want to read it." Stone took Ash's hand and tugged until she sat in his lap.

"Me too." Raiden's bones melted into bliss. Stone pulled off Ash's coat. The fabric hit the floor.

"Blast it, Raiden. Now you got Marion thinking we're staying. I said we're leaving. Get dressed, or you're walking out of HQ naked."

"The deal was that I follow you out there." Raiden pointed to the door. "And you follow me in here." He pointed to the bed. "We are in here." His eyes met Stone's, and the other man grinned. "Take off your clothes, Ash Winsor, king of the trains. I want sex with both my Conpars."

"Such a punk." Ash laughed and then turned in Stone's arms. Stone lifted her shirt off and threw the garment on top of her coat. "Sorry, Stone, I did make that deal." Ash's hands went to the buttons on Stone's jeans. "If you wanna win…"

"You gotta bet." Stone set Ash on the bed next to Raiden and dropped his pants.

Chapter 27

Raiden didn't want to leave HQ. He loved the hot showers and the hot sex with Ash and Stone. He grumbled as he packed, but Stone reminded him that he'd agreed to go. They had promised Ash.

Luna had fully healed Raiden's leg, so he couldn't ask to stay for recovery. Plus, Ash was antsy to leave. She didn't tell them why she wanted to move on, but neither Stone nor he had outright asked her. They didn't want her to lie, and she seemed uncomfortable sharing. Jokingly, he told Stone they would find out tomorrow.

Over the last two weeks, Ashley told them quite a bit about her life on the trains and how dressing as a man had protected her on many occasions. Stone had opened up as well. He admitted he fell in love with all of Ash, not just her gender, but all of her. Watching the two of them let their guard down was beautiful and humbling. Watching them in the bedroom was erotic and exciting. He didn't have one thing to complain about other than the fact he was worried it would all end when they walked out of headquarters.

Raiden tried to be what they needed to connect, and he made up his mind that once they left that was all he would shoot for. When he said things like that to Ash and Stone, they just called him a slush-head.

"This is the train." Ash pointed to *Ketch* when the train arrived in Dallas. Raiden paused and smiled. *Ketch* had private rooms. He was sure Ash would have a key. Stone and he would have her naked.

"What's wrong, Wishbone?" Stone asked him when he didn't move toward the train. "Is it your joints?" He linked his fingers with Ash's. "See?" he held up their united hands, "we're not fighting."

"Yeah, we're holding hands like twelve-year-old girls." Ash laughed and then shoved Stone before straightening her big fur-covered coat.

Raiden laughed too. Truly, his body felt like new. Since the time he spent with Luna and then explaining in detail to Gears about the pain in his body, Ash and Stone had been careful to come to him with any disagreements.

"Nothing's wrong." Raiden followed Stone onto the train. He didn't even worry about their arguing anymore. As soon as the three of them started to have sex, all the pain had eased. Gears wanted a report on whether or not he could still feel snowstorms as soon as they were trekking again.

Raiden got to a private room on *Ketch*, and Ash handed him a key. He grinned at the two of them when Stone punched her on the shoulder. She hit him back.

"What's so funny?" Ash asked him.

"I'm just happy you have a private room." He shrugged. "Maybe you two can practice kissing instead of batting at each other."

"What's the fun in that?" Ash asked him. "You're such a punk."

"Spike just wants a private room so I can fuck him." Stone leaned in. His tongue slid along Raiden's piercing in his ear. He shivered. "I don't need a private room. I'd fuck you anywhere, Raiden."

"I need a private room, ice-for-brains." Ash swatted at Stone's arm. "Open the door. I want to practice kissing."

Raiden got into the room just as Stone and Ash dumped their packs. They had Raiden's bag off his back and his coat to the floor before the door even closed.

Stone kissed him until he was dizzy and then lifted his head and kissed Ash. Raiden nibbled on her neck as Ash loosened his belt. Stone's guns hit the tiles. He caught the scent of coconuts, and Raiden's cock hardened.

A knock on the door sounded.

"*Fanken*," Raiden groaned. "Ash's room sucks."

"Or doesn't suck." Stone let go of him and slid the door open.

A harvester Raiden didn't know stood at the entrance. "I'm looking for Winsor. It's important."

Ash's eyes slanted into a glare. "Why?"

"Someone is asking for you. Said it's an emergency. I was told to get you."

Ash straightened her coat. "I'll be right back."

"I'll go with you." Stone kissed Raiden's cheek. "I need more coconut oil. This is a long trip."

Ash laughed. "We'll be right back, tough guy." She disappeared out the door with Stone behind her.

Raiden sat on the cot and stared at their packs. After a few minutes, he started to pace. Mac had commanded Ash and Stone to keep their guns in their backpacks while at HQ. Stone had strapped his weapons back on as soon as they left, but now they sat on the floor. Raiden wasn't sure if Ash was armed.

Pacing by the door, he stretched his stiff muscles. His shoulders started a sharp, familiar ache. When he bent down to rub his knee, he stopped. What was he doing? He'd felt fine for days at HQ. Other than his ass being a little sore from Stone, he hadn't had any problems. Were Ash and Stone arguing?

Raiden yanked on his coat. If the two of them were bickering again, he would slap them both. The moth, bridge, nanny, or whatever they wanted to call him was tired of their thick-headedness.

After locking the private room, Raiden headed down the hall of the train. When the engines started up, he stopped to gain his equilibrium. The train began to rock. He hit the first train car but didn't see Ash or Stone. In fact, the metal room had only a few people sleeping and lounging. In the next train car, he could hear boisterous noise.

Raiden reached the door to the next car and was met with a wall of people. He elbowed a few harvesters to get through. When his eyes alighted on what was in the center of the group, his jaw dropped.

Forcing the man next to him aside, Raiden moved closer. More people closed the gap, blocking his way. Ash knelt with two men grasping her shoulders. Blood oozed from her nose. Stone was on his knees struggling to rise, but he was dragged to the floor. Three men held him when they got him to his belly. He cussed and fought. In the center of the ring of onlookers was Doug.

"Winsor's reign is over," Doug held up Ash's gun. "No more King Winsor," he bellowed. The group didn't cheer. Murmured confusion fluttered all around him. No one really liked Ash, but Raiden knew most of the harvesters liked her more than they liked Doug.

Doug leaned back and full-on kicked Ash in the stomach. She hit the floor. Stone yelled and fought to rise. Doug spun around when Stone cursed. His eyes slashed over Stone's face. He waved Ash's gun.

"Ash shot me with this gun." Doug leaned closer to a still struggling Stone. "I can show you where you'll start sucking me." Doug petted Stone's face with the barrel. "Before I shoot you in the same place."

Raiden did a quick count: three men on Stone, two men on Ash, and Doug. Six men. He would be fine. He took a deep breath. Raiden didn't like fighting and had often told his mother that, but now he was glad he was so well-taught. No one would touch Ash and Stone for as long as he was around.

Raiden squeezed past a few more men and then stepped to the center of the ring.

"Let them go, Doug." Raiden thought he would try peace. He preferred problem-solving over violence. If there was a solution, he would take it, but if Doug didn't let them go, he would have hell to pay.

Doug spun away from Stone and smirked. "I was wondering if Ash was still leading you around on your leash." Doug pointed to the floor. "Heel, Mutt. Ash can watch you get fucked by the real king of the trains. I've waited long enough for your ass."

Raiden stepped closer and gauged his spacing. He didn't want to get stuck in a tight corner like when Doug struck him near the boxes in the hall. This time he was ready and wouldn't be distracted like when he was caught on the crates.

"No, Raiden," Ash cried out as she tried to rise. Stone thrashed against the men who held him.

"Run, Spike," Stone begged. "Get back to the room. Lock it."

Doug grinned. "Going to run, Mutt? I can just as well fuck you over Ash's bed."

"I'm not running away." Raiden relaxed his shoulders.

"I always knew you were a good dog. Get on your knees."

Raiden took a settling breath as he stretched his neck. Doug tipped his head to the side in confusion. Raiden reached out and snatched the pistol from Doug's hand. Without hesitation, Raiden dropped the clip out of the gun. The magazine hit the floor. The weapon followed.

Doug lurched back in shock. Raiden spun and kicked the harvester in the face. As soon as he struck Doug, one of the men holding Ash let go and dove for him. Doug's friend threw himself forward as if he would tackle Raiden. Raiden sidestepped him easily and thrust the flat of his hand into his nose. The man hit the floor at Raiden's feet.

Like a dancer, Raiden spun toward the man still pinning Ash to the floor. This adversary tried to rise, but he didn't have enough time. Using a series of rapid strikes, Raiden made sure his opponent didn't even have time to let go of Ash to block. As Ash shoved the unconscious man off her arm, she hunted for her gun.

As a child, his mother wanted him to learn different forms of fighting. Raiden switched easily from kickboxing to Jujutsu to Judo. Whatever worked, he used.

Raiden was down to only the men holding Stone. No one had even gotten near him yet. Ash swiped at her bloody face as she looked around for her clip. Dim lights swung from the ceiling casting the room in a dull glow. Men and women still crowded in to see what was happening. Ash's magazine was kicked. The bullets skidded across the floor.

Doug fumbled across the room after Ash's gun, but he didn't rise. One of the men gripping Stone looked at Raiden and then let go and ran. Raiden faced the two men left. Two men were not enough to keep a man like Stone down. Stone got one arm free and began to punch the guy trying to hold his opposite bicep. They wrestled to the floor. The other guy decided to attack Raiden.

The stranger should've stayed with Stone. Raiden was no easy opponent. His challenger threw the first punch. Raiden blocked, then struck back. He used a series of moves that would get him close enough to knock the other man out. With a final jab, his rival hit the floor.

Stone stood and wiped at the cut on his lip.

"Found it." Ash stood with a hop and slapped in her magazine. She held the weapon up, and Raiden thought she stroked the barrel like when she petted his dick. "Still titanium." She smiled as her gaze traveled down to Doug, who sat on his knees.

Doug looked around for help. He didn't have any. Harvesters were exchanging money.

"I'm not living under Winsor's rule anymore." Doug rose to his feet and stumbled backward looking for a way out.

"Open the door." Ash pointed with her gun to a side door on the train. The room crackled with tension. A man to the right of Doug opened the door, and everyone looked at Ash.

"Jump." She pointed her weapon at Doug.

Doug shook his head and then glanced around.

Ash's eyes were steel. She shot, and Doug staggered. He reached for the door with one hand as his other hand went to his chest. She shot again. Doug slumped near the door frame. With a whoosh, the harvester fell out of the train car. Silence descended over the crowd.

"Damn, Cujo." Stone reached Raiden's side and wrapped his arm around his waist. "I didn't know you could fight like that."

"And if I didn't want to be fucked, I would've fought you and won." Raiden's eyes bore into Stone's.

"Okay, Fang. You could fight me and win. I see why Ash calls you tough guy." They both glanced to Ash. She stood in the center of the circle of harvesters. Her chin was raised, and her silver eyes flashed.

"I want to be left alone. Leave Raiden and Stone and me alone, and you won't get killed." Ash addressed the bystanders. "This is my only warning." She slipped her pistol into her holster, and then she joined Stone and him. She took Raiden's hand, and her eyes met his. A touch of sorrow flickered across her beautiful silver eyes. Ash Winsor was softer than she let on.

Ash turned to him and smiled. "You can fight. Does the moth have any more hidden talents?"

Raiden shrugged. "I can do a lot of things. Bridge, moth, nanny." He stepped closer. "Friend, lover, match."

"You want to show us all the other things you know how to do?" Stone pressed closer to his side, as they started back to their room.

Raiden smiled. "Just follow me."

Epilogue
(Marion Stone)

Three months later…

Stone thrust once more and came deep inside Ashley. Damn, she felt incredible as she gripped his cock. Every time he was inside her, Stone thought it was a miracle. In moments like this, he wished he'd met Raiden sooner.

Stone tilted his head back as Raiden kissed his neck. Raiden pumped once more inside of Stone's body and then growled as he climaxed.

His eyes closed, and Stone just felt the flow of the two people he loved. They surrounded him, and he had never been this happy and satisfied before. For once, he wasn't scared he would make a mistake and ruin his life. Ash and Raiden promised him they would never leave. They were the two things he had been searching for. They were his direction.

"You're fucking hot, Marion," Raiden moaned. Stone smiled. Only Ash and Raiden seemed to get away with calling him by his first name. Whenever he tried to correct them, they distracted him, and he ended up forgetting what he was about to say.

Raiden slumped over him, and his boyfriend's softening dick slipped from Stone's body. The loss caused shivers to run down Stone's spine. He shuddered and then curled to the side of the cot next to Ash. She panted, with her eyes still screwed shut. Stone watched her breasts as they rose with each breath. He did have ice for brains. How had he never noticed she was a woman?

He smiled. She was a beautiful woman, too. Ash Winsor was everything he could ever want in a woman: strong, sexy, smart. Actually, Stone didn't even know a woman like Ash existed in the world. And his Raiden was everything he could want in a man. He didn't know how he got so lucky, but he didn't question it. He just held on to them.

"When I asked you to keep me warm," Ash sighed, "that's not what I meant."

"I think you're going to have to be more specific next time," Stone snickered.

Ash used his shoulder as a pillow while Raiden linked his fingers with Stone's.

Stone snuggled Winsor to his side and then glanced at the clock near Ash's British flag. Ash was due to vomit any minute. Her morning sickness always fell at the same time. Raiden had pointed out the puking to him the other day.

"I've gotta pee," Ash said suddenly. She hopped up and vanished into the bathroom.

When the door to the bathroom closed, he looked to his boyfriend.

"She lied again." Stone didn't understand why she wasn't willing to talk about what was going on.

"I know." Raiden grabbed a quilt and flung it over both of their bodies. "You were both doing so well. I don't know why she's lying to us again."

Stone snuggled near Raiden. His boyfriend said he was working it out. Stone was positive Raiden would tell him what they should do next. Stone sat quietly, while Raiden and he listened to her hurling.

"I don't have ice for brains. I'll admit it. At first, I thought maybe the puking was caused by our being too hard on her or getting used to traveling after HQ. Then I thought it was bad water, but then I figured it out. Why doesn't she want to tell us?" Stone asked Raiden.

"I think she doesn't want it to be true," Raiden answered as he stared up at the ceiling.

Stone nodded. They had been gone from HQ for three months. He didn't think she would want to go back there, but eventually, they would need a doctor. He considered his brother Mather. They might head to Water Base Cure.

"She's too skinny. We have to feed her more." Stone was embarrassed anew. "I think she has to gain weight to carry a child."

Raiden turned to face him on the cot. "What happened to calling her fat?"

Stone's eyes dropped. "That was before I saw her naked. It was all the layers." He ran his finger over the spike in Raiden's ear, and then his eyes met Raiden's green ones again. "Do you think she doesn't want to tell us because she doesn't know if it's mine or yours?" Stone pulled up the blanket. "We shouldn't be having sex with her so much. Will we hurt the baby?"

"I want to make fun of you for worrying, but I don't know the answer to that, either." Raiden sighed. "I think we should see your brother Mather. He could tell us what to do." Raiden's brow furrowed.

"I thought of that. But we gotta wait until she tells us first, don't we?" Stone grinned at Raiden. "I'll make you a deal. You bring up the topic."

"And what're you going to do?" Raiden asked him.

"I'll watch and see what happens."

Raiden laughed and shoved him. Stone caught himself from falling off the cot.

"Why won't she just tell us?" Stone said after a few seconds.

"If she has a baby, we'd have to stop moving for a while. She won't want to do that. She gets weird about staying anywhere for too long. It's always move, move, move."

Stone nodded. Ash had always been that way since the first time he'd met her. She seemed to always be hunting for a lost item and hated to stop looking. He assumed the object was the unidentified treasure that she whispered about with Morgan-Roth.

The door opened. Ash appeared. Her brow was damp, and she shivered.

"Do you need a second?" Raiden held out his hand.

"No." Ash crawled in between them again.

"We want to go to Water Base Cure to see my brother," Stone said slowly. His eyes met Raiden's over Ash's head. "We should stop having sex until you're better."

"I'm fine," Ash griped. "It's just a bug. I'll be better soon."

"You'll be better." Raiden sighed. "In nine months?"

Stone held his breath while Ash was silent. He waited for her to lie or say a snide remark. She didn't say anything. After a few seconds, Stone decided the silence was much worse.

"Do you want to find someone who will…" Stone waved his arm and then dropped it. He couldn't even say the word. He wanted the baby. If she decided she didn't, it would be hard for him to accept that. He would, but it would be difficult.

"To what?" Raiden asked.

"Abort it?" Stone forced the words past his lips. He looked away from Raiden so the other man wouldn't see how much that hurt.

"Never, you knackered old bassoon," Ash snapped. She shoved Stone. Again, he just about fell off the cot. Her angry answer made him grin. "It's our baby. I'm keeping it. Go fuck a ferret."

Stone relaxed and curled next to her again. What would he name it? He pictured holding his kid. He could teach the boy all sorts of things. Ash would have to curb her bad language.

"Why not tell us?" Stone asked after a minute. The question nagged at him. "Are you upset because you don't know if it's mine or Raiden's? I don't care." And he truly didn't. If it was Raiden's, the baby was still his in a way. They were tied together. He would love it just as much as Spike would.

"No," Ash groaned. "I'm scared. Big, bad Ash Winsor is fucking terrified."

Stone hugged her shoulders. It was a rare occurrence that Ash ever said she was scared. She got worried sometimes. She talked to Raiden and him about things that concerned her, but she never said scared. She had never run from a problem in all the time he knew her. She always faced things head on.

"Terrified?" Stone asked. He would be there for her. Raiden and he could fix this somehow. They were her shadows. They were anything she needed them to be.

"What's so scary, Ash?" Raiden turned onto his side and stared at her. "Whatever it is, it's not that bad. We love you. There are three of us."

"We'll follow you, Ash Winsor," Stone stated sincerely. He meant that with every fiber of his being. The only people in the world he wanted were here on this cot.

"I had some problems when I had my first baby, and I'm scared that it'll be like that again. You're with me, but are you *really* with me?"

Ash's statement took a few seconds to sink in. When it finally did, Raiden and he reacted at the same time.

"Your first baby?" Stone sat up dislodging the blankets.

"Of course, we're really with you! I'm betting to win!" Raiden sat up as well. Stone almost fell off the cot. He swore they would have to make a bigger bed in their rooms on the trains. They would have to make a place for the baby, too.

"Did you have a baby with Morgan-Roth?" Raiden asked suddenly. "Is that why you were looking for the child with him? Is the baby his?"

"Would that matter?" Ash asked.

"No." Raiden shook his head. "I'm just trying to puzzle this out."

Stone knew Morgan-Roth was looking for his kid. Once he had offered to help him, but Morgan-Roth said he didn't have anything of the child's, like hair, for Stone to hold to use his gift. Without a piece of the original, Stone was useless. It had never dawned on Stone that the child could be Ash's. She should've asked him for his help long before now.

"No." Ash frowned. "Morgan-Roth is looking for Rourke. That's his kid with a woman he had a one-night stand with on the Equator. I'm looking for Kelvin. I had him with Felix."

"You should've told me, Ash. I could help. Do you have a small part of the baby for me to hold? A piece that was a part of him? Hair, a tooth?" Stone asked as his eyes popped to Raiden. Ash had shared with him about Felix. Raiden looked like he didn't know this new baby information. Ash had left the baby part out when she had talked to Raiden as well.

"Of course, I thought about telling you and asking for your help, ice-for-brains." Tears danced in Ash's eyes. "I love my child, but I have nothing, Stone. Nothing. And I didn't want anyone to use the information against me. You said it yourself; harvester trains are dangerous for a woman. It would be even more dangerous if people found out I was desperate to find my child." She sniffled, and Stone hugged her to his chest. "I'm looking for him, but I don't want Felix to catch wind of it. He's unstable. What if he kills Kel?" Ash sobbed, and Stone rocked her. His heart hurt just knowing she was miserable. They would help. Raiden would think of a way to solve this.

"You and Felix had a baby together when he raped you?" Raiden asked.

"No." Ash lifted her head and swiped at her tears. "We had Kelvin when Felix and I were a couple. When Felix left, he said he didn't care about the boy and that I could have him. I loved Kel. After Felix left, I never thought he'd come back. He never cared about our boy. I was planning on taking Kelvin to England with my uncle. My uncle was leaving, and with a baby, I couldn't harvest and pretend to be a man. I planned to go with my uncle and cousins and make a home for Kelvin and me."

"Then Felix came back," Raiden said.

"Yes. Felix took Kel just to hurt me. I fought so hard, but I didn't win." A few fresh tears slipped down Ash's face. "The next day I got my gun, and I swore I would find Kel. I let my family leave without me, and I started to trek with Morgan-Roth. He knew that I had promised my baby that I'd never give up on him. I know he's alive. I can't seem to stop searching for Kel, and if I find Felix, I'm going to kill him."

"Ash, why didn't you tell me this?" Stone hugged her to him and kissed her tears. "I could've been helping you this whole time. We could've looked together."

"You have been helping me this whole time. You've been traveling with me and keeping me safe while I looked for him. I trust you to have my back." She leaned into his chest. "I have to be careful all the time, Stone. I needed you, and after I found out you couldn't help unless I had a piece of the original, a piece of Kel, I just decided I wouldn't risk telling you. Not telling you I was a woman was the first and only cowardly thing I've ever done in my life. I'll admit I was so scared you'd leave if you knew I wasn't a man. I thought I'd disappoint you. You had your heart set on King Winsor. I thought you'd run if you thought you were stuck trekking with not only a woman, but a woman who is fucked up, and searching for her baby with another man. You do tend to run when things get tricky."

"I'm never leaving either of you. You're both exactly what I want." Stone kissed her hair. The strands were getting long again. They would have to cut it. "I heard you once, Ash. You were talking to Morgan-Roth. I knew you were looking for something. I thought you were talking about Kelvin as in a temperature." Stone's eyes caught Raiden's. "I do have ice for brains."

"No, you don't. I love you, Marion." Raiden smiled at him. "And I love you, Ash. This is all okay." Raiden rubbed his hand down Ash's back. "Thank you for telling us. This is a workable puzzle. We will find Kelvin. Even if we can't use Stone's gift."

"It is?" Ash's eyes flipped from Stone to Raiden. "I thought maybe you'd be upset. I can't seem to stop searching for Kel. I just want to know he's alive. I might never be able to stop hunting, and I know it's not fair to drag you two around with me everywhere I go."

"That's what shadows do." Stone nodded. "We can look for him. There are three of us, and I think I remember Raiden saying he's good with kids. Moth, bridge, nanny? We'll help you find Kelvin if that's what you want. We follow you."

"And our baby?" Ash asked.

"I like the sound of *our* baby." Raiden smiled. "We can do this."

"I'll make you a deal. If he comes out as white as me, I get to name him." Stone grinned. Already, he had thought of three names he liked.

"What if I want to name him?" Raiden poked his arm.

"If he comes out all slant eyes like Spike, then he can name him." Stone laughed and pushed Raiden.

Ash glared. "And I don't get to name him?"

"You can name our baby if it's a girl." Stone grinned. "And if it's a girl, then we can really have a twelve-year-old girl to talk to."

Ash shoved him and Stone fell off the cot.

~ The End ~

Thank you for reading
RAIDEN OUT THE STORM

If you enjoyed this book and would like to give back to the author, please consider writing a review! Reviews are a tremendous help for authors. So if you were moved and enjoyed this book enough to write even one sentence of encouragement it would be a huge boon.

https://www.goodreads.com/book/show/39197677-raiden-out-the-storm

Want more of the Ice Era Chronicles? Get a FREE story! Join C.M.Moore's exclusive readers group for a free story, GIVEAWAYS, Advanced reader opportunities and Pre-order notifications!

Join at:

http://eepurl.com/dnoLrr

About C.M.Moore

C.M. Moore is a retired soldier, and a romantic at heart. After being blown up in Afghanistan and receiving a purple heart, he began writing with his wife. Connor's first book *1:05 am* is a mixture of love, sex, and action. Today if you are looking for Connor, you can find him volunteering with veteran organizations, and harassing his military buddies. You can also find him attempting to "hunt" in the woods and ponds of Minnesota. In the event you find him in the woods, don't be scared, he can't hit anything. If you want to contact him message him at c.m.moore.author@gmail.com

Other books by C.M.Moore:

<u>Ice Era Chronicles</u>
1:05 a.m.
2:05 a.m.

<u>Off-the-Rails Ice Era Chronicles</u>
Grinding My Gears

Find out when the next book comes out!
Connect with C.M.Moore:

Facebook:
https://www.facebook.com/profile.php?id=10001044
2116825

Goodreads:
https://www.goodreads.com/author/show/7397933.
C_M_Moore

Pinterest:
https://www.pinterest.com/cmmooreauthor/

Website:
http://www.authorcmmoore.com/

There will be at least 12 novels in the ICE ERA
CHRONICLES and 10 novellas in the OFF-THE-RAILS
ICE ERA CHRONICLES. Want more time in the snow?
Get a FREE Novella! Join the exclusive readers group for
GIVEAWAYS, Advanced reader opportunities and Pre-
order notifications!
Join us:
http://eepurl.com/dnoLrr

Check out the AUTHOR WEBSITE:
www.authorcmmoore.com

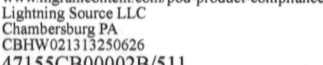